Time and Money

The Old Man with the Pocket Watch
- a novel -

Antonio F. Vianna

authorHOUSE®

AuthorHouse™
1663 Liberty Drive
Bloomington, IN 47403
www.authorhouse.com
Phone: 1-800-839-8640

First published by AuthorHouse 8/26/2011

ISBN: 978-1-4634-3944-6 (e)
ISBN: 978-1-4634-3945-3 (sc)

Library of Congress Control Number: 2011913195

Printed in the United States of America

1

The school bell sounded on time, just as it always did after a fifty minute class. Associate Professor Riley Sullivan raised his voice to finish giving final instructions for next week's assignment, but was barely heard as the students quickly shut down their laptops to hurry to their next class. He continued just the same, "Remember to use at least three references for the paper. There is a two week break, no classes for the next two weeks." He shrugged his shoulders, wondered if the effort was worth it, as students passed by, not bothering to give him a glance.

In less than a minute later he was alone in the classroom. He gazed at the empty seats, and wondered if he'd arrived at a critical time in his life, the itch to switch professions. This wasn't the first time he'd thought about making a career change. It seemed the notion had come up several times within the last month or so. He took in a deep breath and let the air out slowly, and then, without thinking, he shoved papers and the course's textbook into his briefcase to put off further thoughts about the idea.

Automatically, he glimpsed at his wristwatch as a reminder that he had a train to catch. He sped up the robotic motions, and soon he was outside.

The Santa Fe Depot was a short walk away, yet there was enough time for his thoughts to wander. He hadn't gotten over Liz. He had hoped to settle down with her, but she had other plans and dumped him after about six months seeing each other on a regular basis. Maybe he shouldn't have pushed her so much to make a commitment. He thought she was the right one and didn't want to lose her. Ironically, that's exactly what happened in the end. He knew he should move forward in his life, but as much as he tried he kept thinking about her. He blamed himself for the failed relationship and wondered if he'd stay alone for the rest of his life.

The Coaster was just up ahead. Its engines were idled. It waited for the right moment to leave the Depot. Riley quickened his pace.

Once onboard, he took a seat by the window, nodded a few times to other passengers he recognized. He wondered if they were as confused and lonely as was he. At least he had a job that paid the bills, although the salary he earned barely covered his car payment, insurance, rent, and other necessities. All his credit cards were maxed out.

"This is the Coaster, Number 653, ready to leave San Diego with stops at Old Town, Sorrento Valley, Solana Beach, Encinitas, Carlsbad Poinsettia, Carlsbad Village, and Oceanside. All aboard, doors close in five seconds."

The doors of each boxcar closed as the engines revved up. Slowly the Coaster train headed north.

Riley let his head angle towards the window. He closed his eyes and soon realized how tired he was. He felt his chest expand to take in air and then collapse to let it out. Tension in his brow slowly eased before the train reached its first stop at Old Town. He enjoyed the serene feeling for as long as possible, but the calmness had a short life as conversations among nearby passengers cut it short.

Just about forty minutes later, he heard, "This is Carlsbad Poinsettia. Watch your step. Next stop for Northbound Coaster Number 653 is Carlsbad Village. Arrival in seven minutes, doors close in five seconds." The conductor's voice clearly broadcasted the announcement.

Riley grabbed his briefcase, moved into the aisle as quickly as he could.

Now outside, he stood on the passenger's platform, the train's doors closed. Moments later the locomotive's engine revved up. Slowly, the windows of each boxcar passed by, passengers' eyes showed the same tiredness he felt after a long day of work. A loud whistle sounded again, then, slowly it drifted away. With the platform now cleared, he was left alone. Riley remained motionless for a short time. There was no need to hurry. No one special waited for him to arrive at his apartment, not even a dog or cat.

He moved towards the parking lot with a gait and expression that showed little urgency. Few vehicles remained from the crowd of passengers who had hurriedly driven off. He took in a deep swallow of air to savor the sensation. He held his breath for a second or two before he released the colorless gas back into the atmosphere. The move recharged his batteries just a little; greater alertness slowly returned to his consciousness. He reached into his briefcase to gather the keys to his car. He stared at his late model BMW that he couldn't afford, was in need of repair, and soon would need a set of rear tires. He'd like to have something newer but at this point in his life there was no way he could afford it. He still had to pay off this car first along with several other bills. He opened the door, tossed his briefcase on the passenger side floor. Then, he settled into the driver's seat, strapped himself with the seatbelt, and turned on the engine. He drove off, headed towards McCarty's, a local bar where he and his buddy had gotten accustomed to share a few beers.

Off to the right on Highway 1, he spotted someone whose vehicle seemed disabled. He decided to help out the motorist. He pulled off to the side of the highway, parked behind a Nissan Pathfinder, and stepped out. Slowly he made his way to someone bent over the hood of the vehicle. "Having some problems?" He took another few steps forward, unable to recognize the person who remained hidden from view. No one answered. He hesitated, not sure why. A few seconds passed.

An old man stuck his head to the side, "Shit." He wiped a few drops of saliva that clung to his lips, and then returned his head underneath the hood. He continued to finagle with something that Riley could not see.

A few more seconds passed as each man remained silent.

"Got it," the old man's voice celebrated victory. He backed away from the Pathfinder just a step to stare down the opponent. He was satisfied he'd won the battle because that's what life was all about, winning. He took a look at his hands, now dirty from fiddling with the engine.

Without noticing Riley, he walked to the passenger's side, opened the door, and then the glove compartment to grab a rag saturated with a cleansing lotion. Once his hands were cleaned, he tossed the dirty rag on the passenger side floor mat and closed the door. He then circled the vehicle to prepare to open the driver side door to start the engine.

Before he did, he took out a pocket watch to check the time. "Splendid," he said, more approvingly of the London made timepiece than of the time itself. He held one of those grins that could easily be mistaken for a smirk. Suddenly, he stopped as he spotted Riley.

"Do you need any help?"

The old man remained silent, yet his mind ran a mile a minute. He recognized Riley from McCarty's. "Nah, I've fixed it." He hesitated before continuing. His previously stern face changed to a gentle looking appearance as he slowly placed the watch into his pocket.

"Haven't I seen you at McCarty's?"

"Sure, I've seen you too." The old man started formalizing a plan.

"That's where I'm headed, to meet a buddy. You could join us if you want."

It took only a second to answer. "That's good of you. I'd like that. I'll buy the first round ... just because you stopped to offer an old man some help." The old man's grin could have been interpreted as a sincere smile, but he had something else up his sleeve.

Minutes later Riley and the old man were inside McCarty's. Each checked out who was there. No one they recognized. The old man was not surprised since he kept to himself most of the time, but Riley had hoped to spot someone.

He didn't see Graham, a surfer who typically got there before him on Tuesdays. The booth Graham usually took was empty, not even an empty bottle of beer. He wondered why his buddy was absent since this was usually the place and time when they met to drink beer and talk over the events of the day. Maybe something had happened to him; maybe he was only late; maybe it was the good waves.

"What do you drink?" The old man headed toward the bar as he asked the question.

"Stella," Riley answered. "I'm going to take a seat at this empty booth. He sat in the same spot that he and Graham typically used. Then he glanced around one more time just in case his buddy slipped in behind him. No luck.

The bartender gave the old man a smile. "What's up?"

"Two Stella's," the old man said as he pulled out a five dollar bill to place on the bar.

"Two Stella's, coming right up," the bartender dipped his hand into a cooler, uncapped two bottles of Stella Artois, and handed them over to the old man. "Want me to run a tab?"

"That won't be necessary. Keep the change." The old man grabbed hold of the bottles and then he moved towards the spot where Riley had settled in. He sat across the table on the wooden seat.

Riley took another look see if there was anyone else of interest to him. He was disappointed in the selection, so he waited for the old man to start off the conversation.

"Cheers," the old man raised a bottle in the air.

"Same here," Riley replied.

Each man took a gulp of beer in silence.

"Where's your buddy?"

Riley shrugged his shoulders, "Don't know. He's usually here well before I arrive. I guess something came up."

"It is what it is." Then the old man began to weave a tale. "Thanks again for stopping to see if I needed any help. That's pretty unusual these days." He saw Riley shrug his shoulders without uttering a word, so he continued. The old man's face was, in a strange way, grandfatherly looking, as if he would be someone you'd tell your most inner secrets to or agree to partner up with in a business deal. He took another swig of beer, his eyes all the while directed at Riley. "You seem to be a nice fellow."

Riley was not sure what he meant so he let it go. Maybe it was just small talk. He figured the best approach was to hear what the old man had to say. No risk in just listening and having a beer. At least his mind was not thinking about his career, Liz, relationships, and money. He took another sip.

The old man sank his hand into his pocket to pull out the same watch as before, and then after glancing at the time he put it back. After clearing his throat he asked, "What do you do?" The old man seemed interested in knowing something about Riley. "How do you make a living?" He took another gulp of beer. A smile squeezed from his face.

Riley thought the question to be an odd opening question as his mind stumbled to find any importance to it. He came up empty so he kept silent for a while longer.

"Am I getting too personal?" His smile reappeared, this time there was a noticeable crack in its sincerity.

Riley may not have been as experienced as the old man, but he'd had his fair share of ups and downs to develop a sense of caution with some people. This was one such time. He decided to take another sip of beer, so he grabbed hold of the bottle and moved it to his lips. He let the golden liquid slide down his throat. He shifted his eyes away from the old man's stare.

"I don't mean to get personal. I just thought, what the hell, I'd get to know a little about the guy who tried to help me out." He took another sip of beer. "That's really all there is."

Further suspicion emerged. There was something about the old man that unsettled him, yet he couldn't put his finger on it. Riley decided to turn the tables. He straightened up in the seat, "What about you? What do you do?"

"Fair enough," he coughed, and then grabbed a paper napkin from a nearby dispenser to wipe his lips. "Blood pressure tends to boil unexpectedly. Should've never started smoking Camels, had a hell of a time quitting. Damage is done." He paused. "But that's neither here nor there. You asked me what I do." He took in a deep breath as if to prolong an answer.

Riley felt a little grimy. His skin prickled just enough to cause a slight shiver. He glanced away for a split second to take in a time-out, to collect his thoughts before volunteering any information. During the quick look away he thought he saw his buddy Graham standing at the bar, waving him his way. He blinked. The image was gone. His fingers unconsciously tapped the wooden table to an imaginary tune, not stopping to figure out what the message might have been.

"So, what do I do? That's a reasonable question." He cleared his throat. "We're going to need something a little stronger." He glanced at the beer bottles on the table, then stood, and headed for the bar.

Riley remained confused with the old man's actions. He wished Graham would hurry along to join them.

A few minutes later the old man returned with two glasses of scotch whiskey. "Drink slowly." He nodded Riley's way as he took a sip himself.

Riley looked at the shot glass set before him. "What the hell," he said, and then mimicked the movement. He coughed as the booze pricked his throat like needles dancing in all sorts of direction, "Rugged stuff." He pushed the glass away.

The old man gave off a smirk, oddly pleased of Riley's response. He took a final sip of the scotch, puckered his lips as if to make sure nothing slipped out of his mouth. Then he reached for the scotch drink in front of Riley. "Can't let it go to waste." With one big gulp he swallowed what was left. "Ah." He let the word string out as long as possible. He curled his lips. "Son, I'll let you in on an important story." He cleared his throat as if he was about to lecture to a class of students.

Riley thought he was about to get a straight answer, but was disappointed.

"London, England ruled the world in timepieces in the eighteenth and nineteenth centuries. They made self-winding pocket watches so well that the Germans and Swiss stamped the word London on most of their watches because London sold." He grinned, and then pulled out his pocket watch. He looked at it with great pleasure. "Can you believe that over two hundred years ago businesses were making fraudulent products?" He let out a tamed roar. Then, he gave another glance at the timepiece in his hand. "I came across this particular pocket watch many years ago as part of, shall we say, a settlement of a business dispute. It keeps perfect time, and it reminds me that when you take care of special possessions they last a long time. It's a Glashütte Original Pocket Watch No. 1. There are only twenty-five worldwide and each is most likely worth over fifty thousand dollars."

Showing a little curiosity but more with the beginnings

of irritation, Riley said, "That's interesting, but you still haven't told me what you do or what your name is."

"I guess I haven't." He bent forward as if he was about to tell a well kept secret. In a low voice he said, "I buy low and sell high." Without an inkling of a grin, he leaned back against the wooden bench. "That's really all I do. I find deals that are undervalued, negotiate a price, and then re-sell at a higher price." Satisfied he'd said all he intended to say for the moment, he kept his eyes glued on Riley. "That's about it."

Silence took center stage for a short while.

"Oh, I see," said Riley, yet he had no idea what the old man was really about.

"I'm glad you do." The old man knew Riley had no clue. "And now it's your turn. What do you do?"

"I'm a college professor, actually an assistant professor."

The old man waited for more, but when nothing else came he asked, "Is that it? You teach at some college?"

"What else is there?"

"What college? What courses do you teach? Have you conducted any recent research that is noteworthy? Are you published? Come on son, tell me more."

Though feeling embarrassed of only a few accomplishments, Riley admitted, "No, that's about it."

"Hum." He put his hand to his chin. "Are you married with a family?"

He hesitated before answering, but then he said, "No, I'm single, never married."

"A good looking fellow like yourself probably has the

ladies crawling all over you, can't keep them away." He wiggled his furry eyebrows.

Riley's face reddened just enough to be noticeable, "Ah, I wish that was the case." He slowly began to warm up to the question and answer format.

"Oh, I see, not interested in women. Is that it?"

"No, no. I enjoy women. It's just ... well ...." He let the words drift off.

"I think I know what you mean. Relationships are difficult, very sensitive, and there seems to be constant change. One day everything is just hunky dory, and the next day it's hell." He rolled his eyes to emphasize the point.

Riley quickly agreed, "So you've been there as well?"

"Son, we've all been there, some of us many times."

The conversation took a breather as both men gave it time to settle down.

"I'm Riley. What's your name?"

"You can call me Al." The old man waited a few seconds before he said, "Looks like you can use another beer. Stay right where you are, I'll be back."

Before Riley could object, the old man was half-way to the bar. With a few minutes another round of Stella's were set on the table.

"I know I've already said this, but I can't tell you how nice it was to find someone like you who stopped to figure out if I needed help. Not many people do that these days."

Riley shrugged his shoulders again, "Seemed to be the right thing to do."

"Just the same, not many people would do that." He took a gulp of beer, and then he changed the subject. "Can I be honest with you?"

Riley nodded his head with a yes.

"It doesn't seem you're really interested in what you do, teaching." He let the comment settle in.

Riley slowly picked up on the conversation. "It's not that I don't like it. I mean, I actually enjoy teaching. It's, well, the pay isn't great and I seem to have a bigger appetite than my wallet."

"Got bills that you can't seem to cover?"

"Something like that."

"And you can't seem to find the right gal?"

Riley's eyes opened wider, "Yeah." He took a sip of beer as he shook his head to the sides.

"You need some focus in life. At least that's my guess." The old man's voice sounded grandfatherly, but the truth was he was reeling Riley in little by little.

This time Riley was slow to answer, but a slight shake of his head confirmed the old man's assessment.

"Like I said earlier, I know what you mean about relationships because I've been there." He cleared his throat.

Riley nodded his head to agree.

The old man looked away for a few seconds as if to consider something important. Then he reset his eyes on Riley. "I've told you what I do."

"Yeah, you buy low and sell high."

"Correct. I'm a fairly good businessman. I know how to make money."

Riley lifted his head, now full attention toward the old man.

"Hum, I just might have an opportunity for you to make some good money to pay off those bills and get back on track with your life. Would you be interested?"

Riley replied without hesitation, "Yes, definitely."

"It won't take you much time. It'll be worth it." The old man gazed at Riley as if he was looking at a herd of cattle grazing. He cleared his throat carefully after the remark. His look was dead serious, and his voice was low and confidential sounding as if the conversation was a big secret.

Riley put on a smile that shined brightly. "I'm ready to listen." He tugged at his right ear.

The old man coughed. It was either a sign of bad health or just a dry throat. He took another sip of the Stella, set the bottle on the wooden table, and then continued, "I don't tell many people this. I think I can tell you only if you keep this between us ... you and me." He waited for Riley to agree.

"You've got my word on it, just between you and me."

"One of these days I'm going to die. Not sure when, could be many years away, could be today. My doctors seem to change their minds each time I talk with them. But one thing is for certain, it's going to happen."

"Everyone's going to die." Riley was disappointed and confused, not sure what to make of the comment.

"I know, I know. That's not the point," the old man

said with a sound of irritation. "Have you ever thought about what happens after you die?"

"Like, my soul?"

"Hell no, I have no idea what happens to your soul. I don't even know if there is a soul, never met one." He smacked his lips. "I'm talking about all the others who knew you when you were alive, and who are still alive. I'm talking about people's possessions. That's what I'm talking about. Ever think of what happens to those people and your possessions?"

"I don't have many possessions. I'm in hock for most of what I have."

"But if you play your cards right, you can accumulate wealth, lots of it."

"OK, then I'll create a will. Make it real clear as to who gets what." His answer seemed so straightforward that he wondered where the conversation was heading.

The old man thoughtfully replied, "But who will you give your possessions to? Isn't that the real problem?" He paused again for emphasis. "You've promised to keep this between us, right?"

"Of course, I promise."

"OK then." He took in a deliberate deep breath and slowly released the air. "That's the problem I have. Who is worthy of my assets?" He paused, leaned back, and answered his own question. "I can't think of anyone."

Riley now was back into the conversation. "So you want to give away your wealth?"

"It's a little more complicated than that, but yes, that's what I'm talking about."

"What's that got to do with me?"

"You test students, don't you?"

"Of course, I test them all the time."

"Well, you'll do just fine."

Riley was again baffled with what Al was really saying. He was about to ask for clarification but the old man beat him to it.

"Let me be perfectly honest with you." He cleared his throat. "I'm old and could die any day, but I've already told you that. What I haven't said is that I'm divorced with two grown girls. They and their mother don't think highly of me, but they sure would take my money when I'm gone. I don't intend for any of them to see any of it, now or later."

Riley stared at the stone-like expression on the old man's face.

The old man ignored Riley's look. "I want you to test people, to help determine who is worthy of my money, and report back to me."

Riley's frown took center stage. "Give the money to a charity. You must have a favorite one, or even a few."

"Not going to happen. I want real people to have the money, not some organization."

"Where do I find these people? What ideal qualifications do they need to possess? What if no one passes the test? What if more than one person passes the test?" Riley's voice was strained as he tried to make sense of it all. He wondered if the old man was enjoying him struggle. Maybe he was being tested?

"I've got a list. It's taken me a while to come up with

the names, but it will do just fine. There might be more than one person who fits the bill. That's not a problem. The only requirement is for the person who gets my money to spend it wisely. I'll be the sole judge. Your job is to test and then report to me the facts."

"I see," said Riley, but really not fully understanding it all.

"I don't think you do, but you'll soon find out. Maybe you will be worthy of my money?" The old man gave off a grin, although it was not inviting.

"Honestly, Al, I don't think the plan will work."

"I guess we have a difference of opinion because I think the plan will work just fine. I just need you to do what I say. I'll pay you." He paused. "Will you do it?"

Suddenly, Riley's eyes lit up, "How much?"

"You've told me you're in debt and you can't figure out relationships. You admit that you need to focus more." He waited for an argument or any other type of response but nothing came. "I can help out with the money part right away. Later, once the job is done, I'll coach you about the other issues. For starters, I'll pay you five thousand dollars for one to two weeks of work once it's finished. It shouldn't take longer than that. After you complete the job we'll discuss a bonus of some sorts. I'll give you a specific schedule to follow, and you'll have to report to me each day. It will require travel and time away. I hope you're not opposed to a little travel."

It didn't take Riley long to agree, "Deal."

The old man extended his hand to shake. A grin that was more of a snicker appeared on his face.

Riley had no idea the arrangement was all part of a bigger plan.

"When do we start?" He took a deep gulp of air. "I'm in between classes now, and have two full weeks to give you."

The old man gave off a satisfied grin. Calmly the old man said, "I've already identified three people who I'll send a certified letter to. I'll tell each of them that I'm seeking worthy beneficiaries to receive one hundred thousand dollars if anyone can prove to you they are worthy of the money. Of course I won't use my real name, but I will identify you as the bona fide individual who will evaluate their worthiness. I'll include a nine numeric - letter code within each correspondence that you will verify. I'm sure the letters will reach each person quickly, even before you begin. I'll make all your travel arrangements." He paused to get Riley time to absorb the directions.

Riley finished off the rest of the Stella quickly with one big swig. "I'll buy one last round."

By 1:15 PM, two days after meeting with the old man, Riley stopped to fill up with gasoline and get a large Dunkin Donut black coffee. He headed toward Palomar Airport Road East. Soon he was on I-15 North toward Palm Desert. He reached into a collection of CDs to pick out a favorite by The Eagles - Hotel California. "On a dark desert highway, cool wind in my hair." He smiled as Don Henley continued to sing. He liked the free spirit, and in a bizarre way the sadness of it all.

In a little more than one hour he was on I-10 East, closing in on the final destination. Traffic was heavier than he anticipated. Drivers were careless as they disregarded common driving safety practices. He twisted his head to each side, heard a few snapping sounds, then, he shrugged his shoulders. The moves had worked in the past to relieve pressure, and it worked once again.

He felt a little excited when he spotted various billboards of all sorts on each side of the highway. While not the same as Las Vegas, still, there was a cheap thrill in reading the names of celebrities and casinos along the way. He figured he had about another forty minutes before he reached Cook Street.

As he closed in on the exit, he began to rehearse a few lines the best he could. He knew the importance of not trying to memorize everything, but just enough to cover the important points. Too much practice would result in his voice sounding insincere. He didn't want to be perceived as disingenuous. There was too much money at risk for him, yet he had no idea what the real stakes were.

To his right he spotted a billboard announcing open air shopping. It seemed to be some sort of street fair open to the public. Novelties, footwear, art, crafts, and hundreds of items were for sale at bargain prices. He wondered if he might stop to check it out later on. You don't know what you might find that could get an appearance on Antiques Road Show. He took in a deep breath of air, showed a little tiredness from the long drive.

An exit sign indicated Cook Street was one mile ahead. He pulled over to the right lane and prepared to get off the highway. He slowed down. Moments later he stopped at Cook Street, looked to his left, and then to his right where he spotted the Desert Hotel, the place the old man reserved a room for the night. The Full House was only a short drive away.

He turned into the parking lot of the Desert Hotel, found a spot that was well lit and was at a corner. No sense in chancing a dent from another vehicle's car door.

He leisurely walked to the entrance, only one bag in his hand. Inside, he headed to the check - in counter. A good looking woman greeted him with a warm welcome. Her name badge read Cassidi. He wondered if she was related to Hopalong.

"Hi, Cassidi, my name is Sullivan. One night, pre-paid." He looked at her more closely as thoughts of sensual fantasy passed through his mind. He wondered if the woman might be interested in him.

She dropped her eyes towards a computer screen to access room reservations. "Yes, Mr. Sullivan. We have your reservation. Please sign here." She placed a reservation form on the counter top for Riley to sign. "Do you think you'll be charging anything during your stay with us?

He continued to stare at her. Her smile was enchanting. "Uh, no, nothing, I'm only here for the night."

Her professional smile lingered on. "OK. Here is your key, room 207. Can I help you with anything else?"

He shared his true response only with himself. Then he said, "I don't know. What else might I ask for?"

She'd figured him out quickly. "Our dining room is presently open, and we serve breakfast starting at 5 AM." Her smile was now less inviting.

"Thank you. I think I'll just freshen up for now. I have an appointment tonight."

"Fine, let us know if we can be of any further service. Have a good evening." Cassidi held eye contact until he dropped his.

"Thanks." He had an hour to kill before meeting Leah Clare, so he headed to room 207 to prepare.

Not much to unpack for only one night; toiletries, underwear, socks, two shirts, and a novel by his favorite author titled Unintentional Consequences. There was no sense unpacking the other clothes he'd use for the other places he'd be traveling to this week. He'd use the same shoes and slacks tomorrow.

Riley sat on the queen size bed, kicked off his shoes, and clicked on the television. He quickly flipped through channels one after another with not much interest in what was on, just something to pass the time. About to end searching the channel selections, he stopped to watch what appeared to be a commercial.

"Can I help you?" A cocktail waitress held a small tray in her hands, pen poised to write down a drink order. Her face was golden tanned color, lips were succulent looking, and eyes were roasting with sensuality. However, Riley stared at the more prominent part of her body, breasts that begged to be comforted. He heard his stomach growl. The commercial continued. "At Casino Majestic, we aim to please. Come join in the fun. Only minutes away." An address appeared at the bottom of the screen. "Hurry, now. We're all waiting for you."

Riley continued to stare at the screen, now replaced with another commercial, this time promoting used vehicles. He pulled out of the trance, yet he continued sitting on the bed, blindly gazing at the screen. Another fifteen seconds passed until a third commercial appeared. He nodded his head sideways to cut off any further consideration of watching television. "That's enough." He turned off the television, tossed the remote control aside, and then, he flopped back on the bed. He stayed put for about fifteen minutes, then decided to change to a fresh shirt before the first appointment. He moved slowly.

As he passed the check - in counter, he glimpsed to see if Cassidi was present. He was disappointed to find a young guy taking care of new arrivals.

Now in his car, he pulled away from the corner parking space, hoping he'd find a similar spot once he arrived at his final destination. Once on the highway, traffic came to a wretched creep, moved at a snail's pace. What he expected to be a fifteen minute ride was now about thirty minutes. He was already late as he pulled into the parking lot.

As Riley walked into The Full House, he smelled alcohol and tobacco in the air. He stopped in place to take a look see.

The place was essentially a card gaming business that consisted of several gambling tables scattered about. There was one employee per table who acted as the house dealer for a specific card game. Players rented a seat at a table for one hour at a time, thus playing against other players as the house dealer dealt out the cards. Most players lost, the house often won. All the tables were occupied.

Cocktail waitresses strolled about offering complimentary drinks. The waitresses made their living off of tips - legally and otherwise. What you don't know won't hurt you, or so they say. There was a large restaurant with a full bar close by that had an assortment of live entertainment.

He saw several men to his left at the full bar drinking, smoking and talking as loud music gushed from an awful singer and backup band on stage. The unknown entertainer sang an exceptionally poor version of Percy Sledge's "When a Man Needs a Woman." No one seemed to care.

He spotted a couple of women in short dresses and heels waiting at the bar's edge for drinks they'd ordered for the card players. A few women walked around, gave him an inviting look. They were dressed provocatively, probably hookers, looking for work, and apparently not worried about being obvious about it. Nobody seemed to care at The Full House. Riley wondered what Leah Clare did here, the person he had the appointment with. He'd soon find out.

He smelled another aroma coming from some other place. He wasn't sure, but the smell was inviting. The surprisingly pleasant smell suddenly made him feel hungry. His thoughts were interrupted.

"Hi honey. Looking for something that I can help you with?"

He turned in the direction of the voice. He looked surprised at the woman who stood before him. There was nothing about her appearance that he found special, ordinary looking and conservatively dressed. He wondered what she was doing here.

Before he was able to say anything she continued. "I'm Leah Clare. I own this place, first time for you?"

"I'm Riley Sullivan. Sorry I'm late, miscalculated the traffic. Is there someplace we can talk privately?"

"Did you bring me something?" She was not interested in talking about the traffic, weather, or anything not related to the purpose of their meeting.

He looked confused.

"Matching codes, that's what the letter indicated. If we match the code, then we talk. No match, no talk."

"Oh, yeah. That's right." He dipped his hand into his pocket to yank out a piece of paper. "What's the code that you have? I'll show you mine if you show me yours." He thought the comment was funny.

She was all business. "Honey, I'm not much into cute things, and I'm definitely not looking for a comedian at this place."

His face reddened, "Got it." He waited for her to respond.

She continued, "S9MP1T93O."

He looked at the piece of paper, nodded his head. "It matches."

"What else have you got for me?"

He frowned, "I didn't know you were expecting something else."

"Just asking, you don't ask, you don't get." She smiled for the first time, yet her interests were all business. She nodded her head to his right. "Come this way. I've got a private office where we can talk." She headed away from him. He caught up quickly.

Leaving together, they seemed to be two people about

to conduct a normal business transaction, nothing more or less.

Still a few feet behind Leah, he heard, "Want something to drink or eat?"

The surprise question caused him to hesitate. Then he replied, "Well, I smelled something awfully good when I first came in. What was it?"

"Probably, it was our house chili. It's a special recipe I concocted myself. It's one of the regular items on the menu. Everyone loves it. I'm sure you will too. I'll order up a bowl for you. Do you drink?"

"Usually, it's beer."

"Good combination with chili." She opened a door, left it ajar for Riley to follow, and then she headed for a small desk where a phone rested. She picked it up, pressed 1, then 2. "Bring me a bowl of chili with two beers." As she returned the receiver to its cradle she said to Riley, "Only serve Dos Equis."

"That's fine with me," although he'd rather have a Stella. He followed her eyes as she directed him to take a seat opposite her.

As she slowly crossed her long slender legs he noticed for the first time an attractiveness that he had overlooked before. He wondered why.

They stared at each other for a short time until she spoke. "OK, enough of the small talk. What's this all about? I don't have all night."

He didn't have time to look around the room, but if he had, he'd have seen it cluttered with all sorts of things ranging from advertisement signs to odds and ends of broken equipment. A few rags were on the floor. There was a baseball bat against a corner of the room along with piles of paper on top of the desk. It all seemed disorganized, but the truth of the matter was Leah knew where everything was and everything had a purpose. "Should we close the door?"

"I'm OK with it open. I like having options." She paused. "You seem nervous. Relax. I'm not going to bite you."

As if on cue, an attractive server who wore a short dress and heels tapped on the opened door. "Can I come in?"

Leah looked up, "Iris, come in. Set the chili and beers on the desk. Thanks."

As Iris walked past Riley, he got a whiff of a perfume that pleased his senses. Iris left without further interaction.

Leah caught a glimpse of Riley's fascination. "She's off limits." She made it very clear.

Riley felt himself get worked up. It was now time for him to say something. He didn't notice that he smacked his lips while he stared at the chili and beers.

She saved him further embarrassment as she reached for a bottle. "Cheers." She took a small sip.

Unexpectedly, another woman knocked on the opened door. "Sorry to bother you Leah, but a few drunken guys are about to throw some punches at each other in the bar."

Without much fuss, Leah stood. "Excuse me. I've got

some important business calling my name." She grabbed the baseball bat as she walked past Riley. "Chili isn't good when it's cold." She glanced towards the bowl. "Be back shortly. Don't go anyplace."

He was still for a second or two. Then, when he was alone he grabbed the bottle of beer, took a sip, and then reset it on the desk. He reached for a soup spoon to sample the chili. He was amazed at how good it tasted. He ate the entire bowl without much hesitation, wondered about asking for a second helping, but decided against it. Now alone in Leah's office, he wondered about what he might have gotten himself into by agreeing with the old man. He took another drink from the bottle, this time a big gulp. A burp found its way out of his mouth, then a little gas from the other large aperture between his lower cheeks. He tried to settle down. He drank alone for a few more minutes, looked around the office to kill more time.

Leah returned with the baseball bat in hand. "What a bunch of dumbasses. Some people can't handle booze and should stay away from it. A few crazies arguing over which is better, a Camaro or a Mustang." She shook her head, "Who the fuck cares?"

She gently returned the bat to its original position as if the piece of wood was a rare piece of art. Then she looked at Riley, noticed the empty bowl. "I said you'd like it. I tell the truth." She leaned over to grab the bottle of beer closest to her, took another small sip of beer, and then smacked her lips.

Riley was prepared for the next statement, although

he didn't know what she already knew. "Tell me about the letter I received. I'm intrigued."

He cleared his throat. "There's not much further to explain. My client is seeking worthy beneficiaries to receive one hundred thousand dollars if they can prove the money will be given to a creditable and admirable cause. He has little time left to live and wants others to use his money wisely."

"Let me see if I understand this right. Your client, who I assume is a millionaire or at least has piles of money just accumulating dust, wants to give away his fortune to people he doesn't know, but who have some worthy cause. And you are supposed to figure out the lucky ones. Do I have it right, or am I missing something?"

"Well, that's only partially correct. I'm not the one who decides. My client decides. I just gather information and report to him."

"But, if you gather information, you also select which information you share with him and how you share it. I have to assume he will ask for your impressions." She waited to hear his answer.

Riley began to feel uneasiness grow inside. He figured the woman across from him was savvy. He was not able to hold back a grin. "I - I guess that's right. I mean, he is going to ask my opinion for sure, but I don't know how important that will be in his final decision. I really don't know."

"How did he select me? Who am I? Was it random?" The questions seemed innocent enough.

"I really don't know. All he told me was he narrowed

Antonio F. Vianna

the list to three people, and you were one of the three. Honest, that's all I know."

"What's your take in all of this?"

He frowned, not sure he wanted to answer.

She clarified, "I don't care how much money he is paying you." She waved her hand to emphasize the point. "I'm just interested to know why you are involved in this." Her eyes were glued to his. "Quite honestly, you don't seem real comfortable in these types of matters." She continued to look at him realizing his mind was running fast. "I told you I'm honest. I'm also direct. Usually I'm too honest and direct for most people."

He felt himself gasp for air, an emptiness down deep inside his stomach. He wasn't sure why he was experiencing the sensation. His knees began to wobble against one another a little. Fortunately he was still sitting. He had to settle down.

"Are you feeling OK? You've just gotten pale." She leaned forward.

"Yeah, yeah, sorry, something just came over me. Maybe it's the chili, spicier than what I'm accustomed to."

She decided to comfort him in spite of wanting to go in another direction. "Right, the chili gets getting used to."

He reached to take hold of the Dos Equis, took a sip, and felt better surprisingly quickly. "Just a few questions I need to ask, if that's OK."

"Sure, if that's what it takes, the one hundred thousand dollar questions." She smiled broadly. This time it seemed she was enjoying the exchange.

Perfectly looking teeth took center stage. She must have a good dentist.

"How did you get to be the owner of a place like this?"

"That's a strange question. Does this business offend you, is that why you're asking?"

"Oh, no ... it's, well ... not what I expected. I mean ... these places are ... rough. You know."

"Sure, places like this are rough, no two ways about it, but I'm still not following you." She knew exactly where he was headed and enjoyed taunting him for a while longer.

"I mean, don't you think that these kinds of places are more often run by men?"

"So, you're surprised that a woman owns and operates a card gambling club. Is that it?"

"Yeah, I guess I am."

"The world isn't what it used to be."

"I know, but how did you get into this business? That's really my question."

She leaned back in the chair. "When my cheating shit head husband was killed in a hit and run, I took over the business. I figured I could do anything he could do and do it better. This was a rundown place when I got it. Employees were stealing him blind, bills were piling up, and the place was literally falling apart. Within one year I turned it around to a profitable business. I'm an example of a true American entrepreneur. I have twenty full time employees who are offered health benefits and a handful of independent contractors." Her eyes squinted, just enough to underscore how proud she was of the accomplishment.

"I didn't mean to offend you. I...."

"Don't mention it. What else do you want to know, but hurry up because this is a busy night?"

"What would you do with the one hundred thousand dollars?"

Without much hesitation Leah said, "Make sure as many children in America get basic education. I'd probably adopt an elementary or high school in the County and buy books and stuff for them."

"Really, wow, that's great to hear!"

"It's all bullshit." She grabbed the bottle nearest to her, took a long sip as she kept a smirk all the time. She saw the surprise look on Riley's face. "Listen to me. I don't know what your client is up to, but I think he's a wacko. I'm nowhere near being at the top of anyone's list of worthy people. I run a profitable place where people play cards, gamble, eat and drink. I try to stay one step ahead of the bill collectors. I look the other way so people can make a living. I've done some things in life that most people would consider unsavory. I'm at times unpleasant, nasty, and even sleazy." She checked her watch. "Now, it's time to get back to work. I'm sorry you came out all this way. You're more than welcome to stay here and enjoy what I offer." She stood, took one more sip of beer, and then reset it on the desk. She pointed towards the opened door.

"But I've got a few more questions to ask." His voice sounded desperate. He wasn't sure if he'd accumulated enough information to satisfy the old man. He didn't think so. Further, he didn't want to give the old man any reason to reduce his five thousand dollar fee. Mentally he had already spent the money. He opened his mouth to persuade her to answer a few more questions, but he got cut off.

She stared at him with icy eyes. It was clear to Riley the meeting was over. He left without further comment.

Alone, Leah made a call from her cell phone to someone who was expecting an update of the meeting. It took less than one minute, and then she disconnected and left her office.

As he passed through The Full House, he hesitated to wonder if he should have gone back to finish asking the remaining questions. It took him but a short time to decide otherwise. He considered another option. Maybe he'd just hangout a while to see what happened? It could be an interesting night.

Then, all of a sudden, he noticed one of those women he saw before walking around give him an inviting look. She puckered her lips, and then her eyebrows flickered a few times. Come hither, she communicated. She was dressed with little left for the imagination.

His heart began to pump faster. He got a whiff of vanilla as she came closer to him. "Want some fun?" In the background he heard another awful rendition of an oldie but goodie, this time it was Bill Withers' "Ain't No Sunshine."

While he'd never done it before, there was always a first time. He thought about it too long as she concluded he'd be more of a problem than what it would be worth. She moved along to another guy at the bar.

Riley frowned, not sure what just happened, so he too decided to move along. His thoughts then returned to the conversation with Leah. While he hadn't prepared for anything like this, he wondered if there was some truth to her claim. Was the old man a wacko?

He stepped outside into the night. The air was fresh so he took in a deep breath, and then walked towards the car. He checked his watch, figured there was still time for a good dinner. He headed towards the Desert Hotel. The return trip was quicker for some reason. He found a similar parking spot at another corner of the lot, so he swerved into the open space.

At about 7 AM the next day, his eyes opened, he squinted to see the ceiling. Memories from yesterday's meeting with Leah tumbled through his head like pieces of clothes bumping into each other in a dryer. He was not totally sure what to tell the old man what happened so he slowly headed to clean up. Maybe a shower would freshen up his thoughts.

After cleaning up, he was about to make the call to the old man when the room's phone rang. He picked up.

"Where have you been?" The old man's voice was stern as if he was questioning his son who'd stayed out later than his curfew.

"I was tired, and went to bed early. I guess the long drive took more out of me than I thought it would."

"Bull ... shit." He paused, labored breathing split the word. "You're too young to let a two to three hour drive tire you out. Something else happened."

Riley stuck to his guns. "No, nothing else happened. Sorry to disappoint you." He heard the sound of his voice flavored with a little sarcasm. He wondered where that attitude came from and if the old man picked up on it.

"Don't get sharp with me. Remember who's paying you."

Riley was tempted to tell him that what he did on his own time was his business, but decided against it. The truth was he was on the old man's clock. Instead he said, "Do you want to hear what happened with Leah Clare?"

There was a pause between the two men, each deciding what the next move might be.

"OK, have it your way. Tell me what happened with the Clare woman."

"I'll say it as simply as possible. She thinks you're a wacko." He wondered if the old man had a hailstorm of insults to throw back at him, so Riley gave him an opportunity to smack back. He was surprised at what he heard the old man say.

"When I was a boy, much younger than you, I witnessed a pedestrian get run down by a drunken driver, killed on impact. The police and ambulance arrived quickly, but there was nothing they could do. The man who was killed was homeless. He was simply looking for food alongside the road when the drunk hit him. It was all over with so suddenly. They put the dead man in a black bag along with all his possessions that he had been carrying with him at the time. It looked like a garbage bag, what you use to dump your garbage in. I doubt whether anyone claimed his body. I felt this sense of nothingness then, and wondered if that's what I would feel when my time was up, whether anyone would care if I lived or died." He coughed a few times.

Riley stayed silent, staggered by the story, and surprised that the old man shared the early experience with him. He thought how difficult it must have been for the old man when he was young, and could only imagine how the presumably long-buried incident had impacted him now.

He tried to come up with a story of his own, to find something in common with the old man, but came up short in the end. He kept quiet.

The old man continued, but in an even more subdued tone. "I've heard that before, being called a wacko. It's nothing new to my ears. What else happened?"

Riley cleared his throat before he answered. "She owns quite a place, a little rougher crowd than of my choosing, but none-the-less I'd say a much more profitable business in spite of what she claimed. I think she runs it with an iron hand, is constantly putting out fires, but just the same enjoys what it brings."

The old man's tone-down voice quickly escalated to harsh sounding that surprised Riley. "And what do you think that is?" The old man interrupted.

Riley recovered from the change in the tenor of old man's voice. "In one word, challenge, I think she really likes a good challenge."

Riley did not see the old man smile and mumble to himself something, although he heard another cough.

"Would you say she is deserving of my money?" His voice was no longer harsh.

"Not a definite yes or no."

With a raised voice once again, he said, "Boy, give me something definite!"

"Maybe, I really don't know," Riley was not able to more definitive even when pressed hard.

Frustrated the old man said, "Have it your way, I've made up my mind."

"What is it?"

"That's my little secret." He grinned to himself. "The next person is Adrianne Browde. Do you have the address?"

"Yes."

"What about your ticket?"

"Got it, it's right here."

"You better get moving so you don't miss your flight." His voice was stern, and he had a terrible way of being right. "You're on my clock."

Riley heard the phones disconnect. He said out loud into the phone receiver, "You sure know how to take a nothing day and make it worse. What's your problem?" Then, he suddenly felt the urge to even the score so he slammed the receiver harder onto its cradle, glared at the instrument as if it was the source of his anger.

He paced back and forth for a few moments thinking. At least the old man didn't mention his disappointment in the amount of information he provided. Riley thought his fee was still in tack.

Then, without giving it much thought, he flipped on the television to sidetrack his emotion.

"Alert, if you or someone you know has had a hip replacement using JUST products or services call this number to see if you are eligible for a financial settlement. Can now or it might be too late." He stared at the 800 number prominently displayed on the television screen.

Riley shook his head in disgust before he turned off the television. "Everybody is out to get something from somebody."

Suddenly he felt hungry. He decided to have a full breakfast before he set out for the San Diego International Airport - Lindbergh Field.

3

He parked his car in one of those secured distant parking lots, and took a shuttle to the Airport Terminal. United Airlines Flight 707 was scheduled to depart in two hours, sufficient time for him to make his way through security, although inconvenient just the same.

There was a super long line of passengers preparing to be scanned or full body searched. No one seemed real enthused about it all, but you had to do what you had to do. He got in place, reached for his ticket and passport as if the move would hurry along the process. No such luck. Passengers inched slowly along, grumbled all the time. Contrary to a promise he made to himself, he joined in, complained to the next person behind him. He checked his watch, disappointed no more than fifteen minutes had gone by and yet he'd only moved less than five yards.

He stretched his neck to get a better view of the final destination point, the dreaded body scanning machines. He, along with several other passengers witnessed one of those instances that would probably make it to the nightly news, definitely to YouTube, MetaCafe, or DailyMotion, since several people videoed the incident with their cell phones. Malfunctioning electronic equipment, confused and seemingly ill trained T. S. A. Agents, along with uncooperative passengers all piled up into a medley of shouts and screams that was second to none.

An outraged man flung a few barbed comments after he removed his prosthesis that replaced part of left leg. "Here, take it! Inspect it! Respect it! This is what I get for protecting you during the war!" He stared down the T. S. A. Agent, noticeably embarrassed by the scene.

"I'm just doing my job." There was sorrowfulness in his voice as if he would have changed the protocols if he could, but he couldn't. He was just following orders. But aren't we all, one way or another?

Another twenty minutes passed as the line of people, for some reason, seemed to move with greater rapidity. Finally, Riley met his maker.

"Step forward," the Agent said as she waved him through the detectors. Riley hesitated for a split second as if he was thinking of making a scene, then he decided it was not worth it. He stepped into the scanning booth, followed the orders of the Agent, and looked straight ahead. He wondered what the other Agent sitting only a short distance away saw on his computer screen. It all belonged to him, it was his stuff. It was all over within less than fifteen seconds as the Agent motioned him to move along. Riley happily did as he was told. Now that it was all over, he put that stage of the flight out of his mind.

He walked towards Gate 71. Somehow through it all, all travelers made it through the security check on time to catch their respective flights.

The flight, remarkably smooth and uneventful, was just the way it ought to be but rarely was. United Airlines Flight Number 707 touched down five minutes early at the Albany International Airport in Albany, New York.

Riley moved quickly, holding one carryon bag in his left hand, headed for the rental car section on ground level at the far end of the Airport. He maneuvered his way to the Hertz counter much before other passengers arrived. He wanted to get on his way as quickly as possible.

With incredible courtesy from the Agent, he got through the paperwork swiftly. While the Hertz Agent assured him that purchasing extra emergency roadside assistance was necessary, Riley figured it was not worth it. He refused the extra coverage much to the Agent's chagrin. He shoved the paperwork into his carryon bag and took the key for a black Ford Fusion that he was told waited for him in row 21. He drove off.

It was 11:00 PM and he felt weary. Fortunately, with clear directions from the Hertz Agent, Riley found the Albany Airport Inn, only a few miles drive away. He dragged his body to check in. A young looking male was on duty, probably one of those college kids doing his best to pay tuition, books, and fees for the semester. Not much conversation exchanged between the two fellows as each was eager to just get through it all. The kid probably had a few more chapters to read for tomorrow's classes and Riley wanted a good night's sleep before he met Adrianne Browde. He was sound asleep right before midnight. However, his sleep was restless. He dreamed.

Riley ran as fast as his legs allowed, yet it didn't seem to be fast enough as the stranger behind him closed in. He shifted his head just enough around to get a glimpse of the person running after him, but sweat from his brow dripped over his eyes.

"Why am I being chased? Who is the person after me?" He had no idea. He heard his own breathing, first shallow, then deep and controlled, now become thin again. He felt his chest ache and his legs sting. His arms felt tired. He had to go on, to keep ahead.

Then he heard a voice call out his name, a sound that was familiar. He twisted his head to the right, and then to the left, but he saw no one. He was convinced the call must have been from behind, from the person following him. He turned again to get a glimpse of the one behind.

This time he thought he recognized the chaser. "This can't be!" he said. The voice from behind was stronger, louder, closer. "This can't be!" he repeated.

Riley stumbled from the realization. His legs gave way as he fell to the ground. Face down his breathing slowed a bit, but not enough to prevent sucking in debris through his nose. He coughed. Then there was silence. He hesitated to check see if he was alone.

Then, slowly, with a great deal of apprehension, he got to one knee. He lifted his head ever so slightly. Standing before him was an image of himself!

Riley woke up. His body was sweaty. He was too wound up to get back to sleep. It was safer, he thought, to stay awake for a while. He threw the bed cover off his body, and then he stood only wearing boxer shorts. He began a slow pace around the room to calm himself down. It took a great deal longer to wear off agitation than he would have liked, yet the physical activity eventually worked. He returned to bed, resolved to get back to sleep. However, even the best plans are often never materialized. He remained awake for the next few hours. Around 3:00 AM, he finally dozed off even though his sleep was on and off.

Around 7:00 AM, he decided the struggle was not worth it, so he headed for the shower to ready himself for the scheduled meeting.

The sky above was an ugly gray that threatened to provide a heavy layer of rain for the next few days. He gambled he would not need an umbrella in spite of never being good at wagering. Following directions to Route 7 - Troy Schenectady Road, he headed to Post Avenue in Schenectady, where Foremost University was located. The University was one of the four original Ivy League Universities, but when they enrolled students who lived in the South who sympathized with the Confederates, Foremost U got booted out of the League. Go figure.

As he drove, he began to think through the questions he'd ask Adrianne Browde. However, he was distracted by the dramatic differences between the California coast and upper New York State. There were many more mountains and valleys there, and he also noticed the variety of

Dutch names such as Rotterdam and Vanderlyn. He snapped out of that particular train of thought in enough time to organize his ideas for the upcoming important interview.

He parked the Ford Fusion in the visitor parking area at about the time a light drizzle began. He ran as fast as he could to Cropsey Memorial Library and Museum, one of New York State's oldest library and museum that included more than fifty paintings and oil sketches, and over one hundred letters, photographs, and other materials about the Hudson River Valley and Mohawk River Valley. He stepped inside just in the nick of time before the light rain turned to a downpour. He looked around to find a service desk.

A perky female coed greeted him. "Hi, how can I help you?" The curve of her smile and the gleam from her eyes were warm.

"I think I just made it inside in time."

She giggled a little. "We were expecting rain. It's that time of year."

"I see." He paused. "I'm actually looking for someone, Adrianne Browde. Do you know her?"

"Oh, yes. Everyone knows Adrianne. She's been here for ages." Her eyes widened with greater glitter than before. Her name badge read Amie.

"I see. Is she here now?"

"She's actually giving a tour." The coed looked at her watch. "She should be finished up shortly. Care to have a seat. I'll tell you when she finishes." She kept a warm smile Riley's way.

"Thanks, Amie. I'll just stand over there." He pointed to a spot a few yards away.

A loud crack of thunder resonated inside the building. Riley jumped. His face reddened just enough to be noticeable by Amie. He heard her chuckle. A second booming sound had the same effect on him as before. His eyes widened as he turned toward Amie and shook his head. "Do you ever get used to this?"

"Sure, like most things. If you do the best you can do, then the rest is out of your control." She paused. "There will always be another one."

As if on cue, another rumble bellowed out.

"See what I mean?" Another giggle accompanied the comment.

Riley took in a deep breath. "This rarely happens in California."

"Is that where you're from?"

"Yeah, Carlsbad, which is near San Diego."

"I've never been to California ... would like to though ... one of these days ... maybe after I graduate ... maybe not." She raised her shoulders, seemingly not sure about it all.

Riley wondered if the conversation was only meant to kill some time with a visitor, nothing more. He was about to continue when Amie said, "Ah, there she is." She pointed to an elderly woman who was leading a group of people towards the service desk.

"I hope you enjoyed our journey today. The service desk

has a variety of interesting literature about the University and the two Valleys, as well as a good assortment of gifts and souvenirs should you wish to purchase anything. Thank you for your interest in Foremost University, the Hudson River Valley and Mohawk River Valley." Adrianne Browde folded one hand over the other as she held a sincere smile. The guests applauded in thanks as she slightly bowed her head.

As the guests mingled about, she heard her name called. "Adrianne, there is someone to see you." She looked at Amie, who pointed towards Riley.

He stepped forward, and extended his hand. "I'm Riley Sullivan. I hope you've been expecting me." He was surprised to see a slight frown take over her face.

"Yes. I received his letter." Her voice was solemn, not the cheerful type he had hoped for. She knew something that Riley should know but didn't.

"Is this a good time, or perhaps later is better?"

"I suppose I could take a break now." At first she seemed unsure of a decision, but after a pause she turned towards Amie. "Mr. Sullivan and I will be together for a short while in the Dutchmen room in case you need me." Then she stepped away all the while assumed Riley would follow.

Once inside the small room, she slowly closed the door. "What's this all about?" Her voice was more like a mother questioning her son after he'd been found out of doing something naughty. Her back remained towards him for a short time, covering her irritation. Slowly she turned, in sync with a change to a neutral looking facial expression. She forced a smile that was easily deciphered by Riley.

"Did you receive a letter introducing me and the purpose of my visit?" His voice was a little coarse. He wondered if it was from a lack of sleep, the effects of the cross-country trip, or the symptoms of a cold making its way through his system.

"Yes." Her voice was flat. Her face now suggested impartiality, yet below the facial appearance she was predisposed to make this meeting as short as possible. She knew what was going on and had other priorities.

"Do you want to compare each other's code?"

"That won't be necessary. Can you move this along a little faster? I have another tour in fifteen minutes."

"Of course," he cleared his throat. "Then you know that my client has identified you as a possible recipient of one hundred thousand dollars with only a few strings attached. All he wants me to do is to ask you a few questions, and then report to him our discussion." He paused, wondered if she had something to ask. He interpreted silence as a signal to continue. "OK, then. Here is my first question. What would you do if you received one hundred thousand dollars?" A pen was poised along with a note pad to record her answer.

She started off with a grin, figured to give him some morsels of information. She knew who sent him and would rather tell Riley to leave, yet, she decided it might be worth a few minutes of her time to play along. "As you might have noticed, I'm a woman of age, not a young one who has most of her life ahead. I've lived many years, experienced much, and learned quite a lot. I've done just the right amount of wrong." She smiled as if she was proud of getting into a little mischief during her day. "I've been married and then divorced. I decided not to remarry but to move away from California to a more peaceful place as here. I have two wonderful daughters, just about your age. They've developed into two very different types of people, but whom I love very much." She paused again to make sure he'd taken in the information. Then she continued. "I've done very well with investments, and along with a monthly Social Security check I receive on schedule, I'm financially in quite good shape. I travel when I want, take in the theater in New York City along with a few select friends, and offer educational information to guests who come to this marvelous place. So, you might say, I'm a happy camper." She pinched her lips ever so slightly. Eyes were still squarely focused on Riley as he continued to jot down notes. "So, to answer your question, what I would do with the money. That's not as easy to answer as it might seem. You see, I'm not a frivolous person. I take great care to think out what I want to do before I do it. I don't mean to be flippant, but I am a serious woman. You could even say somewhat calculating." This time, she paused for a longer time.

Riley took the temporary halt to ask a question. "So, you don't know what you would do with the money?" He lifted his eyes to meet with hers.

"No, I didn't say that. What I said was I carefully

think through what I want to do and how to do it before I ever do it." Her voice sounded as if she was schooling a child.

"Yes, I'm sorry. I see." He quickly scribbled through a few lines.

"They say never to believe the tears of a woman or the legs of a limping dog." She paused to calculate his response, and then asked, "Do you know what that means?"

Riley stopped writing, and looked up. A frown covered his face. "No, I've never heard that saying. What does it mean?"

"What do you think it means?"

His hesitation prompted encouragement from her. "Take a guess, any guess."

"I really have no idea."

"Then, take a wild stab." Her eyes opened wider than normal. She was getting a little impatient with his lack of cooperation.

"Ah. It could mean to be careful what you see, that what you see might not be true." Another pause, and then he took up again with another possible interpretation. "Symptoms are not causes, so be sure to differentiate a warning sign from a reason." He felt energized, so he offered another option. "Don't let emotions rule decision making. Don't necessarily feel sorry for a woman when she cries or when a dog limps. They both could be very dangerous in defending themselves. They might be hiding something." He beamed with pleasure as if he'd just overcome a big problem.

"Very good," she nodded her head ever so slightly. Yet,

in the end, she concluded he had no idea what he'd gotten himself involved in.

A little disappointed the exchange did not continue he said, "OK, then, let's get back to the question. What would you do with the money?"

"After taxes, I'd only have about sixty seven thousand dollars, maybe less. I might simply donate it to this University's museum and library. There are a few things that could use some renovation."

"OK." He finished off with a few more notes. "Let's move onto another question." He was about to pose a second query but was interrupted.

"This is all the time I have." She glanced at her watch. "I have another tour in less than two minutes." She stood, pointed her hand to the closed door. "I'm sorry. We seemed to have run out of time."

Riley was not deterred. "Can I schedule another time with you? There are only a few more questions."

She answered, "They say you shouldn't believe the sound of another's voice ... but in this case, you should."

"I - I ...." He was desperate to continue. There was more information he wanted to give the old man. Riley again thought about the possibility of losing his fee for the job.

"This way," She said as she opened the door, and then she headed down the hall towards the service desk where another coed who had replaced Amie waited. Several guests hung around patiently for the next tour.

Steps behind, Riley followed Adrianne, disappointed that he had not finished asking all the questions he

, intended to ask. There was not much more he could do if she was unwilling to cooperate. He decided to make sure to include that part in his notes when he reported to the old man. He walked past the service desk, disappointed Amie had been replaced with another person. He'd like to have gotten to know her a little better.

Riley stepped outside in the rain. He wished it would stop. Then he geared up to run towards the Ford Fusion. Without an umbrella the downpour got the best of him. He slid into the driver's seat partially soaked, started the engine, and then he drove towards the Airport where he'd return the car, change into dryer clothes, finish off his notes, and make a call to the old man. The next flight to Albuquerque, New Mexico was not until later on tonight, so he had enough time to think through the upcoming meeting.

If he had made the arrangements, he'd given himself another day in Albany to recover from the cross country flight. It wasn't his decision. The old man scheduled everything.

Tension and frustration intensified as he wondered if the old man was using him to achieve a much different motive than his current assignment. He'd like to pack it in right then, but knew that wouldn't happen. He'd finished two of the three interviews, and soon he'd return to Carlsbad to collect his fee.

He sat in one of those small chairs in the waiting area at Gate 37 that seemed to have been constructed for children. He figured the chair size was meticulously calculated to ensure passengers didn't spend too much time waiting, rather keep them moving along as quickly as possible. It might be his imagination but the airplane seat seemed to be a little snug as well. He moved to more important matters as he reviewed his notes before making the all important phone call to the old man.

He looked around for a phone with a landline, preferred to make a collect call without using his cell phone. Nothing was visible at first, so he took a little walk. Minutes later he found a bank of phones but all were occupied, so he decided to pull out his cell phone to make the call. After two rings he heard the old man's voice.

"Yeah," the sound was not inviting.

"It's me, Riley."

"Holy cow, what a surprise," it seemed the old man couldn't stay away from tossing a sarcastic remark. It was becoming more frequent.

Riley decided it was best to ignore the mocking comment. He was too close to completing the business arrangement, and just wanted it to end with no complications. "I finished talking with Adrianne Browde, a remarkable woman in my opinion."

"How so," the old man seemed to be sincerely interested in knowing more.

"She appears to be quite intelligent with a decent sense of humor. Has done financially well for herself and seems quite happy. I sort of like her, and I wish I had more time with her. I didn't get a chance to ask everything I wanted to."

"Hoop-de-do," the old man couldn't pass up another opportunity. "What will she do with the money?"

"She made that point very clear. She'd donate it to the University's library and museum she works at for some sort of renovation. I find that a decent cause, not selfish at all."

"What else did she say?"

"I'm not sure how important this is but she presented a saying and asked me to interpret it."

"Why do you think she did that?"

"I have no idea."

"Any chance she was testing you?"

"Hum, I never thought of it that way, maybe, but why would she test me?"

"What do you think?"

"I really don't know. I guess I have to think about that some more."

"You do that." The old man coughed. "What was the saying?"

"They say never to believe the tears of a woman or the legs of a limping dog."

"Interesting," the old man said. Under his breath he continued, "I wonder what she is up to?" Then he said to Riley, "What else?"

"I don' think there is anything else."

"How sure are you," asked the old man one more time to be sure.

Riley cleared his throat, "I'm positive, nothing else."

"So, you found out nothing more. Is that what you are saying?"

"Yes, that's what I just said, nothing more. I'm sorry," said Riley, seemingly apologetic.

"Oh, don't be sorry," answered the old man.

"Why?" Riley was confused.

"The fact that you've not discovered anything more means there is much being concealed."

Riley heard the phones disconnect.

Riley's patience with the old man continued to fade. He'd had just about enough of the put downs, cutting remarks, jabs, and digs he could take. He sure wanted to abandon what was left of the job, but then again, he remembered the financial implications. "Why did I ever agree to this?"

He realized he was standing adjacent to one of those coffee carts that sold overpriced and unappetizing beverages and snacks. He took a debit card from his wallet, readied to buy a large black coffee.

"Sorry, we don't accept debit or credit cards, only cash." She appeared uninvolved in the dialog, just repeated a few memorized words that have been practiced again and again.

For some people, it is easy to remain detached.

He frowned. "Cash only?" Another disappointment came his way.

The girl at the kiosk pointed to a small sign barely

visible to customers. She lifted her shoulders as to say *not my rule, just obeying orders.*

He reluctantly dug into his pocket to pull out a five dollar bill, and then waited for a small amount of change. He noticed her eyes shift to a jar labeled, **Thanks for the Tip,** as she dropped a few quarters and nickels into his palm. He hesitated before he let fall everything into the jar. He'd just about given up hope to be around reasonable people.

"Thanks," she said. Then she moved to the next person in line. "Next customer, how can I help you?"

Riley took a sip of the tepid beverage as he stepped away. The disappointing frown on his face explained the displeasure with the coffee and his life in general.

He gazed around to spot an empty seat. He spotted a tall, thin man with gray hair and a full mustache. He was distinguished looking, and he sat in a chair.

Next to him was a woman with red hair that was all tightly wrapped together on top of her head. It looked like a nest for a family of birds. She appeared much younger than him, a daughter perhaps, but more likely someone who was along to keep him company until he passed on.

Riley wondered if he'd get to that point in his life at some future time.

The distinguished looking man and the woman with the bird nest on her head did not seem much interested in each other. They simply stared off into some place in space.

Riley moved his eyes away from the couple, and looked around further. He was not searching for anyone specifically but he noticed someone else in particular. There was another man dressed in black clothes starring down like a priest on his parishioners. It seemed he was trying to smile but the corners of his mouth did not cooperate. He touched his cheek, and then quickly he moved his hand to join the other hand on his lap. His fingers progressed from bead to bead as his lips barely move. Then, without warning, he looked straight up at Riley.

Both men stared at each other for a while before Riley turned and started to walk away. He didn't look back. There was something eerie about the man in black that frightened him.

Sometimes it is better not to look back.

Southwest Flight 1023 took off on time. Riley was securely strapped in seat 17C. It was well after sunset when the plane landed at Albuquerque International Airport.

He rushed to check out a rental car, fatigue was getting the best of him. Then he drove to El Rio Inn for the night. Too wiped out for much of anything else, he headed straight to bed and fell asleep quickly. The next day's wakeup call came too soon.

After a good breakfast, he headed West on Highway 40. The dark blue sky joining the distant desert red hills created a dramatic landscape. He pressed down on the accelerator to hasten the trip to a trailer park just past Gallup. He spotted the place to his right, pulled off the road, and settled the car into a stop as he thought through his next step.

He had an uneasy feeling. Was meeting Flo Hobare in this run down place something to do with it or was it something else? He was not sure, so he gave up trying to figure it out.

He drove into the trailer park, Western Sky. This was his last interview so he decided to finish it off as quickly as possible. He anticipated getting back to the comfort of his place in Carlsbad.

The dirt road was almost too narrow for two way traffic. He was happy no one was coming in the opposite direction. He stretched his neck to figure out the address but that too was difficult as most trailer homes were unmarked. People walked around, looked at him suspiciously. They knew he was not from the area. He tried to give off a smile, but that further created more doubts in their minds.

To his left were two small children who played with something on the ground, an object he couldn't make out. They seemed to be happy.

Further up was a woman who hung clothes on a line to dry. With two wooden clothes pins in her mouth she followed him with her eyes. He almost stopped to ask for Flo's address but decided against it.

Behind him he spotted an old Chevy, without license plates, nearby. He wondered if he was being followed. He

Antonio F. Vianna

wondered if he was safe. He wondered if he should forget about this part of the assignment. However, he moved on just the same. The Chevy pulled into a small parking space in front of a trailer home. One man got out, threw on the dirt what little remained of a cigarette. He paid Riley no attention as he stepped up to open the front door of the trailer home. Soon he was out of sight. Riley continued to search for Flo.

Next he saw a young boy who stood alongside the dirt road as he held an empty bag. The boy looked friendly, so Riley decided to ask for help.

"Excuse me."

The boy smiled. His reddish colored face and dark brown eyes gave him a peaceful look. He remained quiet and still.

"I wonder if you know where Flo Hobare lives." Riley's optimism was dashed when the boy remained quiet, so he asked again. "Do you know where Flo Hobare lives?" His voice was louder this time as the boy continued to stare his way.

"Don't you talk to no strangers!"

Riley turned to the sound of a new voice.

"Get along. A large sized woman dressed in an oversized shirt and baggy pants continued looking at the young boy. She was barefooted. "I said, go now."

The young boy with the empty bag dashed off leaving Riley alone with the large sized woman. She turned to face Riley, but remained silent.

Before he talked he cleared his throat. "Good morning. I wonder if you tell me where Flo Hobare lives."

The large sized woman continued to look intently at Riley, and then said, "You not from 'round here."

"No I'm not. But I am looking for Flo Hobare. Do you know where she lives?"

"You gonna take her away?"

"No. I just want to talk with her."

"About what," she was suspicious.

Riley said, "That's really between her and me."

She gazed his way without saying another word for a few seconds. Then she slowly said, "She's a good woman, means no harm, keeps to herself." She repeats, "Means no harm."

Riley answered, "I'm sure she is. Where does she live?"

The large woman figured Riley was not dangerous. "Two down, this side." She pointed in the direction of a faded green color trailer home.

"Thank you." He drove off as the large woman continued to watch him. He found a place that seemed to be a parking spot next to Flo's trailer, shut off the engine, and stepped outside. He made his way to the front door and knocked twice. At first there was no answer, so he knocked again.

"Comin'! Hold your horses!" The voice was scratchy sounding, perfect for singing the blues but not much else.

Riley waited until a woman about his age opened the door. A screen door separated the two people.

"Who you," Flo wasn't sure who she was speaking to.

"I'm Riley Sullivan. Did you get the letter stating I'd be visiting you?" He continued to look at her. Something was very different about the woman other than her voice. "Can I come in?"

"You gonna pay me?"

"No, I'm not paying anyone. That includes you."

"Then, I got nothin' to say." She shut the door.

"Hey, don't do that. Please."

A few minutes passed as Riley waited outside. He noticed from the corner of his eye the large woman still peering his way, so he turned. "Tell her I'm not going to hurt her. I just want to talk."

"Flo, let the man in, he's got somethin' to say."

Slowly the door opened again, and then she slightly pushed open the screen door to signal Riley to enter. He stepped forward.

By the time Riley was inside the trailer, Flo had made her way to a rocking chair. He looked around, depressed at the squalor inside. She pushed back and forth at a steady pace. He noticed her messy appearance, disheveled at every level. He wondered if she noticed his gawk, but not for long.

"What you lookin' at?"

"I'm sorry. Can I sit down?"

"Make yourself at home." She fixed her eyes on him, wary all the while.

Riley figured the best plan was to jump right into it. "Did you receive the letter, the one that indicated I'd be coming to visit you?"

She continued with the rocking motion, "Yeah." She

figured a one word answer was sufficient for the time being.

"Good. That's good. Do you want to compare the code on your letter with the one that I have? You know, to make sure that I'm legitimate and all."

"Should I?"

"That's only if you want to. It's entirely up to you."

"Nah, let's forget 'bout that." She began to massage her right leg just above the knee. The kneading comforted her, took away some of the pain. She noticed Riley checking it out. "Quadriceps, stepped on one of those IED's durin' the war. Docs say I'll have a permanent limp, less than forty-five degree motion with this leg. The other one got off with less damage." She shifted her unhappy eyes to look at him directly.

"I'm sorry," he said in an apologetic manner.

"Not more than me. Only get three hundred thirty dollars a month from the V. A. Not much to live on, but it's more than zero." She seemed so much older now.

Life's experiences can do that to you.

Riley took in a deep breath. He felt apologetic, for some reason, for her situation but there wasn't really anything he could do to change what's already happened. He decided to return to the purpose of the visit. "So, you know why I'm here." He waited for an affirmative response that was confirmed when she nodded yes. "Great. So, you know that my client is prepared to give you one hundred thousand dollars if he believes you are worthy of the gift. No strings attached, and nothing you have to do. It's yours, free and clear." He waited again for Flo to nod.

"Understand, too good to be true." She blinked a few times. Flo seemed to be warming up.

"OK, then. I have a few questions. Are you ready?"

Without saying a word, she lifted her body from the rocker, turned and headed towards a back room. It took her a while to return all the while Riley sat, confused by it all. Then, suddenly Flo pointed a revolver his way.

He felt a big lump in his throat. His eyes bulged wide. Words were blocked from coming forth, yet he wanted to say *Oh hell.*

Flo lowered the revolver as she returned to the rocking chair. Her body flopped into the seat. "Gotta protect myself from aliens, they're all 'round us. Look like you and me, but they can change the way they look at any time. Have you seen any?" The gun now rested on her lap.

Riley took a deep gulp of needed air. He realized Flo was not only physically injured from serving her country but also mentally impaired. He felt the corners of his eyes get moist, wondered if she spotted the watery appearance. With as quick of a move as he could, he swiped his eyes dry. He figured not to answer the alien question, so he pushed on. He wondered how she would answer the next question, "What would you do with one hundred thousand dollars?"

Her mouth began to slow slight curves at the corners as her eyes looked upward to nothing in particular. "I'd buy me a nice dress and real expensive pair of shoes." She paused as her face broadened to a full smile. "I'd have my hair done just right."

Riley's eyes focused on her lips, seemingly turned

lush and fresh. He returned her smile with one of his own, something she didn't notice. He didn't want to interrupt her revelry, but he did not know what to do, so he remained quiet for a while longer. Then, he noticed the chair stop rocking and Flo's head tilted forward. She seemed to have suddenly dozed off.

As quietly as possible, he stood and walked towards her. He leaned close to Flo, removed the revolver from her hands, and replaced the gun with some of the money he had in his pocket. He put the gun on a table some distance away. Then, he left her peacefully resting.

***

The return drive to Albuquerque International Airport was painful. He couldn't get the image of Flo out of his mind. There wasn't anything he could do, yet he felt responsible for part of her condition. It was after noon time when he pulled into the car rental lot at the Airport. He made his way inside the Terminal to check in, but was interrupted with a phone call.

Before Riley was able to say hello, the old man started it off. "How did it go?" His voice was angry as a coiled snake ready to strike its victim.

It took Riley a while to collect his thoughts before he began. "Did you know she's a disabled veteran?"

"What's that got to do with anything?"

His mind jumped back from the snake's initial attack. Then he readied himself to launch an attack of his own, but quickly decided against it. No sense cooperating in a senseless verbal strike with nothing to gain.

Riley took in a deep swallow, and let some air flow from his mouth. "She got mangled in defending our country. I'd like to help her out, but I'm not sure what I can do."

"Do it on your own time. I'm not paying you to sympathize with her. Now, tell me what happened."

While Riley was close to hanging up on the old man, he knew better than to do that. He stayed on the line, and found just enough strength to continue. "She lives in a rundown trailer park with seemingly meager financial means to stay afloat. I suspect she's mentally impaired, but for sure she's physically disabled. She thinks there are aliens all around us." Weakness suddenly overcame him as he was not able to continue further.

The old man waited a few seconds, and then he started in again. "Is she worthy?"

Riley managed to get back into the conversation. He responded in a soft voice, "Definitely." There was very little gas in his energy tank. At least he thought this was the end of the deal, and he'd soon return home. He wondered if he had served the old man adequately to earn the full five thousand dollars fee.

"I'll consider it." The old man coughed before he continued. "There's been a change in plans." Since he couldn't see the depressed and sullen impression on Riley's face, he hesitated, thought he'd hear some sort of objection. With nothing but silence, the old man forged on. "I've cancelled the San Diego flight. You'll fly to San Francisco instead. A ticket is waiting for you at Southwest's Customer Courtesy Counter. When you arrive at San Francisco International Airport, go to baggage claim where a man will meet you. Follow his directions." Silence returned, this time it was due to the old man who disconnected the phone connection.

Riley kept the cell phone to his ear as if he was impersonating a statue. Then he slowly collapsed the instrument. For a brief time he wasn't sure exactly what had just happened or where he was.

Then consciousness returned when a child bumped into him running after a small ball. He looked down at the young boy, gave him a smile. The boy paid him no heed, too interested in retrieving the cherished play toy.

Riley slowly looked around, spotted a sign, and then headed to Southwest's Customer Courtesy Counter where he verified the original return flight to San Diego had been cancelled and replaced with one to San Francisco. He considered paying himself for a direct flight to San Diego rather than continue on to San Francisco. He figured he had done his part of the bargain and was due the money owned him. However, since the old man had been acting too squirrely he wasn't convinced he'd see any payment if he reneged. He didn't like it one bit, but he reluctantly took the ticket. With things changed so fast, he did not notice there was no confirmed flight to San Diego on the reissued ticket.

4

Shortly, Southwest Flight 12 departed for San Francisco. Exhausted, Riley let his head rest on the seat back and was soon asleep. However, his sound slumber was interrupted about twenty minutes into the flight when the aircraft experienced a sudden drop in altitude. Cascading sounds from passengers accentuated their panic. A woman sitting adjacent to Riley grabbed his arm as if the move might settle down the situation, yet all it did was to draw more attention to the circumstance. He wasn't sure what comfort he might possibly bring to her fear, so he let her hang onto his arm.

"This is your Captain. We're experiencing some unexpected turbulence, nothing to worry about. I'm going to take us to thirty-five thousand feet which should take us out of the disturbance. Sorry."

Moments later, as the plane leveled off at the new altitude, all was calm.

Riley looked at the passenger next to him, "Everything

is OK now." He gave her the best smile he could come up with for the time being.

She remained silent, still clenched to his arm. Then she gave Riley a glance, noticed his eyes switched back and forth between her grip and her eyes. "Oh, excuse me. I - I'm sorry." Her reddened face apologized better than her words could ever.

"No problem." He straightened his body in the seat, decided against making further conservation, yet he gave himself a talking to about using the phrase. He'd never liked telling someone no problem when there really was a problem.

While the rest of the flight went without disruption, he was not able to get back to take a snooze. He used the remaining time to go over what had happened to him in the last few days.

Although he disappointed himself in not getting as much information from the three interviews that he had hoped for, he still had high expectations there would be financial payment once he finished the job. He did the best he could. The real question was if he did it well enough to satisfy the old man.

He convinced himself the old man was up to something else other than giving to a worthy person one hundred thousand dollars. But what that might be was still a mystery.

He would soon discover more about the old man with the pocket watch as the Southwest Flight 12 descended.

Once on ground, Riley made his way to baggage claim where he easily spotted someone holding a sign, **Riley Sullivan**. He headed toward a man dressed in some sort of uniform. "Looking for Riley Sullivan?"

The man in the uniform said, "Yeah, that you?" His voice was not comforting, ruff and harsh. He also seemed impatient as if there was something else swirling around in his head that took more prominence.

Riley nodded, "Yes." He gave the man a smile that did not seem to hit its mark.

Without much acknowledgement, the man asked, "Got bags?"

Riley lifted the one carryon bag in his hand, "Just this one." His shoulders lifted a little, yet that too didn't seem to be of any concern to the man.

The man in the uniform lowered his arms, turned and walked away. "Good, this way." The sign was clenched in his left hand. His pace was rapid as if he was in some sort of hurry either to get done with something once and for all or to make more time for other important matters.

Riley followed the man to a parked black limousine. He had to quicken his stride to keep pace.

The man moved to the driver side, got in, tossed the sign on the front passenger seat, and started the engine. The back passenger door was left closed.

Riley quickly got the drift he was on his own, so he opened the door himself, put his bag on the backseat, and got in himself. As he closed the door, the limousine took off, headed for Hwy 80 towards San Francisco. The drive was without conversation, something that bothered Riley but was not willing to get into. He figured he'd find out sooner or later where the driver was headed and what it was all about.

As the limousine moved off Hwy 80 to Hwy 280, the driver glanced a few times in the rear view mirror to check out his passenger. Then, he took King Drive for a short time, and at Fourth and King Muni Metro Station he took a right. Two blocks on the left was The China Basin Wharfside Building, a pre - 1960's recently renovated building. The driver pulled into a parking lot, shut off the engine, and said, "Follow me." He then got out of the vehicle without saying another word.

The driver quickly walked to a side door of the building. It was metal and had a padlock. He removed a key from his pocket, unlocked the door, and swung it up. He stepped inside in silence with Riley close behind. A small room contained a five foot square table with two white wooden chairs. A chess board with chess figures rested atop the table. The driver took one seat. "That one's for you." He nodded in the direction of the empty chair. There was a slight quiver in his voice, yet it was something that went unnoticed by Riley.

Still quiet, Riley let his body rest on the chair, his face twisted with confusion. Silently he waited for the man to say something. The delay was quite short.

"Do you play chess?"

Riley coughed a little, his mouth dry from his body using up much of his internal fluids. He managed to nod,

"Yes, a little." A frown slowly grew on his face, puzzled by the question.

"Let's decide who makes the first move." The quiver in his voice settled down as if he was more comfortable with what was about to happen next.

Confusion mounted on Riley's face. His voice was barely audible, "What's this about? Why am I here?" He saw the driver's face more clearly now than before. A scar just above his lip and below his nose gave him a shutter. He wondered how it might have happened, but he figured this was not the time to ask.

"If you win, I'll tell you everything." His face remained unfriendly looking.

"What if I don't?" Riley then felt slight perspiration on his upper lip, along with a few water drops edging their way from his nose.

"Well, then, that's entirely different." A grin was prominent.

"I don't want to play." His voice sounded off an early alarm to something. "Where's the old man?"

"He's not here." He took in some air through his nose. "You don't have a choice. I'm just following his orders." The grin seemed to be a permanent fixture, like a statue. "I'm here instead."

Riley was about to stand but changed his mind when the man pulled out a revolver. "Like I said, you don't have a choice. Sit." Only his lips moved. Then he shifted the gun's direction between Riley and the chair.

Riley's knees almost buckled as he slowly returned his body to the white wooden chair. He sniffled.

"I have an idea." The surprised look fooled no one. He pulled out two small bottles from a pocket, placed the two containers between them, and waited just enough time to further torment Riley. Then he continued. "In each bottle is a pill. One is poisonous, the other is not. Pick the right pill and you live to play a game of chess. Pick the wrong pill and you die." He purposely waited to emphasize the point. "That's all there is to it."

Riley stared at the two containers side by side. He felt his heart pick up a beat or two. Then, somehow, he felt a surge of strength. "I'm not going to pick." Riley's voice was suddenly strong and defiant.

"Then, I'll have to end it another way." He swirled the revolver in his hand, then aimed it directly at Riley's head.

Eyes quickly widened, Riley asked, "Why are you doing this?" He took a much needed gulp of air. "What have I ever done to you?" Another needed swallow of the precious substance. "I don't even know you!"

"Don't take this personal between us. I'm only doing my job." His voice was without emotion, eyes glued to those of Riley.

Riley felt his heart's beat pick up, fast and hard. It was as if the organ was ready to implode, to burst inward to cause a violent compression. His eyes glazed over with moisture, as the appearance of the man sitting across the table was now hazy and unfocused. Slight dizziness moved his head from side to side without much control of its direction. He felt as if his entire insides were about to empty out. He gulped once and then a second time, but the acid tasting substance was insistent in making its

71

way to freedom. There was a sudden but brief break in the fluid's advance, and then an avalanche erupted. Unable to restrain any further, a large amount of substance matter poured out of his mouth. He couldn't have been more perfect in directing an assortment of material towards the man with the revolver. "Ah," Riley shouted out with a mixture of pain and relief. His body leaned forward.

The man who sat across from him was equally surprised, but more upset. Unable to defend himself from the blend, he tried to dodge away. The sudden move flung his hand holding the revolver towards his head. Unable to keep his trigger finger immobile, the motion activated the release of one bullet that penetrated his head.

There was only one loud noise, "Pow!"

The gun shot was over quickly as the man fell backward onto the floor. Rich red blood began to pour out of the bullet hole.

They say the fall isn't as painful as when the body hits the ground, but not this time. His death was immediate.

Riley remained motionless and speechless, unable to make out what had just happened. Then slowly, he realized the man was dead. It took him a while to settle down, to collect his thoughts, and to figure out what his next move might be. He immediately thought to call the old man.

He fumbled for his cell phone. Then it dawned on him that the dead man implied the old man was behind all of this. So, why should he call him? He paused to think clearly, but his mind was not working all that well.

Without further thought, he returned to fumble for his cell phone. At first his fingers did not cooperate, so he wiggled them a few times to get them back into working order.

Seconds later he heard the sound of phones connecting, then silence. He waited just a second or two before he said, "This is Riley. The driver is dead. He tried to kill me. What's going on?" Silence continued, and then when he heard a click he realized the phones had been disconnected. His mind went blank. He stared at the device still clenched in his hand. The old man had hung up on him!

There was only one option left. He went through the pockets of the dead man to find the keys to the limousine. Finally, he grabbed a key ring, took one last look at the dead man, and ran to the limousine. He headed to San Francisco International Airport.

He left the vehicle in the section reserved for limousines, and then rushed to Southwest Airlines to make the return flight to San Diego. However, when he checked his packet of tickets to locate the flight number to San Diego, he realized no return flight had been purchased. He stopped in his tacks. Riley realized the old man had no intention to see him alive.

Riley looked around to find the nearest airline ticket counter. He was pleased to find a convenient Southwest Airlines ticket counter nearby, so he rushed to buy a ticket as fast as his legs would take him. He was pleased that there was a departing flight to San Diego soon. With another fortunate experience, this time through passenger screening, he rushed to the boarding gate with five minutes to spare before the aircraft took off. He flopped his body into seat 19 A, a nervous wreck.

5

Inside the San Diego International Airport - Lindbergh Field terminal, he ran towards a connecting bridge that passed over a busy road used for passenger pick-ups. He moved his legs as fast as possible. The quickest way to get to his car was from the courtesy busses that took passengers to and from long term parking.

He lucked out. Just at the time he reached the designated area, a shuttle bus arrived. The trip was short, yet he tried again to connect with the old man. He encountered the same result. "Shit. He did want me dead." Then, another person's name popped into his head, so he quickly dialed a friend. Graham answered.

"This is Riley." He did not wait for Graham to reply. "I need your help badly. I'm on my way to get my car at the Airport. I can be at McCarty's in an hour. Can you meet me there?" He heard his own deep breathing as air was sucked through his nose.

"Where have you been?" Graham wanted to carry

on a conversation in spite of sensing the desperation his friend felt.

"I'll tell you everything when we meet." He swallowed another gulp of air. "Can you meet me?"

"Sure. You sound terrible."

"You have no idea. I'm just happy to be alive. I'll see you in an hour." He disconnected as the shuttle entered the parking lot.

"Number 330 is on the left," The driver announced a parking spot through a microphone whose speakers were in need of repair or replacement.

Riley quickly stood, and made his way to his parked car. Using as much horsepower as the BMW allowed he headed up I - 5 North towards McCarty's. He reached the place in less than one hour.

Still feeling the effects of almost being killed, Riley felt that his entire body was tighter than a drum. With eyes as wide as they've ever been, he looked to the booth he and Graham usually shared. A sense of relief came over him when he spotted his buddy. As he moved quickly in that direction, he noticed two bottles of Stella Artois on the table.

Graham pushed the full bottle towards Riley as his friend took a seat. "You look like hell." Graham had never seen his buddy look so bad.

Riley grabbed hold of the bottle as if it were worth a million dollars, gulped down much of the golden brown liquid, and reset the bottle on the table. He was noticeably shaking, but in a little more time he settled down. He saw a pair of worried eyes face him, and then he gave off as best of a smile he could under the conditions. "I'm really glad to see you." Still holding the bottle, he took another swig. "I've got a lot to tell." There was still a noticeable quiver to his voice.

"I'm all ears." He replicated taking a sip of beer. "Did I tell you that you look like hell?"

Riley shook his head yes, and then said, "Where do I start?" Riley nodded a few times as if the head movement would order his thoughts in some logical way. Another sip of beer, this time more conservatively. He began to feel less tense.

Graham patiently waited, finished off the Stella. "I'll get another round." As he got up to head towards the bar, he clenched his left hand into a fist to tap Riley on the arm. "Don't go anyplace."

Riley stared ahead, only partially hearing the message. He took in several deep breaths of air.

Within a few minutes the two men were together again, fresh Stella's in front of each person.

Riley seemed calmer, but only a little. Without any sort of introduction, he began. "Thanks for being here. I really need someone to talk with."

Graham looked at Riley, "That's what friends are for."

Riley continued, "Last Tuesday, on my way here, I stopped to help out a guy who was having some problems with his truck. He fixed whatever the problem was, and to thank me for stopping to help out he offered to buy me a beer. When we got here, I thought you'd be on your second beer, but that wasn't the case."

Graham interrupted him. "Yeah, I'm sorry about that." No further explanation was offered, nor was one expected. That was just Graham.

"Anyway, when we got here, he and I had a few beers together." He finished off the first Stella, shoved it to the side to make way for the fresh one. He saw Graham's look puzzled. "Yeah, so far everything seemed OK. However, our conversation changed quickly." He took in another deep gulp of air that seemed to calm him further. His voice sounded less anxious. "The guy told me he wanted to give away one hundred thousand dollars to someone who would spend the money wisely. I thought that was crazy, in fact I thought he was crazy."

Graham butted in again, "I agree, really crazy."

"Anyway, he told me he needed some help and that maybe I could lend a hand. He said he had narrowed a list of people down to three who he wanted me to interview. All I needed to do was to tell him which of the three people I thought should get the money and why; none, one, two, or all three. In return, he'd give me five thousand dollars and a bonus at the end." His heart started to race in reviewing the situation, so he took a breather.

Graham thought that by stating the obvious, he'd help calm down Riley, "You know what they say when it sounds too good to be true?" He took a sip of beer.

"I know, I know. But, I have to tell you, the way he said it was very convincing, at least in the beginning."

Graham gave him a quizzical look. "Come on."

"Yeah," The one word was all that was necessary. He paused for a few seconds, and then continued. "Anyway, he told me where the first person lived, and then the second person and the third person. I've either been driving or flying around since last Wednesday, two days after I met him." He cleared his throat as if the next comment was the most important. It also helped him stay calm. "Then, when I was ready to return to San Diego, he told me there was a fourth person I had to meet in San Francisco. So, I flew there. However, a limo driver picked me up at the Airport and eventually tried to kill me!"

Graham's mouth opened wide.

"That's right, someone tried to kill me!" His face turned fearful.

"No shit!"

"No shit," Riley repeated in a softer voice. "But evidently, that didn't happen."

"How did you escape?"

Riley took in a deep breath of air, "I threw up on the guy and his gun accidently went off."

"He shot himself?"

"Yeah, right in the head," Riley pointed a finger at his forehead.

Graham started off with a shallow laugh that wound-up to almost a roar. "You threw up on the guy and he killed himself!"

"Shh," Riley said softly.

"I'm sorry, but you have to admit that this is sort of funny. The guy kills himself as a result of you throwing up on him. Come on."

Riley took in a deep breath. "Maybe later it will be humorous, not now. I've got to tell you I thought I was going to die. I've never felt that way before. It isn't a good feeling."

"Yeah, I can't imagine." Graham settled down and took a sip of beer. Then, he asked another question, "So, what did you do with the dead body?"

"I left it alone and got out of there as fast as I could."

"Did you touch the gun or leave any evidence that you were there?"

"I don't think so."

"But you had to get back to the airport. No?"

"Yes, and...." He paused, "... and my fingerprints are all over the limo's steering wheel and door handle." He puckered his lips. "My name is printed on a sign that he used to find me." He paused again, "I left my carryon bag in the limo!"

"I think you should go to the police to tell them everything. They're going to find the dead man sooner or later and think you had something to do with it."

"They'll think I'm crazy. Come on. I've tried reaching the old man but he doesn't pick up. I think he wanted me killed!"

"Why, what would be the point?"

"That's a great question. I don't know. But the dead guy implied the old man was behind it."

"It's your word against a dead man's word," Graham reminded Riley.

"I am perfectly aware of that little bit of fact." Riley paused. "If I could find out where the old man lives I could get to the bottom of it all. I only know his first name, Al."

"But you do know the three people you interviewed. That's a start. The police could check them out to prove you are telling the truth." Graham nodded to help persuade his friend it was the best advice.

"I'm not so sure."

"OK, then, contact the three people. Tell them you need their help."

"So what do I say? That I need them as character witnesses because I might be accused of killing a limo driver in San Francisco? I don't think they know anything more about me than what they learned from our short meetings. I don't think they even know the old guy who I was representing. I'm really screwed!" Nervousness turned to fear.

"What do you want to do?" Graham's precise question was as potent as it could get.

Riley smacked his lips. "You're right. I've got to contact them, even if it is disguised as a follow up question or two to the original meeting."

"Do you have their phone numbers?"

"No, but I have their full names and mailing addresses. I can search them on the Internet."

"OK, let's start it now." Graham was full of enthusiasm and support, something that his buddy needed most at the present time.

They finished off their Stella's and drove off to the Carlsbad Public Library on Dove Lane where there was free access to the Internet using the library computers.

Graham sat alongside Riley as he entered his password. He connected to the Internet to begin a search. First on the list was Leah Clare in Palm Desert, California. Several entries appeared identifying a few different people, but one current listing shocked both men. Their eyes stayed glued to a story that indicated Ms. Leah Clare, owner of The Full House, was dead. "This can't be!" Riley was dumbfounded.

"Are you sure she is the right one?"

"Definitely, how many people with the name of Leah Clare own The Full House?"

"Try the next one," encouraged Graham.

Riley typed the name of Adrianne Browde along with the City and University names to make the search as narrow as possible. Anxiously he waited for the results. "No!"

Graham stretched his neck to see the findings from the Internet search. He too was surprised. "This can't be! Two of two are dead!"

Riley's fingers stayed atop of the computer keys, unmoving, unwilling to find out the status of Flo Hobare.

"What are you waiting for?" asked Graham.

Slowly Riley's fingers touched each key to set up the last search. Then, before pressing **Enter**, he hesitated. He blinked his eyes, and dropped his right hand off the keyboard. It gently landed on his right knee.

Realizing what was going on, Graham touched **Enter** with his index finger.

The computer took over with amazing speed.

Both men had the wind taken out of their sails from the same end result. A sudden darkness fell.

It took a while for Riley and Graham to come out of the frozen emotional state.

Graham broke the silence. "We've got to find the old man. He lives nearby. He needs to know what's happened."

So far, neither Riley nor Graham had thought about a possible connection among the deaths of these three women but with the attempted murder of Riley the old man might be dangerous.

Riley was slow to respond. "That bastard tried to kill me."

"So said the dead man," clarified Graham.

"One way or the other I've got to find Al. He's got to know what's going on."

"Do you have anything that we can use to track him down?" Graham asked.

"I've got all the airline tickets, hotel room and car rental receipts. He made all the reservations. Maybe we can backtrack by contacting the airlines, hotels, and car rental agencies to see who made the reservations."

"It's a long shot but it's all we've got."

With renewed enthusiasm, they headed outside of the Library to make a few cell calls. Referencing the information on Riley's airline, hotel, and car rental receipts, he began making cell calls. With an unexpected stroke of luck Riley managed to get the full name of the old man with the pocket watch along with an address.

Was it luck, chance, fate, or destiny? It really did not matter. He got what he wanted, and now he and Graham had to hurry or else it might be too late to discover what was all behind the scheme. The old man might have already taken off.

With a sense of desperation, they drove to Escondido, a city just to the East of Carlsbad. The last address of the old man was 1990 Via Scott, someplace between Nordahl Road and Nutmeg Court. Their dialog was far from ordinary. They usually discussed women, surfing, and sports, but not now. It was more serious than ever before. "He's a strange old man. He showed me a pocket watch that he claimed to be worth fifty thousand dollars."

Graham looked over towards his friend, eyes widen a little. "Honestly?"

"Yes and now it wouldn't surprise me if he's been in trouble with the law before."

"Oh, really," Graham was warming up to idea of finding out the real identify of the man. "How old is the guy?"

"Old? I'm not good at figuring out real ages, but maybe in his late sixties."

"Did you trust him?"

Riley frowned. "My instincts told me not to."

"But you did." The obvious comment was not necessary, but among friends, it was OK to say the obvious.

Riley glanced towards Graham, puckered his lips, and frowned. He acknowledged his stupid decision. "Listen, I thought I'd be able to pay off my bills with the money, and for once feel what it meant to be almost debt free. Can you blame me?"

Graham frowned without having to say a word. Then he said, "So, you really didn't know him that well."

"I think we've established the fact that I screwed up by trusting him. Let's move on to something else."

"Sorry." Graham paused for a short time, and then continued. "What do you make of the three people you interviewed?" He shifted his eyes between the windshield and his buddy driving.

"What do you mean?"

"Do you think they knew each other, or maybe even knew the old man?"

"Why do you say that? That's a weird presumption."

"I guess, based on what you've told me so far about this guy, I wouldn't put it past him. I mean, think about it for a second." Graham smacked his lips. "Let's assume he knows all three people, but for some reason wanted to get more information about them. By accident, he bumps into you, thinks you're an honest guy, and therefore decides to use you."

"But what's his motive? What would his interest be in the three people? Why would he want to get me killed? Graham, this doesn't make sense. Come on."

Graham was insistent with his theory. "It doesn't make sense to us because we're not like him. He's a bad dude."

Riley found the whole idea intriguing, but he was not sure of its practicality. He let out a groan.

Graham pushed on. "We found out his name, Alfred Smuts. What do you make of it?"

Riley's twisted face expressed a grimace. "My friend, I think you're reaching."

"You don't think there isn't meaning in a name?"

"No, I agree that names have meanings, but, to be honest, I'm not interested right now. I just want to find the bastard."

Graham realized he was asking too many questions, maybe letting his imagination run riot. Looking out the passenger window he realized they were getting close to the home of the old man named Alfred Smuts. He settled down his curiosity for a while. The rest of the drive was in silence.

Riley slowed down once reaching the 1900 block of Via Scott. He checked out the addresses of each house. Suddenly, he stopped the car, unable to speak for a while as his mind stopped processing information.

Graham shouted out, "What the hell?"

"What happened?" Riley chimed in.

They saw to their left a mostly vacant lot with what appeared to be the remains of a burned building. All that remained was a cement foundation, a chimney, a few scorched trees, along with the driveway and a sidewalk. There was a sign that read **Caution. Do Not Enter**.

"What happened here? Where did he go?" mumbled Riley.

"Pull up and park the car. I think I see a phone number on the sign."

Riley responded without words. He moved the car.

"Let's get out," said Graham.

"I'm going to knock on a few doors. Maybe someone knows what happened here and where he went."

As Graham walked towards the sign to get a closer look at the phone number, Riley moved to an adjacent house. He knocked on the front door. Within a few minutes a young boy, about thirteen with a silver necklace around his neck, answered. He stared without any noticeable facial expression.

"I'm sorry to bother you, but I'm looking for the person who lived next door, in the building that used to be there." He nodded his head in the direction of the vacant lot.

The young boy continued his statue-like stare. Then he asked, "Who wants to know?"

"I do. I'm Riley Sullivan. I was supposed to meet him today."

"Too bad," the kid said.

"What happened to the house?"

"Cops torched it, had all kinds of dangerous materials to make bombs and stuff."

Riley was stunned. For a moment he was without words.

Graham joined to make it a trio. "The phone number belongs to the police. What else do you have?"

The young boy looked suspiciously between Riley and Graham, not sure what to make of it, so he decided caution was the best tactic. He remained quiet.

Riley picked up the conversation. He asked the young boy, "What was his name?"

"I thought you had a meeting with him? You don't know his name?"

"OK, his name is Alfred Smuts. Is that the same name?"

The young boy raised his shoulders without comment.

Graham whispered to Riley, "He wants money. Give him a few bucks."

Riley frowned, and then he reached into his pocket to take out some money. "Here's two dollars. Can you confirm his name for me?"

The young boy smiled for the first time, "I don't know his name."

A second question came from Graham, "Do you know where he is now?"

Another silent look from the young boy signaled his reply.

Disapprovingly, Riley handed over another two dollars.

"He's in jail."

"Which one," Riley asked.

There was another silent response that prompted Riley to unwillingly give over the last of his singles, two more dollars.

"Don't know." He figured he'd probably ended the rip-off, so the boy turned and closed the door to leave Riley and Graham alone on the front steps.

Suspecting Riley was reeling with anger, Graham

tapped him on the shoulder. "Let's go. We'll contact the cops to find out what happened. They should know what jail the old man is in." Riley's reaction was slow in coming, so Graham said, "Come on. We're not going to get anything more here."

They moved to the parked vehicle without conversation. Then, using an electronic Tomahawk Navigational Map, Riley located the nearest police station. He pulled into the street, made a U - turn, and drove off all the while steaming inside.

"It'll all work out," Graham said as confidently as he could. Yet, down deep inside he was worried that his friend was chasing nonexistent clues.

The comment seemed to calm down Riley a little. "Why did he pick me? Why did he want me dead?"

"He's an evil hearted lying guy. You were in the wrong place at the wrong time."

"I was smarter when I was younger. I get more stupid as I get older."

"Don't be so hard on yourself."

Enough said for the time being. The rest of the drive was without talk.

Minutes later the car was parked in one of those few parking spots reserved for visitors. Both men exited the vehicle at about the same time, walked towards the entrance without conversation. Riley entered first. They looked around, first time for them both in a police station.

Someone in uniform passed by, and then stopped to ask a question.

"Can I help you?" A warm smile on her face diverted their attention from the stack of papers held tightly in her fists. She seemed sincere.

"Ah, I want to find out about where someone might be. Can you help me?" That was about the best Riley had to offer.

"Do you want to file a missing person's report?" She looked straight into his eyes without blinking.

"Well, not exactly. You see, I went to see him today but it seems his house burned down. I don't know where he might be." He rewound the answer in his mind, shook his head in disapproval. It all sounded weird to him now that he'd said it aloud. Too bad he couldn't take it back and start afresh.

Still holding the smile, she wondered what his real motive might be. "Take a seat and I'll be back with you shortly." Without waiting for his answer she nodded towards a few wooden chairs in the corner. As she walked away, the two men each took a seat without talk between them.

Only a few minutes passed before she returned. "I'm Detective Cabo. Now, tell me who you're looking for." While appearing relaxed, she was mentally on her game. Glances between Riley and Graham began the profiling process. She patiently waited.

Graham remained silent while Riley talked. His voice had a slight quiver. "I've been doing some business with Mr. Alfred Smuts, and just returned from a business trip. I used my cell to contact him but, well, there wasn't an answer, so I ... we ... this is my associate ... decided to visit him." He slightly shifted his head towards Graham, and then continued. "When we arrived, we discovered his house completely burned to the ground. A neighbor said the house was torched by the police, not much more. That's why we're here. We need to talk with him. It is quite urgent."

"I see." She paused, recognized the man's name immediately. "What type of business might that be?"

Riley squirmed, not sure how far he ought to go. Graham decided to contribute.

He used business-like words that surprised him and Riley. "It's a non-profit. Mr. Smuts asked my partner to identify creditable benefactors who might be able to put to use a sizeable financial donation." It was too late to reconsider his involvement. The cat was out of the bag.

"I see. So, could you give me your names, and the name of the non-profit organization?" She figured they trapped themselves. Now she'd wait for them to dig the hole a little deeper. Cabo was enjoying the game, a sort of weird pleasure by law enforcement personnel.

The two men fought off glancing toward each other. They knew what just happened. While the temperature inside the building had remained constant, their body temperatures had risen. The longer they waited, the more anxious they became.

Common sense suggested they should never lie to the police; don't mess with law enforcement.

She waited just a little longer before she continued. "How are you feeling? You don't look well." More pleasurable taunts came their way as she switched looks between the two men. She figured another few seconds left before one of them would relent.

"OK, there is more to it." Graham shifted his eyes away from Cabo toward Riley. "You've got to tell her everything. You haven't done anything wrong."

She waited another few more seconds, looked Riley's way, and then added, "You don't want to have a loose relationship with the truth. The more lies you tell me the more difficult it will be for the both of you." She gave Graham a quick look.

Riley gave Graham a fleeting look, and then said to Cabo, "I met Smuts only a short time ago, a little over a week, at McCarty's. He offered me an opportunity to interview three people so that he could decide who would receive one hundred thousand dollars." He noticed for the first time a slight surprise on Cabo's face. "Yes, that's right. He told me he wanted to give one hundred thousand dollars to a worthy person. All I had to do was to interview these people, and then brief him on how it went. In return he would pay me five thousand dollars and a bonus once I finished." He took a deep breath of air. "Can I have something to drink, water or something?"

"Sure." Cabo left the two men to get bottles of water. She figured her departure also would give them an opportunity to get their story straight.

"It's the best way," Graham said. "I'll back you one hundred percent."

Riley remained quiet, a little peeved at Graham for

opening up the can of worms, but down deep inside relieved not to continue in the cover up.

She returned in less than one minute, and handed over the water bottles. "Go on. You left off explaining your fee for all of this."

Riley unscrewed the cap, and took a big gulp of water. He continued, feeling remarkably better. "So, I interviewed the three people, and told him my opinions over the phone. Then he said there was one more to meet, a fourth person. I was a little annoyed at the sudden change in plans, but I agreed." He shrugged his shoulders, "Hey, it was a job he was paying me to do." He took another swig of water all the while Graham remained silent. "But the fourth person was a big surprise. He tried to actually kill me." Riley felt his heart tick a little faster with only a brief mention of the near fatal incident. Fortunately, that guy accidently killed himself before he could kill me. But before he shot himself, he implied that Smuts wanted me dead. I don't know why anyone would want to kill me." He paused to take in a deep breath of air, and then another gulp of water. " Anyway, I ran away, drove myself to the airport, and when I arrived in San Diego, I called Graham. Now, I'm looking for Smuts." He felt relieved that it was all out. Breathing returned to normal. A small tap on his shoulder from Graham congratulated him for doing the right thing, yet he wondered why Riley omitted talking about the three dead people he interviewed.

Detective Cabo processed the information. While it all seemed strange, she'd heard stranger stories during her career. She concluded there was sufficient truth to the account, so she began a line of questioning. "Let's move to a more private room. I have a few questions."

One hour and twenty minutes later, Detective Cabo ended the interview. "I appreciate your cooperation." She closed her note pad, gently placed her pen on the table top. "You've been through a lot. I hope you understand that I've got to check all of this out, including, I might add, the both of you." She saw their eyes widen. "You wouldn't expect me to believe just anyone who comes here with a story like yours, would you?" She saw them nod their heads in agreement. "I don't want you to do anything foolish. Don't leave the area. I need phone numbers and street addresses where each of you live. I'm pretty sure we'll be talking again soon."

"What about Smuts?" Riley asked.

"What about him?" she answered in a matter of fact manner.

"I want to know where he is, why he chose me, what the three people really meant to him, and why he wanted me killed. I've got a right to know." Riley got all worked up again.

"I can see you are upset about all of this, but in due time, not now." Her voice did not leave any room for negotiation.

Riley had no intention to let this go. "I demand it!"

She gave him a firm stare, forbidding in some ways. "Don't do anything stupid."

About to take the disagreement to another level,

Graham chimed in. He grabbed Riley's shoulder, "We understand. He's just very upset. You understand."

Cabo understood perfectly well realizing Riley was not letting go. While there was not much else she could do, she gave him one last word of advice, "This is now a police matter. Don't interfere. Let us do our job." She kept an intent look directed at Riley to leave no misunderstanding of her message. She finally said, "Now, give me your contact information." She looked at both men as she reopened her note pad.

Once Riley and Graham were inside the car, Graham looked at his friend. "Just let it go. You're safe. Let the cops do their job."

Riley was not so sure. He was still quite upset. He turned the ignition key, heard the sound of the engine, and drove off all the while trying to figure out a way to find the old man with the pocket watch. He figured he'd do it alone. Better to keep his buddy out of harm's way. "Yeah, just let it go."

Graham was not persuaded.

After he dropped off Graham, Riley headed towards Poinsettia Blvd, and then he got on I-5 North. The destination was not as important as some time he needed to figure a few things out. He had no intention to let the old man get away. He had to know what the scheme was all about. The BMW struggled to reach 65 MPH. The car badly needed a tune-up. A light rain started to fall that set off the automatic windshield wipers to sway back and forth. The blades streaked the windshield in a zigzag pattern, they needed replacement as well. No music, only internal thoughts to make some sense out of what next to do.

It was after midnight when he pulled into the driveway. Rain continued falling at about the same pace as before. No one waited for him, no hurry to get home. The garage door opener responded to his command. He wondered if there were any messages waiting for him on his answering machine, but deep inside he knew the answer. After he turned off the engine, he stepped out of the vehicle and pressed another button to instruct the garage door to close. He stepped inside his modest place and slowly walked towards the answering machine. No blinking light, no messages, just what he thought. He shrugged his shoulders to head upstairs. He felt dirty for some reason, so he decided to take a shower.

Once in his bedroom, he took off his clothes, walked towards the shower, opened the glass door, and stepped in without waiting for the water to heat up. The cold spray startled him just a little but he endured it realizing comfort was on its way. He put his head underneath the water's jets to wash away any clogged thoughts. After reaching for a bar of olive oil soap, he lathered his body so that he was completely covered with soap suds. The water, now warm, felt soothing. With closed eyes he took in a few deep breaths of air. He remained in a statue-like position for at least one full minute until he decided to end the self-indulging treatment.

After he turned off the shower, he stepped out. He grabbed for a large blue towel that was hung close by. He wiped away all remaining water from his body, and then he glanced at a full length mirror. He thought he had aged since just a short time ago. He wished he had someone to talk with, to put her arms around him, to kiss him, to make him feel good. He knew relationships don't just happen. You've got to make them happen. And that's been his problem ... he'd never been good at it.

Suddenly hungry, he wrapped the blue towel around his waist to head for the kitchen. He opened the refrigerator to find it mostly empty. No surprise but it was worth it just the same. He stared at the meager contents as if to see if something of interest magically appeared. Disappointed, he grabbed a Stella Artois and a canister of grated imported Parmesan cheese from Italy. With beverage and protein in hand, he placed both on a counter. Then, he stepped towards a cabinet door that contained a box of Orville Redenbacher's Microwavable Gourmet Popping Corn. He took one bag out of the box, and with the other hand he grabbed a bottle of Lucini Extra Virgin Olive Oil. He was now ready to put together something to satisfy his hunger.

He opened the Stella to begin the process, took a sip, and then removed the cellophane from the popping corn. He placed the bag of Redenbacher's in the microwave, set the timer, and let the machine take over. Within a few minutes the job was done. Carefully, he opened the bag as fumes puffed out. He poured just the right amount of olive oil over the popped corn, and then sprinkled adequate cheese into the bag. He settled down to a late night snack. It took two Stella's to adequately satisfy him.

He looked at the clock on the microwave; 1:12 AM. He slowly moved away, towards his bedroom, to force himself towards a dreamless sleep. However, it didn't happen that way. He dreamed.

He saw someone in the distance, but couldn't make out who it was.

The night's partial moon and cloudy sky prevented him from seeing clearly. He narrowed his eyes hoping the move would help out. He looked sideways and then straight ahead. He strained to see what was up ahead. He was not sure if the object moved closer to him, or if he moved closer to a stationary object.

None-the-less, there was someone with pale, translucent skin, milky looking. The sight was not comforting to him. There was horror in his thoughts.

He yelled out, "Who are you?" A no response frightened him even more. "What do you want with me?" Another silence accentuated his fear.

Then he heard, "Imagine the worse, so you won't be surprised." He took in a deep breath that he thought was his last.

He tossed and turned in bed until the day's sunlight cheered him on to get up. With a sigh, he stretched his arms over his head, rubbed his eyes, and slowly moved his legs from beneath the covers to start the day. He'd figured out what he had to do, so he hurried as much as he could in spite of some sleep deprivation to get on with it.

Twenty-five minutes later he left the driveway to return to the lot without a structure. He parked the car in about the same spot as before and made his way to the place where he talked with the thirteen year old kid. He knocked on the door. The wait was not long.

A rather large woman appeared before him, baggy eyes. She puffed on a cigarette that dangled from her mouth, close to tipping off her lips. The suspicion like expression told Riley all he needed to know for the time. She looked around him as if to scout out who else might be hanging around outside.

"I'm sorry to bother you. I'm Riley Sullivan. I spoke with your son a few days ago. I wonder if I could talk with him again." His voice was not at peak performance, a combination of last night's erratic sleep and nervousness he presently felt.

"What's it about. He's a good boy." The cigarette between her lips moved up and down with each spoken word.

"I'm sure he is. He helped me out before. I need his help again." His eyes were the worrisome look that pleaded for a little understanding.

Her look remained distrustful as she calculated the odds to taking the conversation further.

"If he helps me I'll pay him."

Her eyes lit up.

"It's all legal," he decided to add.

Without turning, she moved her right hand to remove the cigarette from her mouth. She'd taken the greatest advantage of the smoke; anymore puffing might burn her lips. "Diego, get over here!"

Within a few seconds the young boy stood alongside his mother, silent, speculated if he'd gotten himself into some trouble with the police. Then he noticed Riley, remembered him from a short time ago. The kid wondered if the man was complaining about their recent financial transaction. He remained quiet, best to wait for his mother to take the lead.

With continued eye contact with Riley, she said, "Is this the same man you told me about?"

"Yes mama. He's the one." His voice was more timid than Riley remembered.

"He needs more help." She took her eyes off Riley's face to scan his body like a metal detector ascertained a level of safety. It seemed she was satisfied, nothing was revealed to concern her at the moment. "Tell me what help you need." She flipped the burned remains of the cigarette on the sidewalk.

"I need to know the whereabouts of the man who lived in the house next door, the one that is burned."

"He's in jail," she said.

"Jail," Riley repeated. "Yeah, that's what your son said."

"That's what I said too." She paused, and then continued. "He was making some sort of bombs. Police found out, arrested him, and then decided to burn the building. No other safe way. That's what they told us. Paid us a few dollars for the hassle, we had to go to a motel for a few days."

Riley wasn't much interested in knowing about the inconvenience. "Can you describe the man to me?"

She turned to Diego.

"Tall white guy, about forty, wore glasses, kept quiet."

Riley clarified, "Not an old man, wrinkled face."

Diego nodded, no.

"Did he own the house or rent it?"

"An old man owned the house, rented it to a lot of

folks. Only saw him when he came around to pick up the rent money. Paid us a little now and then to keep a watch on the place," she said.

"I see," Riley looked back and forth between the woman and her son. "Do you know where the old man lives?"

"No." The flat answer was all that the boy said.

"Listen, I've got to find the old man. It's really important. Can you help me?" The desperate sound in his voice verified how he felt.

The woman jumped back into the conversation. "We can do that for fifty dollars, pay in advance."

Riley figured there would be a charge for information but not that much. "All I've got is twenty-five dollars on me. I'll give you twenty-five now and then another twenty-five when I find him." He doubted if the negotiation would succeed, but there was nothing lost in trying. He figured if you don't ask, you don't get.

The woman extended her hand to reach for Diego, pulled him closer. Suspicion seeped into her psyche. "What do you do?"

The question surprised Riley. It was the same one Smuts asked him. He was hesitant then to answer, but not now. He needed help real badly. "I'm a teacher."

"Thought you were some kind of schooled man," for the first time, she gave him a smile. "Deal is this. Give me twenty-five dollars now. Then after you find the old man, you teach my boy how to read proper. I don't want him to be like this for the rest of life. He's a good boy, he can learn." She squeezed Diego closer to her side.

"Sure, I can do that." Riley was in favor of the deal.

"Get dressed proper. Your mamma and Mr. Sullivan got some talking to do. Now hurry." She gently pushed Diego away from her. "Come in," she said to Riley.

As the young thirteen year old boy walked away, she made her way to a chair that was in much need of repair. Riley followed her, tried to avoid looking at the run down place. He took a seat, and waited for her to begin.

"What's your problem with the old man?"

"I never said I have a complaint with him. I just need to find him, that's all."

She waved her hand to the side, smiled a little as if to tell him she knew more than what he'd already said. "OK, none of my business. Don't you put my son in any danger, hear me."

"No, no. I would never do that. I just want him to help me find the old man. That's all, I promise."

She nodded, realizing there were secrets everyone must keep. "No police involved in this."

"Not if I can help it. That's another promise."

There was a brief silence before Diego returned, dressed neatly in dark slacks, white long sleeve shirt, and black shoes. He stood a few feet from his mother, waited for her to signal him to advance.

She noticed his presence. "Go with the teacher."

Riley stood, prepared to leave, but was stopped when she said, "You forgot something."

He turned, saw her extended hand, palm up. "Oh." He dipped into his pocket, and handed over twenty five dollars.

Riley and Diego left the house.

Diego looked at the car, not impressed at all. Words were not necessary.

With both inside, seat belts in place, Riley said, "Where to?"

About fifteen minutes later, Riley parked a few blocks away from Riviera Funeral Chapel. The walk was made in silence. It was jammed with family, friends, neighbors, and business associates of a deceased person. A group of teenagers, about the same age as Diego, stood by the door of the Chapel. There were both girls and boys. A few recognized Diego with a nod of the head. They all gave a quizzical look towards Riley that made him a little uncomfortable. Overhead, the sky was bright but the air was dead quiet.

There were no announcements in the newspaper, not necessary since the people in this community were very close to each other. They knew who came and who went. That's just how it was. Word got around fast, informally, and accurately.

Diego moved inside the Chapel, Riley close behind. They walked to a midway point, not too close and not too far away. The closed casket was mounted on a raised area at the front of the Chapel. The religious service was conveniently short, conducted by Pastor Siqueiros, an elderly man who wore a long white robe with a religious purple shawl draped around his neck. His speech was soft, especially difficult to hear by everyone who sat more than three rows away from him. A few words were sparingly heard. There were several people, most likely family members, who sobbed throughout the ceremony. A few cried loudly in an uncontrolled manner.

Finally, the Pastor said, "Thank you all for coming. Go in peace."

Most people stood and made their way out of the Chapel. Family members lingered for another few minutes before they too left.

Riley gave a glance towards Diego for the next move. It came shortly after the Chapel was empty. Riley followed the young boy to the front who found an inconspicuous entrance that led to a small room. Pastor Siqueiros stood with his back to the unexpected visitors although he heard their footsteps announce their presence.

"Pastor Siqueiros, may I talk with you." Diego's voice was soft and respectful.

The Pastor recognized the voice, smiled, and turned to face the young boy. His grin turned worried at the sight of Riley.

"I'm not in trouble, so don't worry." Diego understood why the Pastor might be concerned.

The comment relieved the religious man of further worry, yet he wondered what to expect next. He was surprised.

"This is Mr. Sullivan. He's a teacher. He needs your help."

Pastor Siqueiros frowned just a little thinking how strange it was for a boy to bring a man to see him for religious guidance. Stranger things had happened. "Yes, what is it that I can do?" He switched to look at Riley.

Riley believed it was best to be direct and get to the point fast. "I'm looking for someone."

The Pastor turned to Diego with a puckered brow, taken off guard with the request.

The young boy clarified, "You know everyone in the community. My mama thought you could help him."

"I see," he said, although he was still quite confused about it all. "Who is the person?"

Riley interjected, "Alfred Smuts. He owns the building next to Diego's house that burned."

"Oh." He couldn't imagine why the teacher wanted to find the owner. "What is your purpose?"

"It's a private matter. I'd rather not say."

"But, if I am to help, I need to know."

Riley gave it some thought, looked away for a split second, and then towards Diego. He promised the boy's mother he wouldn't get Diego into trouble. He was going to see to it that he kept his promise. He reset his look at the Pastor, "Can I talk with you privately?" Then he glanced toward Diego who showed off a look of disapproval, "I'm sorry."

The Pastor said to Diego, "Mr. Sullivan and I need to have a short confidential talk." He motioned with a nod of his head to direct the boy to allow them to be alone.

With little resistance, Diego begrudgingly left.

"Thank you. I appreciate that." Riley took in a deep breath. "Smuts is responsible for three deaths, and almost my own. He owes me money and has gone into hiding.

I told the police all about this, but they don't seem to be much interested in finding this guy. I want to know why he chose me to be his patsy and why he tried to kill me. I want him to pay me what he owes. I'm not interested in harming him. I'm really not."

"I take it you don't like him very much."

"Correct, but it's not about whether I like him or not, it's about finding him."

He looked directly at Riley, sized him up as much as possible. "I make many visits to various hospitals in the area, seeking those who need or want spiritual guidance. I recently visited St. Anthony's where you will find Mr. Smuts. He's suffering from a heart attack, and I suspect he does not have much time left to live before he passes on. Do you know where St. Anthony's is?"

"Yes." Riley kept looking at him and felt a gush of exhilaration so intense that it almost took his breath away. He put his hand on the Pastor's shoulder. "Thank you."

"Keep Diego out of your affairs. He is a young and impressionable boy."

"Yes, I completely understand."

"Go, my son, in peace."

Diego sat quietly inside the car, thought about how he could improve the vehicle's appearance and engine power. His inner thoughts were temporarily interrupted when Riley arrived.

"Thanks for bringing me here. You've helped me out more than you know." Riley glanced towards the young thirteen year old boy. Then he continued. "I owe you reading tutoring lessons."

At first Diego didn't hear the words, he'd returned to previous thoughts about doing a total make-over of the vehicle.

Riley continued. "When we get back to your home, you, your mom, and me will schedule the times and dates. I'm not sure what your grade level of reading is, but I'll figure that out pretty quickly. How does that sound?"

A no response got Riley to say it again. "How does it sound to make a plan with your reading tutoring?"

"Sure. Whatever." The kid was not enthused about the entire idea, yet knew down deep inside it all made sense. He didn't want to wind up like his father and uncles, too short lives with not much to show for.

"It'll be fun. Trust me on this one." Riley gave it his best, but he knew the performance fell short of getting the kid inspired. There was an awkwardly long pause before he continued. He decided to get a commitment from the boy now. "When do you get off from school?"

Diego kept silent for only a short time, and then replied. "Three. Momma wants me to get straight home, don't like me hanging around, getting into trouble."

As Riley headed towards Via Scott, he said, "That'll work for me. We can start next month, the first Monday, whatever that date is, at three thirty."

"Go back to the Chapel." Diego had something else on his mind.

Riley turned to Diego with a frown on his face. "Not going home? I thought you said ...."

He was interrupted. "Got to do some work for Pastor Siqueiros, I forgot about it."

"Oh, OK." He returned to the Riviera Funeral Chapel. It was only a short time before he got there.

Riley stopped in front of the Chapel. Without further talk, Diego got out of the car, started to slowly walk away.

Riley watched the kid for a few seconds, and then he said, "Remember, the first Monday next month, three-thirty."

He saw Diego nod his head in agreement.

Then, he drove away.

"What's up?"

Diego recognized the voice, not happy with its owner. He'd rather ignore the comment but that was not how it was done around these parts. Showing respect was important for survival. He turned toward the older boy. "Not much, just going to help out Pastor Siqueiros with a few things."

The older boy was now surrounded by a few more boys and girls, some his same age, but it was not that easy to tell them apart. As he stepped closer to Diego, the others remained packed together. "Who's the white guy driving you around?"

Diego knew where this was headed. "It's not what you think. My momma wanted me to take him to meet the Pastor. That's all it is."

The older boy did not believe him, suspicious

something else was going on. He stepped closer, and then he gave Diego a shove that pushed him on his heels. "Shit no. Don't lie to me. He's a cop, isn't he?"

"No, he's a teacher. I'm telling the truth, just wanted to talk with Pastor Siqueiros." His voice cracked enough to be noticeable by everyone."

"About what," the older boy was angry.

"Don't know. The Pastor told me to leave." His eyes widen, anticipated the situation to go from bad to worse. He swallowed deeply.

The older boy smacked Diego in the face with his fist, toppled him back so that he fell to the ground. "Don't lie to me!" His voice, now louder than before, oozed with anger.

The others watched, waited for an order to kick the kid flat on the ground.

Now standing over Diego, the older boy shuffled some dirt on him with a swift move of his foot. "Stay away from him." The order was clear, no need to be more precise.

Diego knew better than to argue with the older boy. The odds were too much against him to try to defend himself, so he kept quiet.

Without further talk, the older boy turned away as the others followed him like a herd of sheep.

Later the same day, Diego respectfully listened as his mother gave him a harsh scolding. "You've been hanging around them again. I told you to stay away. They're no good." Her eyes bored sharply.

"I - I just went to help Pastor Siqueiros with a few things. They told me to stay away from him."

"The Pastor, they want you to stay away from Pastor Siqueiros?"

"No, the teacher, Mr. Sullivan, the man who's going to teach me to read," he wanted his mother to understand.

She thought for a moment, and then asked, "Why would they do that?"

"They want me to be part of their gang. They don't want me to have no other friends except them."

She'd always understood the harsh realities of the neighborhood, the gangs, their turf protection tactics, and their recruiting strategies. She'd really like to move away, someplace where there would be a better chance for her son to grow up with positive opportunities. Sadly, she'd most likely not find another decent paying job elsewhere. She figured just a few more years to get her son through high school, and then if he was lucky to a community college. Just a few more years' time was all she thought she needed. Her face softened as she looked at her son. Then, she grabbed him close to her bosom. "I love you baby." A few precious moments passed before she gently separated him from her. "What time did Mr. Sullivan say he be around to teach you?"

He gave his mother a warm smile. He knew her toughness was to keep him out of trouble, but he wondered why she didn't trust him just a little more. It would make his life easier, or so he thought. "Three-thirty, when I get home from school. He wants to start next month, Monday."

She returned his smile with one of her own. A warm feeling ran through her body as she thought to herself that this might be something very special for her son.

***

The Oceanside Pistol Range was located in a sparsely inhabited part of the city. A few rare pieces of vacant acreage stretched out to the North and East. There was a bar to the South, and a stripper's joint to the West. A western breeze made its way off the Pacific Ocean on occasion to clean up the pungent odor cast from the establishments. Camp Pendleton, a U. S. Marine training base, was nearby.

The Range was founded in 1960 by a couple of combat Marine veterans, been around for a long time. Little had been done to refurbish the concrete exterior walls except to paint over graffiti that occasionally was the result of a few peaceniks' labor of love and demonstration.

Entering the building was like crossing into a different time dimension that dated back to days of the Viet Nam War. There were worn out arrows on the cement floor to lead customers to different destination spots, and the walls were stenciled with ads from a while back. The retro look was much in evidence. The deeper one moved into the building the stronger was the smell of gunpowder and tobacco smoke.

There were ten shooting stalls that allowed customers to shoot their own pistols at targets with a bull's eye or an imaginary mugger. Beyond paying an hourly fee of $49 and using their own ammunition, each person was required to show a valid proof of gun ownership and a current certificate from an approved shooting course. The Range offered a ninety-nine minute safety course for $99. While a large sign indicated it was a first come first serve system, old timers often reserved shooting times in advance.

The customer base was more varied than you'd think. While military personnel made up the majority, some came to let off steam from a hard day's work, some did it mainly for personal protection, while others secretly lathered in pleasure that was never mentioned to anyone else. Not many customers came to communicate with each other on a social or business basis. In places such as this, there were always the hard cores. For some, shooting was better than running a few miles, pumping iron, or spinning on a cycle. Several even thought it was better than sex. The most common expression after an hour of squeezing the trigger of a hand gun was relaxation. Go figure.

Riley turned into a parking spot on the road, and twisted around to face Graham. "I hope this works."

"Me too, a few surfers told me it's worth your time and money if you're thinking of owning a gun."

Riley wiggled his eyebrows as he turned off the engine. "Let's go see."

Both men made their way towards The Oceanside Pistol Range for Riley's first safety class in pistol shooting.

Graham reminded his buddy of something important. "The old man might be old and in the hospital, but from what you've told me about him, you've got to protect yourself. You've never fired a gun before, so this safety course makes sense." He waited for Riley to agree, but there was no response.

Riley had not been in many dark and dingy places before, so entering The Oceanside Pistol Range was a totally new experience. It took a little while for his eyes to adjust. A few timely prompts by Graham helped him move along.

Suddenly he felt a little shiver, and then he wondered if it was a signal of what was next to come, or might it be a reaction to the low-sixty degree temperature inside. He noticed several customers wearing sweaters and a few others with leather jackets. He wanted to ask Graham why his buddy hadn't let him in on the temperature conditions, but then reconsidered when he rechecked to see both were wearing short sleeve Hawaiian shirts. A few feet ahead a sign indicated to stop. He and Graham complied.

A guy with a mustache sat in a chair, separated from the two men with a wired mesh window that seemed strong enough to protect anyone from entering the area. His head was covered with a ski-like wool hat and a tattoo on his left arm that showed off an insignia that Riley couldn't make out and didn't want to ask about. The cold temperature didn't seem to bother the guy. Riley took a quick look around the guy to check what was inside the room. He saw, what appeared to be, handguns, ammunition, cans of oil lubricant, and lots of paper stacked messily in various places. Riley thought he'd reached the right location.

The guy behind the wired meshed window lifted his head ever so slightly. "Yeah," his voice was rough sounding as if he hadn't figured out how to stay away from smoking and drinking. His eyes gave off a gloomy appearance. His larger-than-life left hand held onto a half smoked cigar, while his right hand rested on top of a counter.

Riley spotted an embroidered name written on the man's military fatigue uniform, Shady. He hesitated before saying anything, somewhat intimidated by Shady's persona.

"What's up?"

The simple phrase seemed to break the silence.

"I've registered to take the gun safety course." Riley's voice was noticeably nervous sounding.

"You've come to the right place." Shady took a long puff from the cigar, blew the smoke off to the side, and then looked down at a piece of paper, "Name?"

"Riley Sullivan."

Shady nodded his head as he placed a check mark alongside Riley's name. "Your friend, an escort," he lifted his head to look at Graham.

Graham twisted his nose from left to right, prepared to correct the man, but decided otherwise, "Yep."

"Ninety-nine dollars cash, no checks and no cards." His eyes moved back to Riley. He continued sitting on a wooden stool, and then glanced at the two men alternatively.

As Riley took out just the right amount of money, Shady filled out a few pieces of paper.

"Sign where the X's are and date it today." Shady slid

the papers underneath the wired mesh as he grabbed the money. While Riley signed the documents, Shady counted the money. The simple transaction was done in silence. After Riley finished his part he returned the papers by shoving the papers towards Shady.

Satisfied the paperwork was in order, Shady handed Riley a slip of paper. "Take this to the room down the hall. You're ready to go." He took another puff from the cigar. "You've got to stay here. No pay, no play." The message was directed towards Graham.

A few minutes after one PM, Riley emerged from the room. His face was a mixture of relaxation and excitation. He tilted his head to the side as he walked the hallway. Then he stopped at the window with the wired mesh.

Shady sat on the same stool as if he had not moved once since the first contact with Riley. He gave Riley a head nod, and then looked down at the small space between the wire and counter top that was used to slide money and documents back and forth. He saw Riley's hand move the same slip of paper he originally gave him, this time it indicated Riley had successfully completed the safety course. Shady initialed the slip of paper, and then dropped it into a metal basket. "Sacramento will send you your official certificate within ten days. Then, you can buy a pistol, not before."

"Really," Riley acted surprised.

"That's how it is."

"Just one more thing," asked Riley.

"Can you recommend a good place to buy a gun?"

"What's your purpose, protection, collection, or something else?"

"Protection," there was no hesitation with the response.

Shady turned towards his right, shuffled through a few pieces of paper to his side, and finally found the one he was looking for. "Here are the ones I recommend. Honest people, good selection, reasonable prices." He slid the paper underneath the wired mesh.

"Hey, thanks for everything."

"Come on back for practice. You know what they say."

"Yeah, catch you later." Riley turned to walk, but then stopped to ask another question. "Do you know where my buddy went?"

"Probably outside, there's no room inside the place."

Riley nodded and then walked away feeling a strange increase in self-confidence for some reason. Outside he spotted Graham.

"How did it go?"

"I can't tell you how great I feel. Man ... it's ... well ... a fantastic feeling."

Graham puckered his lips, and then said, "Hey, I'm starved. Let's get something to eat. You can tell me more about it then."

The next day Riley received a surprise phone call. "Mr. Riley Sullivan?"

He wasn't sure who the caller was, but the voice was familiar. "Who's this?"

"Detective Cabo, got a minute?"

He wanted to answer with *got a warrant*, but decided against it. "Sure, what's it about?" His grin quickly turned more somber.

"I understand you completed a gun safety course the other day."

"Yeah," he cleared his throat, and then said, "How did you know?"

"A little birdie told me."

"What?"

"Local law enforcement is notified anytime someone buys a gun or takes a gun safety course. It's the law."

He glanced around the room, quickly lost the self-confidence he felt just yesterday. He took in a deep breath before he said another word. "I see."

"Does this have anything to do with Alfred Smuts?"

"Why would it?" A little confidence mixed with more defiance appeared. He was getting a little tired of all the questions. He wanted answers.

She realized he was trying to play a cat and mouse game that he'd surely lose. Cabo decided to stop the match before it got out of hand. "Listen, I'm only doing my job. I'm trying to make sure you don't do anything foolish that would get you into trouble later on."

Riley had not figured it out. "What kind of trouble?" He thought he was outsmarting her.

She laughed outright. "I don't believe you are that naive."

He pushed on. "It only makes sense to know how to properly use a gun. Don't you agree?"

"What type of gun are you planning to buy?"

The surprise question threw him for a loop. Without thinking he replied, "I've got to shop around. I don't know yet." Then he realized he'd said too much.

"If you buy a gun, you know that it too will be registered. There is a sixty day wait period to check your background. Law enforcement will be notified. You won't be able to carry a concealed weapon." She paused, and then continued, "You do know all of this, don't you?"

"Are you worried?"

"Yes I am." She took in a deep breath, "Just routine, nothing more."

"Yeah, sure," It was his turn to pause before he said anything more. "Is there anything else, or are we finished?"

"How old are you?" She asked unexpectedly.

The question took him by surprise. "Why do you want to know?" He was not about to tell her anymore.

"I was just thinking that you seem to be the same age as one of my friends, but you give the impression of being much younger."

"How old is your friend?"

"About your age," she was beginning to enjoy matching his wits.

He did not see her shake her head in disappointment.

She continued, "I was hoping you'd be more cooperative."

Beneath his breath Riley said, *no kidding*. Then, louder

for Cabo to hear, "Thanks for the call. Is there anything else I can help you with?" There was no mistake with understanding the sarcasm.

"I thought we could handle this over the phone, but I guess I was mistaken." She waited for Riley to say something. She shook her head with displeasure when he kept silent.

Riley wondered if he was getting too deep into something he knew little about.

She did not see him frown. "I want you to come down to see me today. There are some things we've got to clear up."

"What about," he wasn't giving up being difficult.

"We found the three people you visited and we found the dead limousine driver." She paused. "Did you know the three people you interviewed are also dead?" She waited to hear his response.

His voice rose to almost one higher octave. "I - I...." He let the words drift off.

"They were killed." She let the words settle in. "Did you have anything to do with it?"

"You don't think I killed them, do you?"

"Did you?"

"Hell no," he felt cornered with no way out.

"But you knew they were dead before you talked with me."

Riley cleared his throat. He knew he'd been caught. "Yes. When I couldn't get in contact with Smuts, I did a little research on the Internet where I read about them. I should have been honest with you."

"Should have ... could have ... would have ... I hear too much of that these days."

He heard disgust and disappointment in her voice.

She waited for a reply, but he kept quiet. "Come on down today. We'll clear it up."

He wasn't happy with how this was turning about, but figured it was probably better to cooperate than to resist. "OK, I'll be there shortly." He hung up the phone without giving Cabo a chance to say anything further. He told himself to back off trying to battle with her. He knew he was out of his league.

Riley rolled into the parking lot of the police station in less than an hour later. He made his way into the building still feeling a mixture of anger and nervousness with it all.

"Thanks for coming in." While her voice seemed pleasant on the surface, she was much different. "This way," she said as they walked down the hallway towards the same room used before when he and Graham first met the Detective.

Once settled in seats, Riley said, "I'm sorry I didn't tell you everything before."

She heard a noticeable quiver in his voice. "Right," she let out a whiff of air, and then she continued. "We now know all three people you interviewed were shot with a .32 caliber rifle. That would be Leah Clare, Adrianne Browde, and Florence Hobare. We can't tell if the rifle is American made or from another country, but it shouldn't take us long to find that out. The limousine driver put a bullet into his own head as you already claimed. His name is Alexander Bahiminia, and he had a long criminal record ranging from minor robberies to attempted murder. You were lucky he didn't finish you off as intended.

Silence, and then Riley said, "The old man is behind all of this"

"Could be, maybe not." She continued to look directly at him.

"Who else could it be?" He looked away for a split second and then back to Cabo. "The limo driver even implied it!"

"It's your word against a dead man's word." She frowned. "But you can still help out."

"I don't know anything more about the old man than what I've already told you. We both know he's a patient at St. Anthony's Hospital, so why don't you interview him?"

"He's had a heart attack and is in intensive care. The doctors don't think it's safe to talk with him now. There is a guard posted 24 - 7 outside his private room making sure everyone who enters and leaves is approved. I don't want some wacko ending his life before I have the chance to talk with him. He's our only real person of interest at this time."

Relieved to hear some positive news he said, "So, I'm not someone you suspect?"

"No, not presently," the words were said without emotion.

He took in a deep breath of needed air. Another

silence, and then Riley said, "You know, I wonder what the connection might be among the three women."

"Smart thinking," she gave him a little smile. "They're all related to each other."

"Oh," he was surprised to hear the news.

"And they're all related to Alfred Smuts."

"No!"

Cabo explained. "Adrianne Browde was his former wife, while Leah Clare and Florence Hobare were his daughters."

He was almost unable to take in some fresh air. "Why does anybody do stuff like that, murder three women?"

"The world's full of crazy people. You tell me. But remember, there is no evidence Smuts had anything to do with the murders, and your attempted murder. He's innocent until proven guilty."

Riley knew she was correct, but just the same didn't like it. "I told you before that I don't know anything else. I'm still trying to figure out all of this."

"What about the driver?" She was persistent. "Did you know him before?"

"No, that was the first time I met him."

"There's one thing I found out about Smuts," she said.

Riley shook his head, "What's that?"

"He didn't care much for his former wife and two daughters."

"How do you know that?"

"The divorce papers are filled with all sorts of things

that I can't share with you." She wiggled her eyebrows, "Only on a need-to-know basis. You understand."

"So it was messy."

Without saying a word, she nodded her head to agree.

He asked, "Messy enough to make him kill them?" He couldn't believe what he was hearing himself say.

Another silence, this time she kept her response confidential. Then she continued, "Do you remember when you first met him?"

"Sure."

She reached for a file folder, opened it, and readied to take notes. "Tell me what happened, and give me your impressions."

Riley cleared his throat. "Well, nothing at first seemed odd. I mean, after I stopped to help him, he had fixed whatever engine problem there was. Then he offered to buy me a beer at McCarty's as a thank you for stopping."

"Do you remember the type of vehicle?"

"Yeah, a Nissan Pathfinder," he seemed convinced of the type of vehicle.

"What about the color, year, license plate, or anything else that would identify the specific vehicle?"

He thought for a while, "Black color. That's all I remember."

She continued to write a few notes as she said, "Go on."

"Well, we had a few beers. Things were going along fine, just two guys passing the time." He paused to think about something, and then continued. "Then we got into a deeper level of conversation about death and who would inherit what when you die. At first it seemed strange to talk about these things, but, well, that's just how it went."

Cabo asked a question. "So, there wasn't anything about him or the conversation that was troubling to you?"

"Not at first. I can't remember exactly how it happened but it seemed all of a sudden he told me he wanted to give away one hundred thousand dollars to someone who would spend the money wisely." He paused, "Oh, yeah, he did mention that he was divorced with two girls who were intent on inheriting all that he owned, but he was equally intent not for them to get anything."

She shrugged her shoulders and said, "That's a possible motive." She nodded his way to encourage him to continue.

"Then he somehow got me to talk about myself." He stopped.

She looked up, "Go on. There's something important you want to tell me."

He looked away for a split second and then he picked up the conversation again. "I told him I was a college professor, and I might have told him that while I enjoyed teaching there wasn't much money involved. It could have been then that he offered me the job, you know, to interview the people." He shook his head to admonish himself. "That's when he offered me five thousand dollars and a bonus once the job was done."

She continued writing and kept quiet since he was doing exactly what she wanted him to do.

"He showed me a pocket watch that he claimed was worth over fifty thousand dollars." He looked away and then returned to look at Detective Cabo. "I'm still not sure why he showed me the watch." He took in a deep breath. "I guess I really didn't know much about the guy who I decided to do business with."

"How could you if he wasn't about to be honest with you." She paused, "He conned you, pure and simple."

"So you think he wanted me to get into trouble with the cops?"

"It appears to be more to get the heat off of him. You were simply convenient."

"I've never killed anyone! I pay my taxes! I obey the law!" Riley said passionately. "Do I need to have a lawyer?"

"Do you think you need one? I've already said you are not a person of interest in this case."

Silence returned.

"Nah, I haven't done anything illegal."

"OK, then, let's go on. What other impressions?" Her voice was softer than before, comforting in a way to encourage Riley to share more information.

"Each time I talked with him on the phone he got more and more irritable with me. He was sarcastic. I almost quit."

"Why didn't you?"

"I guess I figured if I could just finish the job I'd have five thousand dollars to pay off bills, maybe a little more since he mentioned a bonus of some sort at the end of the deal. The money would have really helped me out." He puffed out a breath of air. Then he continued, "I'll lay odds he knew exactly what he was doing." He smacked his lips together. "He figured me out as a good guy, a sort of patsy in a way, whom he could use to do some of his dirty work. And I fell right into it."

"Probably didn't care who he hurt along the way," she added.

"Probably didn't think anyone would make the connections. And, we almost didn't!"

"But there still isn't any proof that he did anything illegal."

Disappointment covered his face.

***

His downfall started well before he saw it coming, too engrossed in making money, swindling people out of their nest eggs. He had always been that way, even as early as a teenager at eighteen. Nothing else really mattered to the old man, even before he got the pocket watch. At times he would close his eyes, smile, count the people he'd harm as rolls of hundred dollar bills floated before him. The old man didn't worry because he never thought it would come to an end.

Few people knew he was wealthy, and that was just the way he wanted it to be. He wore clothes that made him appear to be poor.

His third wife, Adrianne Browde, divorced him and financially took him to the cleaners. She was clever enough to convince a judge that their prenuptial agreement was invalid so that she was due one-half of his assets. Her two children from a previous marriage, Leah Clare and Florence Hobare, each married and divorced themselves, shared in the proceeds.

He had always had a breathing problem, asthma, developed when he was quite young. That didn't stop him from smoking and drinking heavily while putting off any form of physical exercise. Once he reached his sixties, breathing became even more difficult. He vehemently denied acknowledging he was getting old, yet his stamina lessened as weariness increased. He even dreamed at times he was dying.

He went to doctors around the country to give him a magical elixir that would return his youthfulness. It goes without saying that he never found anyone who could give him the miraculous potion. While he never gave up seeking the perfect mixture, he became angrier and angrier, determined to get himself into better health.

Then he convinced himself that everyone was out to get him. That paranoid led him to go after those closest to him. First on his list were Adrianne, Leah, and Flo. He had no real plan before he unexpectedly met Riley. At first, everything worked fine, but then it all changed to a different story after the massive heart attack.

The old man laid flat on his back in St. Anthony's Hospital recounting his life. He was determined to make the remaining time much different than those already gone.

It was tougher than imagined. Riley Sullivan was the only one who could help him, but in a much different way. The old man had to convince Riley he was sincere in spite of the unsuccessful hit he ordered on him. In some way, that failure might be a pathway to making atonement for the ruthless deeds he committed in his life.

He guessed he had less than one year left, but that was only a guess. The doctors determined the time was probably much less. There was no stream of well wishers who visited him. With 24 -7 guard at the entrance of the private hospital room, the old man seemed to be sealed off from doing anything. In fact, the betting odds were he would die alone in this very same room before any likelihood to make amends.

Another week passed as did the chances of any sort of reasonable recovery from the massive heart attack. Intravenous liquid dripped into his thin purplish veins. Bed sores started to form since movement was next to impossible. He began to suffer more than he ever imagined possible. Eyes shut, his mouth contoured in the only way he knew how. "Ah," he moaned. "Ah." He felt the most helpless he'd ever felt. He thought to himself, *Isn't there anyone who cares just a little about me? Don't they know what's happened to me?*

The fact of the matter was the world had not stopped to take notice of his situation, nor did it seem to care, except for the Hospital clinicians who dutiful attended to him the best they could.

Seldom experienced tears formed at the corners of his eyes. He tried to cry but that too was unsuccessful. He felt as if he was experiencing his own funeral.

7

"You've been preoccupied with something for the past week or so since you finished the gun safety course. Want to talk about it?" Graham sipped a Stella from the bottle. Surf conditions were not suitable, waves too small and infrequent. He held onto the bottle with his hand.

Riley quickly recovered from his self-imposed thoughts. He murmured at first. "I went to the Hosptial where the old man is. There's a security guard right outside his room. Impossible to get in." He mimicked Graham's sip of beer. "Nurses' station won't let me close to him unless my name is on the list of relatives." He glanced away. "Strange that when I asked to see the list, I was told there weren't any names what-so-ever."

Graham shrugged, "I guess no one is really interested in whether he lives or dies."

"Seems to be the case."

"That's it, nothing else going on?"

"The good news is Diego is coming along nicely. I'm

surprised he's gotten into reading so quickly. It's like there was all this built up passion to read. All he needed was the opportunity." Riley smiled, happy to be part of the kid's education. He looked at Graham who seemed surprised. "Oh, I guess I forgot to tell you. I'm helping the kid to read."

Graham shrugged his shoulders, not much interested in hearing about it. He had something else to ask, "I wonder how the old man feels?"

Riley thought Graham's question to be strange. He shook his head as though to say he was not really interested in talking about it.

Graham was persistent, "Come on, don't you want to know?"

Riley felt his emotions build. "OK, OK, I hope he's in pain! Is that what you want to hear?"

"Don't ask me. Is that what you want to say?"

A little out of control Riley continued, "Hell, the old man tried to kill me! How should I feel?" His eyes widened.

Before Graham lifted the bottle to his lips for another swig, he said, "Feel whatever you feel." He took a long gulp and then reset the bottle on the table not showing much emotion one way or the other.

Riley nodded and was a little more settled down. "I really want to talk with him, to know why he wanted someone to interview his ex and two daughters. I don't think he had any intention of giving away his money. What's also driving me crazy is if he was going to kill them, why did he want someone to interview them first, and why me?" He felt his breathing accelerate just thinking about it all.

"But you don't really know if he killed anyone, and if he is responsible for trying to kill you. It's just your guess."

"When I asked the limo driver where the old man was, he told me he was replacing the old man, that he was just doing his job."

"Did you tell the police this?"

"Yeah, but the limo driver is dead so there's no way to prove it. Just my words." Riley raised his shoulders.

"OK, let's assume he's responsible and you find out his reasons, then what?"

The question stumped Riley for a short time. He was lost in thought. "I don't know. I just don't know."

"So why did you take the gun safety course?" Graham asked. "Aren't you planning to buy a revolver?"

"I don't know. It seemed the right thing to do at the time. I was all worked up. I'm not sure anymore."

This time Graham shrugged his shoulders. Then he looked down. "Up for another?"

Riley said, "Sure, why not." He paused. "I'm up." He stood to go get two more Stella Artois beers.

Standing at the bar, he ordered two more beers, and then Riley turned to his right. There was a sign, **Lunch Being Served**. Margo was working the lunch counter as she did most every day until two in the afternoon when she was not attending nursing school. He gave her a wave. She returned with a big smile. He stared at her for an awkwardly long time, and suddenly wondered why he'd never asked her out. She was sure attractive enough, single, about his age, and friendly. Maybe it was time.

"Two Stellas."

His thoughts were interrupted as he turned his attention elsewhere. "Yeah, right." Slowly, he took the two bottles, hesitated for a few seconds, and then he decided to return to the booth where Graham sat.

Still on his mind, he asked Graham, "What do you think of Margo?" He placed both bottles on the table, continued to stand to wait for a reply.

Another shrug. " Why?"

"I don't know." He took a seat on the booth. "When I looked at her just a second ago, I wondered for the first time why I never asked her out."

"There's only one way to find out." He grabbed one of the two bottles. "Don't ask, don't get." He took a sip.

"How come you've never asked her out?"

"Who says?" Graham wiggled his eyebrows.

"Really?"

"Once, a while back. She wasn't interested." He took another sip.

"Maybe I will." Riley lifted the bottle to his lips. "Maybe I will," he repeated. He glanced her way as Margo wrote down on a piece of paper a customer's luncheon order.

"This sure is a strange way to start out on a first date." She looked at Riley, turned once around. "How do I look?"

Riley smiled, enjoyed what he saw. "Perfect. You look just like a nurse."

Hoping for a bit more of a personal compliment, she said, "That's it?"

He was not sure what she meant so he shrugged his shoulders. Better to keep quiet than to say something that he'd regret later on. He looked at his watch. "We should be going now."

Margo grabbed the keys to her apartment door to notice Riley was already in the hallway waiting for her. She wondered if she had misjudged him. She moved as quickly as she could to meet up with Riley, closed and then locked the door. She gave him a smile that most men would die for, to change the evening's plans by immediately returning to her apartment for the rest of the evening.

This was not the case then. Riley had something else more pressing. His steps were both longer and quicker than Margo's as if it was some sort of race he must win. He stood by the passenger side door, and opened it. His good manners were noticeablly more pleasing to her than his impatience.

She slid into the seat, quickly looked around to figure the interior had recently been cleaned. She heard the door click shut.

He rushed around the front of the car to get into the driver's side, started the engine, and drove off. "This shouldn't take us long. It'll be over with quicker than you think." There was a jumpiness in his voice, a sure sign of tension.

"I'm OK, but you seem nervous." She looked his way. There was a slight concern on her face. "Are you all right?"

"Sure." The one-word answer was quick and sounded jittery.

"Riley, are you sure you're all right. You're a bundle of nerves." She tried to console him at the same time being candid. "Are you this way all the time?"

He took in a deep breath. "I guess I am all worked up. I'm sorry, but this is very important to me, and I really need your help."

She patted his right hand that held onto the manual shift stick. "I'm by your side. I won't let you down."

A smile broke out on his face. He gave her a glance that showed his gratitude. "I feel better already." He took in a deep breath. "I told you about the old man, how he tricked me into a scheme, and then how he tried to kill me. I've got lots of questions for him." He was still convinced Smuts was behind everything.

"I know, I know. You went over that with me before." Her voice was soft and soothing. Margo's hand still rested on his. She gently squeezed his hand. Then, she changed the topic. "Is this the only reason you asked me out, to help you with the old man?" She immediatley felt his hand tighen underneath hers. She realized she'd taken him by surprise. There was no way to rewind the tape.

He paused, then with remarkable self-assurance he clarified. "Not all guys are confident with women. I'm one of them who is actually a little shy. I'm better when I'm around a group of people than one-on-one. I think that might be one reason why I'm pretty good teaching a class of twenty to forty students." He hesitated for a second and then he continued. "Graham is probably my best friend. He's different from me in interests, but he's real easy to talk with. No pressure. We just say what's on our minds."

"You're doing all right with me." She felt his hand loosen.

"I guess so. Hmm." He glanced towards her with a smile.

"I'm glad you asked me out." She gave his hand another gentle squeeze.

"So am I." He couldn't think of anything else to say.

The next several minutes were driven in silence, both comfortable with taking a break in the conversation. There'd be time for more of this talk in the future, not now.

He pulled into the driveway of St. Anthony's Hospital, followed the sign to Visitor Parking. There were several spots available so he picked one at the very end where there were no nearby vehicles that might accidently nick his vehicle. "Just to be safe," he said aloud thinking she understood the reason.

She wanted to say, *doesn't matter*, but simply let it go.

He felt himself start to get jittery all over again, so he took in a deep breath. This time, he grabbed her hand for support. He started to settle down.

Margo decided to resume a conversation to get things back on the right track. "This is easy. It'll be over with soon and I'll meet you in the lobby." She leaned over to kiss him on the cheek.

He felt like a million dollars, invigorated that everything was going to work out as planned.

———————————

She snapped on an improvised name tag to indicate she was a visiting nurse from another hospital, something that was common among reciprocal hospitals such as St. Anthony's.

Separately, they entered the Hospital lobby. Riley took a seat alongside a magazine rack, grabbed one, and started to read an article while Margo walked in behind him dressed in an official nurse's uniform.

She proceeded to the bank of elevators, checked out the floor level of intensive care patients, pushed a button labeled **5**. Margo waited as the elevator descended to ground level. "Bing," the elevator announced its presence. Confidently, as if she was a nurse reporting for her shift, she let the elevator take her to the fifth floor. Fortunately, with no one joining her on the elevator, it ascended without stopping. "Bing," the elevator announced its presence again.

With assurance, she stepped out onto the floor, looked around, and found the nurses' station. She headed straight for the place without looking around. It all seemed normal, nurses everywhere going into and out of patients' rooms. Margo was pleased there was a good level of activity to help mask her true identify. She blended in without others taking notice. Quickly, she surveyed the nurses' station to pick out the clip board containing patient names and room numbers. She spotted what she was looking for,

Alfred Smuts, room 518. She walked down the hallway without being noticed by others.

Now, within a few yards of room 518, she spotted a security guard slouched on a wooden chair. He seemed bored who would rather be some other place. She had the right solution for his predicament. Margo slowed down her pace, took longer strides and strutted out her chest. Now, in front of the security guard, she stopped, and gave him a big juicy smile. She quickly spotted his name tag. "Hello Harvey." She kept her pose so he could take in the view. "Having a long day, huh?" She waited for the expected surprise.

He straightened up, pulled his extended feet close in. "Uh, hello." He paused, unable to think of anything else to say. His eyes moved from her face to remain glued on her chest for an awkwardly long time.

She let him enjoy the view for a little while longer. Then she continued. "I've got to check Mr. Smuts' medications. It should take me about five minutes. I can prolong it if you want to get a cup of coffee. I'll wait until you return." She kept her pose for as long as it took.

"I - I shouldn't leave."

"I won't tell if you won't." Margo gave him a seductive smile. She wiggled her eyebrows.

While he was thinking of something other than a cup of coffee, the break and beverage sounded awfully tempting at the moment. "OK, I'll be back in five minutes. Don't leave before I return."

"I wouldn't think of it. Now go." She kept the smile directed his way.

With the security guard out of sight, Margo entered room 518. She felt excitement grow. Quickly, she moved her eyes around the room. It seemed like most other patients' rooms she'd been to during her field studies. She spotted the clip board at the foot of the bed. She noticed Smuts sleeping, breathing was labored. He looked like death warmed over. She held a stare longer than normal and then moved closer to grab the clipboard to review his condition, prognosis, and medications. Her eyes moved purposely. It didn't look good that he'd survive much longer. She wondered how anyone could do the things that Riley said he'd done. She arrived at the same opinion of Riley that the man was no good, through and through, and yet, she had no proof of anything, just Riley's words.

She took a few more seconds to stare at the documentation, and then another look at Smuts. She shook her head. Then, she took a digital camera out of a pocket, focused it on the man in the bed, and clicked off a few shots. She reviewed them quickly to make sure she'd captured the essence of the patient. She replaced the camera in her pocket. She looked around the room as if she was surveying the patient's room for the first time, to pick up anything that might be useful. Nothing of significance struck her attention. It appeared she was about finished, when Smuts let out a loud sound.

"Ah."

She froze, and then there was silence. She stepped closer to him to check if he was still breathing. Satisfied the utterance was nothing more than a natural sound, she backed away. About to go, Margo took one more look at the room. Putting aside the role she'd placed herself in by helping out Riley, she felt a sense of joy that soon she'd be a practicing nurse in a short time. She'd like her mother to be proud of her, but was quite sure that wouldn't be the case.

Dispensing with the agreement she made with Harvey just a short time ago, she stepped away from room 518, and headed for the elevators. However, her departure was temporarily interrupted.

"Code Blue, Room 527," the announcement came through loud and clear over the floor's address system. A backup pager system simultaneously sent the same message to the necessary personnel who might be inside other patients' rooms. The Code signified that an emergency was occurring, specifically a cardiac respiratory arrest.

It did not take Margo long to resolve what she must do. Believing she was not adequately clinically prepared to be of any help to the patient in room 527, she kept her pledge to do no harm.

***

She left the fifth floor to meet up with Riley. The elevator ride stopped at every floor, prolonging reuniting with him.

Finally, she stepped off the elevator, spotted Riley in the same place she left him, and then she walked past him. Under her breath so only he could hear, she said, "Follow me."

They met outside next to his vehicle.

Antonio F. Vianna

She was the first to speak. "Everything went perfectly."
She grabbed his head in her hands to plant a long kiss on
his lips. He didn't resist.

"Let's celebrate."

"Finally," she gleefully said.

Harvey returned from the cafeteria with a cup of
coffee in his hand, unaware of the emergency. A Code
Blue team provided necessary resuscitative efforts to save
the patient in room 527, a few rooms away. He looked
through the door window of room 518 to check if the
attractive nurse was still inside. Except for the sleeping
patient, she was nowhere to be found. He brushed off the
nurse's absence as probably attending to another patient.
He plopped his oversized body on the same chair, sipped
his coffee.

They arrived at The Fashion Show, a new club on
Carlsbad Village Drive. The place was packed with people
from diverse backgrounds, dancing and drinking to a
live band, Guilty as Charged. The loud music made it
difficult to talk, but for now, that was exactly what Riley
and Margo were looking for. There would be time for
conversation later on.

She didn't change the nurse's uniform. The dress
code was almost non-existent that allowed for a wide
interpretation. People were dressed in all sorts of clothes,

except it seemed most women were dressed in two sizes too small.

"I didn't know this place existed. How do you know about it?" Riley almost had to yell to get her to understand the question.

"I guess you don't get out much." She smiled, grabbed his hand, and took him to a table where there were other people talking and drinking. There were two empty chairs. She shouted to the people who were sitting, "Are these in use?"

A nod indicating they were available was all she needed. She took a seat.

Riley followed. He pulled out a chair and sat down suddenly realizing he was tired and that his muscles were tight. "What do you want to drink?"

"Let's dance first. Come on." She stood, grabbed his hand, and pulled him onto the dance floor. The music was fast and without words, only the instruments told the story.

He didn't have a chance to tell her he was not a good dancer, but it only took her a few seconds to figure it out. She thought he was cute and definitely appealing. They remained on the floor once the dance ended. Then she deliberately yelled out, "Precious Love!" She was quite familiar with this band, aware they knew the oldie. It had a slow and easy going beat, a better fit with Riley's dancing ability, at least that's what she hoped for. The music started again. She pressed her body close to him, felt his response. She'd made a good decision. She grabbed the nape of his neck with her hand, and then slowly blew warm air into his ear. She pleasured in the automatic reaction from him. "Oh yeah", she whispered, "Oh yeah."

He didn't try to pull away, but when the dance ended he secretly was thankful.

"I'm ready for that drink," she faintly said.

"What'll you have, beer, wine?" Riley was surprised with her answer.

"I think I need something stronger." She smiled directly in his eyes.

They left The Fashion Show a little after one in the morning and arrived at Margo's place a short time after. He parked in an empty space. They remained quiet for a short time until Riley spoke.

"I had a great time." He couldn't think of anything else to say.

A grin lingered on her face. "Great? I thought it was incredible." She let her body relax as her head touched the seat's head rest. She closed her eyes. "I wasn't really sure what would happen tonight, you know, first date and all. But I must say you are a real gentleman."

Riley closed his eyes for a quick second, and said to himself, *Good grief. Here comes the let's be friends part.*

She continued. "There aren't many gentlemen these days. You're one of those special ones." She turned to face him. "I hope we can see each other again. Really I do."

He did not pick out the hesitation in her voice. Why would he, she's got him hooked. "I hope so too." He leaned over to kiss her. They stayed embraced for a while longer. Then he said, "We still need to talk about what happened at the Hospital."

"Yeah, I know. But to be honest, Riley, I'm exhausted right now. Can we talk about it later on?"

He wondered if he should hint about staying the night with her. He swallowed, about to say something, but she beat him to it.

"I'd love to ask you in, to stay the night, but I don't think that would be right. I hope you understand. Another time, later on," her look was sincere and final. There was no room for negotiation. She didn't want to come across as being easy.

"Margo, while I'd love to try to convince you otherwise, I think you're right, another time, later on." He took a pause. "I actually was getting nervous about which way it would go. I'm glad you took it head on."

"I'm sure you would have if I hadn't."

"I guess so."

"I've got classes tomorrow, so I won't be at McCarty's. Mid terms are almost here so I've got to study. However, if we can agree to see each other again, I'd love it."

He smiled at her. "I won't let you get away. What about next Thursday?"

She nodded, "That works for me. I'll make lunch at my place, say at noon." She waited for his answer.

"Great," he was very pleased with the outcome.

Later on after he left Margo, Riley got in bed, face was towards the ceiling. His hands were placed under his head as he thought about the evening. No longer was he tired, just the opposite. He was restless, almost to the point of being hyper. He could have fallen asleep if he really tried, but he preferred to think of her. For the time, Smuts was out of his mind. He figured to take one step at a time. He hoped she felt the same way about him.

Monday morning of the following week Riley was awakened at seven with the sound of an alarm clock. He rolled over to switch off the buzzing noise. Yawning, he stretched his arms over his head, arched his back to loosen his back muscles that had stiffened during the night. He rolled out of bed to prepare for the day.

He went through his normal robotic hygienic motions before he stepped downstairs to make breakfast.

He had purposely doubled up his teaching schedule with two different courses at two different universities during the same week to get his mind off of Smuts. That plan was not working out as well as he had hoped.

Today was the first of nine consecutive Monday morning classes at San Diego International University. Students from Europe, Asia, and South America competed to earn the right to attend this prestigious academic institution. He felt privileged to be a faculty member with them.

Last week's University's correspondence informed him of the class size and origins of the students. Thirty-five students were selected, mostly French and German, with a few Chinese and Brazilian who were all in their early twenties.

It took him a short time to prepare and eat breakfast. Within an hour after he woke up, he pulled out of the garage, headed for the Carlsbad Poinsettia Coaster Station. Departing time was nine thirty-four. After he parked in the free parking lot, he headed towards the ticket vending machines to buy a round trip ticket. He made sure to have the correct amount since he was not interested in collecting coins.

He waited on the passenger platform along with only a few other commuters who were also headed South. Earlier passengers were already busily at work. He checked his watch, and then heard a train's whistle. He looked to the North to spot an Amtrak coming his way. It moved quickly without stopping, sharing the same tracks as the Coaster. A delayed breeze of air swooped on his face after the train passed by. In six minutes, the Coaster #644 stopped at this station. He stepped aboard, and then quickly the doors closed. The compartment was empty except for two other passengers whom he recognized. Words were not exchanged as they read the morning newspaper. He was pleased that some people still enjoyed information that was printed on paper. He found a seat, West side, facing the Pacific Ocean and settled in for the next forty-nine minutes that gave him time to think about what had been happening in his life.

He'd never been good with women, sharing his feelings and accepting differences. That's probably why he'd never settled into a long term relationship. Maybe it'd be different with Margo.

The whole situation with the old man still had him baffled. To begin with, he was still amazed he fell for the old man's scam. He'd always thought he had more common sense to avoid opportunities that were too good to be true. Maybe if he hadn't been in such financial distress, he'd have thought more logically, maybe not. Further reflections were interfered with when he heard the conductor announce the next stop was Encinitas.

Riley finally arrived at the University with twenty minutes to spare, just enough time to offer a few cordial comments to staff members and pick up the student roster. Everyone seemed busy to make sure all students were properly credentialed and assigned to their particular course of study. This was the first day of a new group of foreign students. Last minute adjustments were expected. He checked over the roster, grabbed a neatly bundled package in clear plastic that contained copies of the syllabus for each student, and headed for the United Nations classroom. He felt very comfortable in the academic setting where the environment was more structured and expectations were clearly spelled out.

As he walked into the room, most students were already seated and several were busily e-mailing friends and family about their expectations. He smiled to everyone, "Hello. Welcome to San Diego." There was an English-only rule during class time. He heard a few mumbles.

He suspected they had already asked former students about him, as they did with all professors. Some were probably already worried even before the course started that they might fail. That's what reputations did, for better or for worse.

As he looked out into the class he too began a preliminary assessment in a way. The correct word probably was stereotype, for better or for worse. Riley thought he'd already spotted the French students. They were typically dressed most fashionably. Then there were the German students who were organized. The Chinese students were more easily identified from their physical appearance, but if that couldn't be determined, then those students who were most respectful would fall into this category. Finally were the fun-loving and care-free Brazilians, who probably hadn't yet shown up.

He placed his briefcase, the student roster, and the syllabus packet on a desk. Then, he stepped out for a brief minute or two to get a cup of coffee from the faculty lounge and to say hello with anyone else who might have been hanging out before they started their classes.

As he walked into the faculty lounge he heard, "I don't buy that. That's just propaganda to frighten us." He nodded his head to acknowledge the presence of a man and woman arguing over something that he was not interested in getting involved in. He walked past them without comment. He heard, "Here's another example of what I'm talking about." Riley diverted his attention to pour a cup of coffee and then he left as quickly as he could before he was brought into the debate. He was pleased to leave the lounge without any verbal interaction.

He headed back to the United Nations room to begin teaching the course.

⸻

At fifteen minutes to three in the afternoon, Riley started to review next week's assignment. With just a few questions from a German student to clarify how the written paper should be organized, the class ended right at three. He began to pack up to catch the return Coaster to Carlsbad when two Chinese students approached him. Riley stopped to look at them.

The taller student politely said in clear but not perfect English, "Professor Sullivan, we enjoy class very much. We present something from our country." They bowed their heads as the shorter student offered Riley a small box.

Riley understood that expressions of respect varied among cultures. He bowed his head, and accepted the gift. "Thank you very much. I am honored."

They waited for his next move, so he lifted his head and began to open the gift. Inside was a wooden key ring with a carved emblem that signified the province of their home country where they lived. "Thank you again."

They exchanged another round of head bows to end the informal ceremony.

As other students left the classroom Riley offered a friendly smile.

Finally when he was all packed up, he left the United Nations room to head toward the Santa Fe Depot.

8

Riley and Margo began seeing each other as frequently as possible during the next several weeks. He felt good about the relationship, and thought she did too.

Alone, he stood in front of a large window in his place as he gazed at the rain falling, slow but steady, something unusual for this part of Southern California. He'd always enjoyed the rain, a sort of a cleansing, a washing away of unnecessary stuff.

He imagined how differently his life might have been if he had gotten to know Margo sooner. Maybe he wouldn't have fallen for Smut's deception. She seemed to be an almost perfect fit for him. And now, they were talking about moving in together, a big step for her, but a much bigger step for him. He'd not proven to be good at close relationships, better at keeping people at a fair distance. He was almost certain this time would be different, but how can anyone be sure of anything. Unintended consequences happened all the time. His body jumped when the phone suddenly rang. He moved to the black landline telephone on his desk. He felt secure with a few traditional items nearby. He picked up the receiver, not expecting a call from anyone at the moment. He almost did not recognize the voice.

"Riley." Her voice was full of pain and with emotional grief. She began to sob.

"Margo?" It was the only thing he could think of saying. "What's happened?"

She continued to cry, yet managed to say, "It's my sister. She's been in an accident. I've got to go away for a while to be with her."

Up to this point Riley had not been aware Margo had a sister. They really hadn't delved much into each other's family matters. That was one of the purposes for their upcoming live-in arrangement. He wondered if their plan would be put on hold. "I'm sorry. What happened?"

She sniffled, and then continued in spite of the difficulty. "She's always been the wild one in the family. Three girls, she's the second one. Always looking for attention, but rarely getting it." Margo paused and then resumed, "I guess she's going to get the attention now." She didn't answer Riley's question. Was it on purpose or was it an unintentional effect of her distress?

"I'll come right over."

"No, don't bother. I've got to pack a few things to take with me."

He was taken by surprise with her reply. He asked, "Where are you going?"

She paused, "Chino. That's where she lives. It's where I grew up too."

"Are you sure I can't do anything?"

"I'm positive. It's all so sudden." There was deep sorrow in her voice.

"Do you know when you'll return?"

"I don't know. It's all so sudden," she said repeating the message again. "I'll miss you."

"Yes, I miss you already."

"I've got to go. Love you."

He heard the phones disconnect. "I love you too." Gently he replaced the receiver on its cradle. There was absolutely nothing he could do about it. It was what it was. He suddenly felt emptiness deep inside. He looked outside the same window as before. Rain drops continued to beat against the street with much greater ferocity than just a short while ago. He had some crazy notion that more gloom waited for him. He told himself to stay involved with the academic courses he was teaching, and to find a way to get to the old man. Maybe Margo's absence was a gift to keep her away from his concerns with the old man. He had to deal with him in his own way.

Later that night he stretched out in bed to watch the nightly news. There was a story about a crime in Beaumont where an old looking man robbed a bank earlier in the day. The authorities thought the guy disguised himself to look older than his real age. They wondered if it was the same robber who'd gotten away with several other bank robberies in San Diego and Riverside Counties within the last few months. Obviously someone was creative in getting away with the thefts.

He stretched his hands over his head, let out a yawn, and then twisted his neck. He heard a cracking sound that relieved some tension. He repeated the process again. His thoughts switched to Margo. He already missed her. Laying there he suddenly felt a chill overtake his body. He shuddered a little, and then he felt down in the dumps. He knew what was nagging him, and he tried to get it out. He could feel his emotions emerge as he started to cry. He couldn't seem to keep her out of his mind. He was in love with her.

"I really don't love him. Maybe like him to occasionally see him on and off, but no, not in love." Margo was not surprised of the conclusion in spite of telling him something quite differently. Hadn't she already agreed to move in with him?

"Why don't you just tell him?" asked Sandy, her sister. "I thought you were going to move in with him."

She ignored the question. "There's something about his eyes, the way he smiles that's just not for me. It's like he is not really looking at me, but off some other place."

"You've never been able to settle down with one guy. That's your problem."

"Don't be such a creep." Margo said.

"I'm not the creep, you are. You're luring this guy like you've done with every other guy, and then you drop them after they get too close to you. Kind of a bait and switch," Sandy paused, and then continued. "You know I'm right."

"He's got the weirdest laugh."

The youngest sister ignored Margo's comment. "How many weeks has this one lasted, one, two, or longer?"

Margo remained quiet. She knew where her sister was headed and didn't like it. Too often the truth bothered her.

Sandy shrugged. "What about in bed? How's his stuff?"

"Yeah, that's another thing! He's got a lot to learn."

Sandy put a positive spin on the situation. "So, you have the opportunity to teach him. Show him what to do. If this guy loves you, then he'll obey your every command." She gave her sister a smile.

"Come back to the real world. It doesn't work that way." Margo shook her head. "You either got it or you don't." She took in a deep breath. "He doesn't have it."

Sandy reminded her of another guy. "Remember Marshall a while back?"

Margo frowned, wondered what he had got to do with anything.

"He couldn't keep his hands off of you. You said you loved it, but eventually you found something that led you to dump him as well." She hesitated. "Do you remember what that was?"

"I don't want to get into that." Margo's face turned stern, too much truth at once.

Sandy was persistent. "And now here you are again, reeling another one in and then letting him loose to go back into the water ..." She paused. "... and a little more damaged after you've tossed him away."

"Let's change the subject. I'm here to be with Elie."

It was the look on Margo's face that changed the topic. "Drinking and driving. She'll never learn, almost killed herself this time." Sandy's voice was solemn.

"You didn't tell Mom, did you?"

"Hell no, even if I tried, she wouldn't understand."

"She's still drinking, huh."

"In a stupor most of the time," Sandy's voice sounded depressed.

Margo and Sandy looked at each other in the hospital waiting room. Words were no longer needed to express themselves. They reached out to each other for a long hug. They wondered when their family dysfunctional cycle would end and who would be brave enough to break it?

Three days passed and no call from Margo. Riley wondered if something terrible had gone wrong, so he mulled over whether to give her a call on her cell. He knew that family matters of crisis often took longer to resolve than expected. After a few more moments of indecision, he decided against it. A call from him just might complicate matters. Then he reconsidered.

On the other hand, he wouldn't want her to think he didn't care. At least she would know he had been thinking about her.

Finally, in the end, he decided to wait it out. That was it, nothing more to think about.

He switched his thoughts to Smuts. Critical condition or not, he had to talk with the old man. While his buddy Graham might be of help, he had someone else in mind. So, he drove to the home of the young kid who he was tutoring.

Diego was surprised to see him. "What's up? Don't have tutoring today."

Riley stood on the porch, reconsidered the idea. He was about to turn around and walk away but slid back to the original plan. "Is your mom home?"

"No, still at work, boss-man asked for more hours." He liked how Riley treated him. Not like a kid, but as an adult.

"Can I come in? I've got something I need your help with."

Diego's eyes lit up. He stepped aside.

A short time later, Riley explained the situation. "You already know the old man whose house burned down is at St. Anthony's."

Riley wasn't interested in hearing from the kid now, but Diego nodded his head just the same.

Riley continued. "A friend of mine is a nurse. She visited him recently. He's not doing well." As the conversation became more specific he thought once again if it was a good idea to bring the kid into his plan. However, with little self-restrain he forged on. "I really need to talk with him about a particular situation, but with him still in intensive recovery nobody can see him except for the doctors and nurses, and of course, family members."

He saw confusion on Diego's face, so he got more directly to the point. "I need you to pretend to be someone. Can you do that?"

Confusion still rested on Diego's face, yet he was getting keyed up just the same. It sounded so mysterious to the young boy. "I don't get it. Pretend what?"

Riley cleared his throat before he talked. "I want you to pretend you are from a community center who is delivering gifts to patients. I'll buy a few things that we'll wrap. I'll come along to act as your adult supervisor. When we get in his room, I'll take over. That's all there is to it."

Diego's confusion turned to a grin as he began to figure it out.

"But you can't tell anyone what we're doing. It's got to be between you and me, no one else."

The kid's grin broadened. "When do we do it?"

The next day Riley stopped by to pick up Diego. He waited in his car for the young boy to join him as planned. He checked his watch. Ten minutes passed after the agreed upon time. He wondered if something had changed, so he puffed out a few breaths of air to settle himself down. Another ten minutes passed and Diego was nowhere to be seen. He tapped the steering wheel with his fingers. He was nervous. Finally he got out of the car, and walked towards the front door. He knocked a few times. The door slowly opened as Diego's mother stared straight ahead at him.

"I thought you were a good man helping my boy read." She seemed in controlled but was furious inside.

"I - I can explain." He felt his entire body shake. His face turned red in embarrassment.

"You got plenty of explaining, but I don't want to hear any of it." She was about to close the door in his face but stopped when Riley tried to explain.

His mouth was suddenly dry. What he'd do for a cold Stella right now. "I'm sorry." He looked away. His face became a paler shade of white.

"My boy tells me you want him to lie. I don't bring up my child to lie to nobody. I trusted you."

Riley said to himself, *I don't believe this is happening to me.* He thought if he spoke he would sound screechy, so he kept quiet until he could simmer down. He was surprised she had not slammed the door shut in his face. Maybe there was time to turn it all around.

The pace of his speech was faster than normal. "The old man tried to kill me. He's already killed three people, his former wife and two daughters. He set me up to do his bidding. I just want to know why he did it. That's it. I just want to know why he did it. I'm desperate but I shouldn't have asked Diego for help. That was wrong. I'm sorry."

The curve of her lips remained flat, yet she chuckled to herself of the absurdity of it all. She didn't believe him for a minute. "Is that right?"

"Whew." Riley turned his neck to loosen the grip his collar had on his neck. He mistakenly believed she understood.

"I worry there are people like you teaching young

ones." She shook her head in disgust. "Don't come around here no more. Stay away from my Diego." She shut the door.

Riley stood alone on the porch. It all made sense to him why he did what he did, but still, why didn't she see it the same way he did? She was mistaken!

───────────────────

Graham and Riley sat at their usual spot at McCarty's.

"You OK?"

"Yeah, I'm fine." His voice told Graham another story.

"You don't sound fine, and definitely you don't look fine."

Riley made a face. If he could see himself in a mirror he too would have been worried. He took another sip from the bottle of Stella Artois. The beer did not taste the same as it once did. He was not sure why, but it didn't.

"How's Margo?"

Riley shrugged his shoulders.

"I haven't seen her around here for a while."

Riley rolled his eyes.

"It's OK if you don't want to talk, but I think it'll help."

"Yeah," he winced, and then took another sip of beer.

"How's teaching?" Graham figured that was one sure topic to start up a conversation.

"Same."

They both remained silent for a short time. Then, Graham said, "Had a good shit lately?"

Suddenly Riley let go a big laugh. "That's exactly how I feel."

"And your point is ...."

Another loud laugh from Riley got Graham into the same reaction. Several seconds passed before they settled down.

"The truth is I'm burning my options. I'm no closer to getting to the old man than when I returned from conducting the make-believe interviews, and almost got killed myself. Margo is still away and I'm beginning to wonder if we'll ever be together again. I offended Diego's mother, and I'm sure the kid himself. I seem to be screwing up every which way I turn."

"Your voice always sounds formal, academic-like, when you feel frustrated and confused. Did you know that?"

"You're kidding me."

"No. It's just how you sound until you figure things out." Graham took a sip of beer. "It seems you have a full plate these days."

"Yeah, I've got a lot on my mind with no answers in sight."

"What about the Detective. What's her name?" Then he remembered, "Cabo, isn't it?"

"What about her?"

"I'm just wondering if she could help out. I mean she's probably got the same or very similar interests in talking with the old man as you do. Maybe you two can work together." He took another sip of beer. "Just my two cents worth," he wiggled his eyebrows.

"I'm not sure we actually see eye to eye on most things."

"It can't hurt to try again. I've toppled tons of times from my board, but I keep getting up again."

"Got a minute?"

"All depends?"

Riley grinned. "I thought we might work together."

Detective Cabo kept a neutral look. "What's the mutual interest?"

"Alfred Smuts."

"How can you help me?" Cabo lifted her shoulders. "That's how it works. You help me, and I help you."

"We both want to know why he did what he did. Maybe when he sees me alive, standing in front of him on his death bed, he'll talk. You get a confession and I find out why he did it."

"Who told you he's on his death bed?"

"I just know."

She continued. "Why would he confess? If he's dying as you say, what's in it for him?"

He had no answer, so he kept quiet.

"I guess you don't know." She shook her head.

"Know what?" If he sounded desperate, he was.

"Did you know he's no longer at St. Anthony's?"

"What?"

"I guess you didn't know that little piece of information."

Despite the way she'd been treating him, he couldn't help admire her toughness as a cop. She was obviously not going to be shoved around or fooled. *I guess,* he said to himself, *that's what it takes to make it in police work.* He decided to soften his approach.

"Is there something I can do to help you?"

"Got any ideas?"

"Not now."

"When you get something, come on back."

"Right," he was about to turn away, and then he politely asked, "Where did you say Smuts is?"

She gave him a cold stare, "Nice try."

"You've looked better," Margo said to Elie in the semi-private hospital room.

"Close one, didn't think I'd make it." She puffed out a whiff of air through her partially blocked nostrils that were battered when she went head first into the dashboard. "Got to remember to wear those freaking seat belts," she tried to put a little humor into the conversation, but failed to get her two sisters to buy in.

Sandy, the youngest, chimed in. "You've got a death wish on yourself, girl. It's going to happen if you're not careful."

"Looks who talking about being careful," she glanced between Margo and Sandy, and then she settled on the youngest of the three. "A kid with no father," she shook her head. "Yeah, tell me about being careful."

"She might not know her father, but I love her, and always will. At least I've got someone who loves me and who I love." Sandy started to get riled.

"Whoa girls, let's not argue. There will be plenty of time for that later on." Margo tried to settle things down. Then she looked at Elie. "You don't know how worried I was to hear from Sandy of your accident. I got up here as fast as I could." Tears came to her eyes that she tried not to hide. "I love the both of you." More tears as she began to cry.

"Now now, it's going to take a lot more than a roll over to put me down." Elie's unsuccessful attempt to dampen the air was lost. She tried another approach. "So, elder of them all, how's your love life?"

Margo looked back and forth between her two sisters, and then she dropped her eyes to the floor.

Elie picked up on the movement. "Love them and leave them, same old, same old?" She looked at Sandy. "When is she going to understand that she's not getting any younger?" She turned to face Margo. "You've got to grab the man now for future use when you can't roam the fields anymore. Haven't I taught you anything about men?"

"She's got a guy. Sounds like he treats her fine, but, well she doesn't want to stay with him." Sandy said as she looked back and forth between Elie and Margo.

"Is he good-looking too?" Elie asked.

Margo tried to laugh it off, "Am I that shallow?"

There was silence.

Then Margo continued, "Not worth talking about. We're here for you, not to get an update on me."

"Sounds like you need some talking to, old lady," answered Elie.

"Right," that's about all Margo could think of at the moment. Then she said to Sandy, "You're so thin. What's going on?"

"Relax sis. I'm fine."

A brief silence cut through their conversation until Sandy spoke up again. "Remember when we were kids, when we used to make a pack?" She saw Margo and Elie look at each other with a frown. "Yeah, sure you do." She paused. "Each of us agreed to do something positive that would help ourselves and also help each other. Remember?" She was getting excited about the childhood memory.

"Go on," Elie said with a noticeable peak of interest.

"I think I know where this is going," added Margo. "But, go on. This is your idea."

"Each of us agrees to change our ways, to be better in some way. In return, we are stronger as a family."

Elie added, "And we get out of this fucking downward spiral."

"Exactly," agreed Sandy.

"OK, I'll go along. What do we change?" asked Margo.

Another round of silence before Sandy chimed in. "I promise to go back to school to get my degree in social sciences." Her smile was both broad and sincere. She looked at her sisters as a sort of challenge to outdo her commitment.

Surprisingly it did not take long before Elie put in her idea. "I ...." she started to cry uncontrollably for a while.

Margo leaned forward to console her, but Elie held her off, "I'm OK. Let me finish." She took in a deep breath of air. "I commit to stop drinking starting right now. I'm going to turn my fucking shitty life into something to be proud of. I don't know what, but I'm not going to get myself killed. Maybe I too will go back to school." She turned to Sandy. "Why not social sciences, I can do that." She sniffled. "That's a promise."

Tears in Elie's eyes flowed down her cheeks as her two sisters rushed to her side. As in unison, it seemed they wailed the same melody. A few more moments were needed to transition to the elder sister. All eyes focused on Margo.

She cleared her throat. "This guy, Riley, is probably the best guy I've known. He seems truly committed to me. I'm sure he loves me." A pause separated the next comment. "I promise to give it a chance with him." She felt a sense of relief tossed off her shoulders. "I promise."

Margo and Sandy moved closer to Elie, now sitting up in bed.

It seemed they knew what was about to happen next. Each sister extended their right pinky finger to create one uniform link with each other. Now, bound and determined to turn their lives around they said in unison, "I promise."

Jack Bilcini cleaned off a white Ducati 848 Superbike with a soft cloth in his garage as Riley walked away from a nearby mail box where he'd just deposited a few bill payments and picked up mail.

"Hey. How's it going?"

Jack lifted his head, "Good, how's it with you?" He kept the cloth in motion all the while.

"OK." Riley paused. "Got to keep them clean, they run better." He smiled.

"I know what you mean." Jack dropped his head to look at his prized possession, and then he lifted his eyes towards Riley to keep the conversation moving along. "Haven't seen you around for a while," he folded the cloth in half so the clean side had a fighting chance to do its job.

Riley shrugged his shoulders, not sure how much to get into it. He stepped closer to Jack. "Normal stuff, you know." He hesitated before going on. "I used to ride in high school, had a green Honda motorcycle. It seemed I spent more time taking care of it or having it repaired at the shop than riding it. I finally gave up and sold it for a few bucks."

"No comparison between a Honda and a Ducati."

Riley nodded in agreement, "Yeah." He looked at the middleweight superbike as Jack continued caressing it with the soft cloth. "My mom didn't much like me riding either."

Jack kept his hands in motion all during the conversation. Finally, he stepped away, gave the motorbike a glowing look for a few seconds. "Missed a spot," he moved towards a Ducati logo on the right side to sweep off a smudge. It seemed he was finished.

"I've got a question for you."

Jack looked towards Riley, "Sure."

"Remember when you told me about your dad. You know, when he was ...."

Jack knew what he was referring to, "When my sister and I had him enter hospice at the end of his life. Yeah, I remember." His face was earnest and his voice sounded sincere.

"Well, how was it for him?"

"Hmm, I thought your parents already passed on."

"Yeah, they have. I'm, well, just interested in how it was for him and how you got him into hospice."

Jack knew there was more to it than simple curiosity, but he decided not to take on that conversation. "A lot of people don't understand hospice. It is used when someone is terminally ill, usually six months or less to live, and the person doesn't want treatment for a cure. It's usually a doctor who makes the referral to hospice. Then an assessment is done along with creating a plan." He paused, "So far so good?"

Riley nodded his head yes. "Where do you find these places that offer hospice care?"

"I'm not sure, but I suspect there are data bases and organizations on the Internet. In the case for my dad, the doctor knew of a few places. So, my sister and I made appointments to interview them. You know, to check them out. Medicare paid for everything."

"I see."

Jack waited for another question, but Riley kept quiet. "What else can I tell you about hospice?"

"Are there any locations in Carlsbad or the North County?"

"Sure, there are a few. Just look them up in the phone book or on the Internet. But my sister and I didn't use a facility."

Riley frowned quizzically.

"We could have used a nursing home, a hospital, or a dedicated hospice facility, but we decided to use his home. The professionals provided all the services right in his home. I'm sure it made him feel more comfortable than any other place." Jack grinned, "Anything else?"

"No, you've given me enough. Thanks."

"I'm sure you'll find the right place for your friend."

"What?" Riley asked.

"For your friend who's in need of hospice care, I assume that's why you wanted to know about hospice."

"Yeah, for a friend," Riley's voice trailed off.

There was a short silence.

"One thing I should tell you," Jack said almost as an afterthought.

Riley asked, "What's that?" His eyes were opened wide, ready for an important message.

"Most people are afraid when they enter hospice. They know their days are literally numbered to less than six months."

Riley wondered if Smuts was in a hospice care facility. He recalled Margo told him Smut's chart at St. Anthony's indicated he was terminally ill, and Detective Cabo said the old man was no longer at St. Anthony's. With limited hospice services in North County Riley figured he could easily narrow it down to one.

He returned to his place to get connected to the Internet. Before he reached the front door of his home, Riley scanned the few pieces of mail in his hand. There were two bills, a couple of other envelopes, and something else in particular that popped out. It was a confirmation from Sacramento informing him he had passed a certified gun safety course and now was eligible to purchase a handgun. He thought Shady told him it would only take a week or so, but it was well over that time now. He looked at the official document and wondered what he would do.

───────────────

Flat on his back in bed at Serenity House, Alfred Smuts contemplated what was next in his short life that remained. As hard as he tried to think of something, nothing came to mind. His eyes, now failing, caught glimpses of shadows that traversed across the ceiling. Sometimes he heard them whisper things that he could barely hear, but not understand. It was as if the creatures spoke in a foreign language. His breathing was labored in spite of oxygen mechanically feeding his bodily system. There was a catheter appropriately inserted to facilitate urination. Suddenly to his right he heard a familiar voice.

"How are you feeling today?"

Tired of hearing that question he did not offer any reply.

The caregiver came closer. She was attractive.

Now close enough to see, he gave her a smile, the best his body could come up with for now. He thought to himself, *She's got the looks and I've got ill health. I'm going to run out of my health before she loses her looks.*

She moved closer to him, checked a few pieces of medical equipment, and then touched his forehead with her warm hand.

He said something that only he understood. "I'll die with regrets."

"Excuse me, what was that?" She kept a positive attitude keeping in mind her purpose; to let patients live the remainder of their lives in as much comfort as possible. Her smile remained in place.

He gave up trying a second time.

She moved to the foot of the bed, checked off a few items on a chart, and then replaced it to its original location. "I can arrange someone to come in to read to you if you want." She saw his head shake with a no response. "A little television," she asked as she waited for him to answer.

He closed his eyes to tell her not to bother.

"OK, I understand. I'll come back in an hour to check up on you." She evened the bedspread before she left to visit another patient.

He flashed back to an earlier time in his life, something that had become a frequent occurrence. He remembered laughing, eating, and drinking.

His hands worked to cut off a piece of meat that he efficiently fit into his opened mouth, and then chewed. He reached for a wine glass filled with a vintage Merlot to flush down the food after he minced it into small pieces. Each bite and each swallow were divine as they acted in unison to give him as much pleasure as possible. He found time to crack a few jokes, mostly vulgar. People around him laughed just the same. They did not want to anger him. He could dish it out, but he was not good at taking it himself. For a while he continued to eat, drink, and talk to satisfy his own needs, not concerned about others. That was their problem, not his. Why should he worry about them?

Slowly his eyes closed. He fell asleep.

Riley stepped inside his place, tossed a key ring consisting of house, car, and mailbox keys on a nearby table, and then he quickly shuffled through the rest of the mail. There was one from San Diego International University. It looked official so he opened it. He skimmed through the introductory remarks to get to the main message. He read it.

SDIU requires all faculty members verify their employment eligibility by completing Form I-9. While you might have completed and submitted this Form in the past, we are now required to do it at the start of each semester. The Form itself is included in this envelope. Please visit me before you start your current class and bring with you the appropriate documentation as indicated in the instructions found on the Form. I'm sorry for any inconvenience.

"Shit, more paperwork!" He tossed the letter and Form I-9 alongside the key ring. "I've already started my class!" While he'd like to argue about it, he knew he'd be wasting his time.

He walked to his den where he worked and turned to his desktop computer to begin the Internet search for hospice locations in North County. There were several, so he jotted down on a piece of paper the phone numbers and addresses of them all. He intended to call each one by introducing himself as the nephew of Alfred Smuts who wanted to visit his uncle. He had high hopes the plan would work.

However, he quickly found out patient identity was kept confidential except for those who were officially registered as family members, friends, or who had some verifiable government business with a patient. Pleading with otherwise helpful personnel led him nowhere. He was at a roadblock and not sure what to do next.

The rest of the day he spent correcting student papers yet he couldn't get his mind off finding Smuts. Margo, for the moment, had taken second chair. The next day, however, brought him an unexpected gift.

Inside the office of the Director of Faculty Services at SDIU, Riley completed Form I-9 satisfactorily. He smiled at her, yet all the while he felt yesterday's irritation after he read her memo. With a class about to begin in thirty minutes, he had to get over it. "Anything else I need to do?"

She gave him a polite smile all the while recognized his annoyance. Riley was the fifth faculty member she had seen today and all of them were peeved. Both she and the faculty knew there was nothing they could do about it except comply. "Nothing, thanks for coming by. I'm sorry to have inconvenienced you."

The mere acknowledgement from her helped Riley skip over the aggravation. He felt a little embarrassed and said, "No problem," although he hated saying the phrase. "I'm sorry if I've been rude. It's just ...."

She waved her hand to stop him. "It's just part of life today. Have a great class."

He left her office without further comment, now headed to the faculty lounge for a cup of coffee.

"Riley, how's it going?"

He turned to spot another faculty member, Nicole Chaff. As always, she looked impeccably dressed. He'd always had an eye on her for social things, but he'd just never pursued it. He figured she'd probably say no anyway, so why bother. She taught in the College of Social Sciences and was a practitioner in the field. "Hi." He stopped to continue the conversation.

"Got a class this semester?" She took another step his way.

He smelled vanilla as she moved closer. "Yeah, I guess you do as well."

"Sure do, but not today. I've got to complete Form I-9. Did you get the letter?"

Riley grinned, "Oh, yeah." He rolled his eyes, "Just finished. No big deal."

They looked at each other in silence as if to wait for the other person to fill in the stillness.

Suddenly Riley's eyes widened with an idea. "I just thought of something!"

She clapped her hands, "Bravo!" Her eyelashes fluttered a little.

Riley's face reddened and turned serious looking. "I think you can help me with something important."

Nicole became calm. "Sure, what is it? I'll help if I can."

He cleared his throat before he made up a story. "I just heard that my uncle, whom I haven't seen in ages, is in hospice care someplace in North County, but I don't know the specific location. I've called around to various places to find out where he is but no one will give out patient names. I don't have any way to prove that he's my uncle, but I sure would like to see him before he passes on." He looked at her for a few seconds.

"And what specifically do you want me to do?" Nicole frowned. She had a clue what he was about to ask.

He cleared his throat again. "I might be acting out of line, but I wonder if there is a way I can find out what location he's at." He tilted his head to the side.

She got it. "You know you're asking me to violate both Federal and State laws." She frowned.

Riley lifted his shoulders without comment.

"I can get into real trouble."

He thought the silent treatment was working so he stayed quiet.

"Let's go the faculty lounge so I can access a data

base." She moved away from him. "Come on, follow me."
She waved him her way as she walked towards the faculty
lounge.

There were two other faculty members inside the
room. No one was currently using any of the three
desktop computers. Nicole took a seat, logged into one
of the computers, and turned to Riley who sat alongside.
"What's your uncle's name?"

"Alfred Smuts." Excitement almost prevented him
from getting the full name out of his mouth.

"Turn your back. I don't want you to see this." She
pressed several keys to locate a secured website. She gave
him a glance to make certain he was not able to see the
computer screen. "You owe me big time for this." She
didn't see Riley grin. "OK, your uncle is at Serenity House
in Vista." Then she quickly logged out of the site, and
turned to him. "Like I said, you owe me big time." She
gave him a big smile, just the kind that drove most men
wild."

"I'll pay up. You won't have to worry about that." He
felt a little giddy like a school boy on his first date.

"Visitors' hours end in fifteen minutes. Thank you."
The message was transmitted into each patient's room at
this time every day.

Elie looked at her two sisters, "Time for my two sisters
to do something better." A noticeable sadness channeled
from her lips.

"Don't talk that way. We'd rather stay here with you all night," chimed Sandy.

"Just like a sleep over," added Margo with a sudden childlike expression.

Elie rolled her eyes. "Sure, but just the same, thanks for cheering me up. It's been a blast."

"We're coming back tomorrow." Margo looked at Sandy as if she was confirming something with her sister.

"Tomorrow during the day isn't good for me." She wished she had happier news to tell. "I'm working." She paused as if to think of an alternative. "But I could bring Katie here in the evening for a short time."

Elie said, "I'm not so sure you want your daughter to see her Auntie Elie banged up like this. It's not a pretty site." She pointed to her facial abrasions. "And, not a real positive message to give her."

"I see what you mean."

Margo said, "We could say that another driver hit you, and end it right there." She shrugged her shoulders.

"We could. Yeah, I like it." Sandy nodded her head. "Katie and I will come by around six."

"I'll be here earlier in the day," Margo said.

A caregiver stepped inside the room. "Sorry ladies. Your time is up."

Margo and Sandy each gave Elie a kiss on the cheek, said their goodbyes, and left her alone.

During the short walk to the elevators, Sandy said, "Time goes by fast." Her voice had a ring of sadness.

"One day it's all over."

Sandy had an idea. Her face lit up. "Katie is sleeping over at one of her school friend's home. I'm, well, solo for the night. What about the two of us check out Saddles, just for old time's sake?"

"You're kidding, aren't you?"

"Hello no. That's where we broke the hearts of many guys. Remember. Come on, it'll be fun."

Margo saw excitement build up in her sister but wasn't so sure it was a smart idea. "We were a little younger then, had no responsibilities. Hey, you're a mom now. It's not right."

"Don't be so all grown up. You have no idea how miserable it can be living in this town with little prospects for a really good job or meeting a good man. Sometimes I think I'm going crazy. This is no place to raise a kid either. I dread of thinking that this is where I might live the rest of my life, and die right here."

Margo stared at her sister. She had no idea Sandy felt that way. She began to feel sorry. "OK, let's mosey over to Saddles!"

"Where you'll get the ride of your life," added Sandy, now in high spirits.

The drive was short to the only bar in town that had live music and decent chicken wings. Sandy found some parking spaces behind the spot. Margo pulled up alongside. They got out of their cars and walked towards the loud music. While Sandy was all pumped up about reliving being a single woman with no child, Margo still wasn't sure this was a good idea. Yet, they strolled together into the place.

It didn't take long before they were spotted by a man drinking shooters at the bar. He waved the women over towards him as he pointed to a few filled shot glasses on top of the bar.

"Didn't I tell you we still had it?" Sandy was wildly delighted over the immediate attention. She stopped for a second as she maintained eye contact with the man. Then she pointed to herself and to Margo with a quizzical expression that seemed innocent at first glance.

He waved again to join him. While his eyes were partially closed from drinking, he was eager to push the envelope.

"Follow me. Let the good times roll on." Sandy stepped forward.

"Here you go, ladies." He handed each of them a shooter of tequila.

Margo wanted to say no thanks, just water, but she felt pressured to go along with her sister.

In unison, they all dropped a shot into their mouths.

He passed over a lime to each of them, popped one into his mouth, and sucked the juice.

The two women almost choked from swallowing cheap liquor.

Margo whispered to Sandy, "Are you sure you want to do this?"

"No, but I'm not about to change my mind."

The man's shaky hands shoved another round their way. He was way ahead of them, but he might not be able to drink much more on an empty stomach. Eyes glassy, he mumbled something that even he couldn't understand. Then he popped back his head for a fifth shot. He staggered from the motion and almost fell to the floor.

"Whoa," said Margo. "Don't you think you've had enough?" She grabbed his arm in the nick of time to steady him.

"Want to have some fun?" The words were slurred, almost incomprehensible. With the back of his hand he wiped away saliva that formed at both corners of his mouth. He was almost finished, but had no idea. He tried to reach forward to grab hold of Sandy but missed by a yard. His vision was off considerably. He almost fell again but this time he caught himself as his right hand took hold the edge of the bar. "Oops." His smile was all twisted.

"Let's get out of here. This is a waste of time." Margo's suggestion didn't change her sister's mind.

"This is Sandy's time. I'll do what I want." She stepped closer to the now drunken man. "Let's dance."

Before he could answer, she moved him away from Margo, toward the dance floor. Soon her arms were wrapped about his neck as she awkwardly moved him somewhere close to the beat of the tune. Their uncoordinated movements seemed to fit in well with the other clumsy couples on the floor.

Now from a distance, Margo shook her head in displeasure.

"Want to give it a try?" A good looking man, about her age and seemingly sober, stood next to her. He nodded towards the dance floor.

"I don't think so." She brushed him off. She didn't even bother to look his way.

He didn't take no for an answer. "I'll make sure you stay close to them in case they need your help." He crossed his heart. His eyes were sincere. "I promise."

She looked towards him, and then reconsidered. "What the hell." She stepped forward to lead the way.

The slow dance ended shortly after Margo and the good looking guy got into step. "Thanks," she said, prepared to walk away.

"We got cheated, just one more." His looked plead for her to think again. "Only one more, I promise."

The music started up again, another slow one. She gave him a smile. "OK, only one."

"So what's a nice girl like you doing in a place like this?" He thought the corny phrase was funny, just right to loosen up their conversation.

She found the expression a little amusing. "Just helping my otherwise grounded sister have a good time." Margo was not interested in giving out more information than what was necessary.

He waited for a similar question from her, but Margo kept quiet. "I'm Jerry Lessons. Do you live around here?"

Margo mulled over how to answer, imagined coming up with something over the top. Common sense chased away a trumped-up story. "Used to live here, now someplace else, just visiting family." She questioned if she'd given away too much information. Too bad, it was out in the open.

"I understand." Jerry's words were flat. "Keep it point on, nothing private. You don't know who's crazy and who's not."

"Nothing personal, you understand." Her voice was almost apologetic, but not quite.

"I completely understand."

The music finally ended as she pulled away from Jerry. "Thanks. Have a good night." She moved away leaving him alone on the dance floor.

By this time, the drunken man sat slouched in a chair, head drooped to where his chin touched his chest. Sandy stood, and looked at him disapprovingly. "Pathetic." It was the only word that came to mind. She sensed someone watching, so she turned to find Margo by her side. "Let's get out of here. It wasn't a great ride."

Margo put her arm around her sister's neck, gave her a kiss on the cheek. Together the two sisters left Saddles.

9

The class ended on schedule, but it seemed to Riley it was much longer. He'd been thinking about more important matters the entire time, and wondered if the lack of attention to the students was noticeable. He packed up his things without the normal chit chat after class, and then walked the short distance to the Santa Fe Depot to catch the afternoon Coaster at three-forty.

The train ride was uneventful, yet during the entire trip he felt a certain amount of anxiety build. While he'd thought carefully about the questions he wanted to ask Smuts, there was always the unknown that crept into most situations. He strained himself to stay in control. He was not thinking about Margo.

The car ride to Vista took him about twenty minutes. He spotted Serenity House just as Nicole described. He pulled into the visitor parking area, and then he walked into the building.

A small lobby occupied most of the first floor. To the right was a shop that offered an assortment of gifts that visitors could buy for the patients. Riley was not about to buy anything for Smuts. He walked directly to a circular desk where two neatly dressed women greeted visitors. A variety of flowers seemed to be everywhere. He got a whiff of the aroma that seemed to calm him down a little.

"Hello." His voice quivered a little. He took in a deep breath, and then let out the air to settle down. "I'm looking for Alfred Smuts. He's a patient, and I'm his nephew."

The woman who faced him could be the same age as his mother if she were alive today. He, for the moment, wondered what it would be like to talk with his mother. He gave the woman a warm smile.

She looked down to a registry of patients for the name. After she found the correct entry she looked up. "That would be Alfred Smuts?"

"Yes." The pitch of his voice rose with anticipation.

"Mr. Alfred Smuts is comfortably living in room 427. The elevators are just behind me." She kept a warm smile. "You have to sign in." She handed over an official looking document.

"Yes, of course." He completed the form with mostly truthful information, not all, and then with a smile of his own, he returned the form to her. He was amazed at how simple it all was to get around the legal protocols, just act as if you belonged and appeared to know what you were doing.

She glanced to make sure all columns were filled in, and did not consider someone would intentionally misrepresent themselves. Then she said, "Have a good day with your uncle."

"Yes, thank you." His legs felt a little elastic as he moved away towards the bank of elevators. A door was conveniently open, waiting for his arrival. He stepped into the compartment, and then pressed the button for floor four. The doors closed within seconds. Quietly the hydraulics took over as he ascended alone to meet up with Smuts. He felt his heart want to take off beating faster and faster, so he focused to relax.

"Bing." The elevator door faintly opened. He immediately stepped out into a hallway. Signs directed him to room 427. As he walked he felt some tension in his face, so he twisted his jaws to loosen up. It seemed to work.

He hesitated outside room 427. The door was closed. Another needed breath of air gave him sufficient fuel to enter. He slowly pushed open the door, and stepped inside.

To the left he spotted Smuts on his back in a slightly tilted bed that allowed him to watch television comfortably. As he stepped forward he realized Smuts was unaware of his presence. Riley made his way to block full view of the screen, and stood put without saying a word. He waited for some sort of reaction from the man who tried to kill him. He was surprised at the old man's response.

"It took you long enough to find me." The old man's voice was weak, yet easy to hear.

They played a game of who would blink first.

The old man won within only a few seconds. "Take a seat. We've got much to talk about."

While anger and tension still remained a part of his feelings towards the old man, Riley became aware of unexpected curiosity that took center stage. He told himself it was not supposed to be this way. His feet did not appear interested in cooperating with the old man's offer. He stood motionless.

"The visiting hours are limited. Don't just stand there, take a seat or say something."

Riley shook out of the daze-like condition to move towards a chair that was off to the side.

The old man's face hinted of a smile, but that was not for certain. He shut off the television with a remote control device that he kept in his hand for a short time. Then he tossed it on the bed, alongside his right leg. "Good." He cleared his throat before he continued. "Pull the chair closer. My voice isn't as strong as it once was."

Riley agreed.

"If you're at all interested, I don't have much time left. Nothing I can do about that."

Riley was not interested in any of that. He was more interested in asking a few questions, "Why did you set me up, why me?"

"Oh, I see. So this is all about you."

"You had them killed, and then you tried to take my life. Why did you do that?"

The old man kept a frozen look, unwilling to admit to murdering or attempting to murder anyone. He may be old with a short time to live, but he was not foolish. He had another agenda. "Do you remember the first time you wiped your ass after taking a crap?"

Riley's surprised look needed no further explanation.

"I do." The old man smacked his lips. "I found that occasion to be quite liberating, no longer dependent on someone to do something for me." He looked off for a split second, and then reset his eyes on Riley. "Today, someone I don't even know has got to wipe my ass. I'm once again dependent on someone to look after me." He coughed a few times as his eyes watered a little. "Hand me the Kleenex," he said as he pointed to a box set aside to his left.

Riley handed over the box without much sympathy. "For you, this is good. You won't be harming people anymore. You'll die right here." His voice was full of fury.

"You've got a good point. I have to give it to you." He coughed up some phlegm into a piece of tissue. Then he carried on. "But I still can think and use my own money anyway I want." He pointed a finger at his head and then rolled his thumb over his index and middle fingers to emphasize the two points.

Riley sensed the old man felt empowered, and he was not glad about that. "Tell me about the women."

The old man rolled his eyes. "She never gave me a chance to show I could change."

"Who," Riley snapped.

"Adrianne Browde, one of my former wives." The

answer was said in a matter-of-fact manner. "If she only gave me a chance, but she didn't."

"You've been married more than once before?"

He shrugged his shoulders as if the fact was unimportant.

"So you had her killed?"

The old man shook his head, no. "No one told me she died, too bad."

Riley thought otherwise. "What about Leah and Flo?"

"To rub my face in the dirt, she took away from me the two girls."

"Leah and Flo?"

The old man looked quizzically at Riley.

"Of course," Riley added. "You got so pissed off at them you had them killed!" He paused. "So why did you send me to interview them if you were going to murder them? That doesn't make sense."

"As I said before, I did not kill anyone." He coughed again, but this time with a greater problem than before. He wheezed almost uncontrollably.

Riley waited to say something. "Sure." He knew the old man wouldn't confess to anything. "What about me? Why did you need me, why did you pick me, and why did you want me killed?"

The old man continued to cough throughout Riley's questions. Then, he grabbed an extension cord with a button at the end. He pressed it a few times. In about twenty seconds a caregiver entered the room and rushed to his side.

The caregiver said to Riley, "You'll have to leave now. Mr. Smuts is not feeling well. Come back another time, perhaps tomorrow or the next day."

She attended to calming down the old man.

Disappointed, Riley left the old man in room 427. As he walked to the elevator he asked himself, *Maybe, I shouldn't care about any of this. He's going to die soon and won't hurt anyone else.* His rubbed his eyes to try to get himself to agree, but it did not seem to matter. There was more he needed to know.

The drive home and his mind ran slowly, both not fully in gear. Maybe this was a time to slow down. The fast lane wasn't always the quickest way to your destination.

He looked off to his right, and noticed a colorful sign spread across a retail store window. **Buy 1 Get the Second for 5¢.** BevMo was promoting a five cents sale on selected wines in their store. He thought about it, and then he lifted the turn signal lever upward. A green light blinked on the car's dashboard. He safely drove into a parking lot.

Inside the place, he saw stacks of wine boxes, one on top of the other. Various posters marked off a wide assortment of choices. He took his time examining the selections. The appraisal process seemed to help him temporarily forget the short talk with Smuts. Riley picked up one bottle at a time, read the back label and then set it back in place. He was not yet ready to make a decision.

He saw a bowl of free cashews that was offered to

customers as a way to keep them interested in the shopping experience. He grabbed a handful and moved on.

Finally, he made his way to the far left of the store where signs indicated specific countries. He spotted **France** right off the bat, so he looked see what was available. Another few more minutes of perusing got him even more confused. Finally, more out of bewilderment than anything else, he grabbed a bottle labeled Château De La Meulière, Bordeaux. He'd always thought Bordeaux's were red, not white, such as this one. He read the back label, satisfied it was a good buy. He grabbed two chilled bottles, figured he couldn't go wrong.

At the counter he pulled out his BevMo member card, and handed the checkout lady a twenty dollar bill. The rest of the transaction was completed quickly. He was back in his car driving home as thoughts returned to the old man.

On one hand, he was hugely pleased in finding Smuts, but on the other hand he had to be careful the old man didn't con him again. He swore to himself he'd do whatever it took to get all his questions answered.

Within a short time Riley pulled into his garage. He grabbed the two bottles of Bordeaux and headed inside. After he dropped off the keys on the kitchen counter he found a cork screw and a wine glass. He half filled the wine glass, took a sip, and smiled. Holding the wine glass in his right hand, he looked around the kitchen for something to snack on. It didn't take him long to find a bag of Orville Redenbacher's Microwavable Gourmet Popping Corn. Within three minutes of popping, he took the bag of popcorn out of the microwave, and then he repeated the same process he'd used many times before, added Lucini Extra Virgin Olive Oil and grated Italian cheese. Satisfied, he moved to the living room to think things over.

Sitting in a comfortable cushioned chair, he took another sip of wine as he set the bag of popcorn on a coffee table. Thoughts wound up thinking about his parents for some strange reason, not of Alfred Smuts. He did not fight the unexpected change, but let it happen naturally. He wished they were alive to give him advice. Their short lives came to an end too suddenly as a result of a car crash. He took another sip of wine as the popcorn started to cool off.

He remembered someone told him at one time that most people could remember early childhood experiences when they were as young as two years old. Not Riley. He could only go back to as early as five or six.

His thoughts drifted to a time in the ninth grade when he had a huge crush on Rozanne Pardinello.

She was the most popular girl with the boys in his class, yet she only had eyes for someone else who attended another school. No one had a chance. Dave Seratucci was her man.

Riley felt sorry for himself because he tried every angle to get her attention, but nothing worked. He figured she should have given him at least one date based on his creativity and persistence. Rozanne cared less about how he felt.

One evening during supper, his parents asked why he

seemed to be moping. That was all it took to bear his innocent soul. He didn't see them cover up some laughter over his predicament. They were that good with him. Laughing at children during impressionable years could create all sorts of havoc later on.

His father started out the conversation by saying he should be more concerned for people, and less concerned about himself. That guidance didn't make sense to him until his mother clarified when she said he should give love to others rather than take it from others. He remembered, even today, when his mother told him that if he and Rozanne were meant to be together, she would come to him as well, and they would meet in the middle. He'd done all he could do.

Riley took another sip of wine, and then he looked at the popcorn that had not been touched. He figured he was not ready for it just yet. Another sip of the wine, and then there were more memories.

It was in his junior year of high school. Things were going better than the first two years, freshman and sophomore. He was told by the upperclassmen that was how it would turn out, yet he wasn't sure it would end up that way for him. They were right.

Rozanne and Dave were still together, but she was pregnant. At first no one wanted to say anything to her, that it was a taboo if anyone mentioned it. However, Riley thought she handled it just right.

She made an announcement one day in the cafeteria during lunch recess. One by one a round of applause erupted from the student body. Riley remembered thinking how self-assured Rozanne must have felt to tell it like it was. His regard for her appreciated significantly, even though the chances of them hooking up went to zero.

He scolded himself, even today, for not telling her how brave she was. He wondered if it was still too late to praise her.

He finished off the wine, stared a second or two at the stale popcorn, and then he decided to refill the glass. He went to the kitchen and then returned to the cushioned chair with the bottle. He poured another half glass of wine. He tilted his head back and reflected some more.

He flashed to the first month of his senior year when all the academic counselors in his high school pushed students to commit to making a career choice. Like most high schools at that time, a full week of career planning was set in motion where representatives from several colleges talked about their school's academic curriculum and professionals from various fields told the students what it was like to work in a specific job.

Most of the time, most of the students were bored. They had no idea what they wanted to do in life. It all seemed too fabricated for Riley and his classmates. How could a teenager figure out what he wanted to do in life with so little experience set in a controlled environment?

He concluded all the pressure to make a final determination was bogus. His parents agreed and, further, told him to take his time. They said they would support him whatever his choice.

He sniffled a little, and thought how important his parents were to him. He missed them very much.

He took another sip of wine, and then leaned over to grab a handful of popcorn that he placed into his mouth. Riley grimaced. There was almost nothing worse than cold popcorn. As badly as it tasted he chewed the food, and swallowed it with another sip of wine. Maybe it was a guy-thing to never toss out food from your mouth. Once it was in, it stayed there.

The wine without food made his head a little dizzy, so he rested the glass on the table and let his head toss back. He fell asleep and soon dreamed.

Riley drove a high performance sports car someplace on a winding road. He felt energized as if he was on top of the world. Carefully he downshifted as he took a sharp curve. The high-powered engine quickly responded to his command. The road up ahead was straight, so he accelerated. The roar of the engine cheered him on. He pressed the accelerator further down. His hands tightly grasped the wheel. His heart's beat grew faster with each increase in speed.

Suddenly, he spotted a large rock in the road. It appeared as big as an enormous boulder. Riley shifted to a lower gear as he prepared to swerve away. The rock appeared to shift along with his maneuver. "How can that be?" he exclaimed to himself. He and the giant rock appeared closer to each other. Riley wondered if he had time to overcome the obstacle. He was so close to the rock he saw various colorful embedded granules.

Suddenly, he saw a hand come from nowhere. The gigantic rock was lifted high above him. Riley drove through. A glossy white cloud-like image struck him in the eyes.

Throughout the dream his cell phone buzzed. Margo called him but when there wasn't an answer. She decided not to leave a message. She figured whatever she said could be misinterpreted. She disconnected.

⸻

Graham called Riley the next morning after a few hours of surfing. The waves were not cooperative today, unpredictable, just like a woman. He sat back in a chair on the wooden deck of the apartment he shared with two other surfers, much younger than him but able to pay their share of rent and utilities. He stared out at the Pacific Ocean. Its waves were still tranquil. Tomorrow might be different. "Hey, what's up?"

"Huh." Riley was not yet fully awake. He resolved to stick with beer.

"Where are you?"

"Inside a comfortable bed," the sound was low and muffled. Riley was not totally awake.

Graham was curious, "Alone or with someone?"

"What's your guess?"

"Sorry about that." He took a second to pause. "The sun is out, but the waves are hiding, thought we'd have breakfast."

"Coffee included?"

"Be serious."

"Found Smuts, even talked with him a little."

"No way," his voice sounded surprised.

"I'll fill you in at The Nook."

Graham stood up, ready to go, "How long?"

"I'm not teaching today, so it shouldn't take me long. Twenty minutes, tops."

"Good. I'm eager to hear what the old man had to say."

Riley nodded his head. "Will do," he paused, "by the way, I also had a weird dream last night."

"Juicy?"

"Unfortunately no, but I'll fill you in. Maybe you can help me figure it out."

"Interesting, see you in twenty."

They disconnected at about the same time.

Riley slowly shifted his weight to plant his feet on the floor. He stood, stretched his arms over his head, and then scratched his groin. Unhurriedly he made his way to the bathroom to pee. Then he got ready to meet his buddy.

"I still can't believe you found him."

Riley sipped black coffee. "Purely by accident," he set the mug on the table top. "I had to do some paperwork at SDIU when I bumped into Nicole Chaff, another faculty member."

"Oh, yeah," Graham said. "How come you've never asked her out?"

"She'd probably turn me down, so why bother, just another disappointment to live with." He rolled his eyes, and then continued. "She works as a counselor and teaches in the College of Social Sciences." He noticed a frown on Graham's face, so he clarified. "I tried to locate the old man, but each time I called a hospital or other health care facility I was told patient information was private."

Graham moved the coffee mug from his mouth and said, "So you sweet talked Nicole to go through the back door, in a way." His eyes widened.

"Yeah, something like that. Anyway, she found the location, and after class I gave him a visit." He lifted the mug to his mouth for another swallow of coffee.

Graham stared at him. "Go on, don't leave me in suspense. What happened next?"

"I was hoping to clear everything up with just one visit, but he gave me a lot of stock answers, not much to go on. Then, he had a coughing spell. A nurse interrupted us and told me to leave."

"Bummer," he sounded disappointed for his buddy.

"I was hoping to end seeing him once and for all. Now, I've got to return."

"Yeah," Graham continued sensing the let down.

"There is just too much I don't know about all of it."

"When are you going back?"

"I figure today is as good of a time as any, right after breakfast."

"Mind if I string along?"

Riley was pleasantly surprised, "Unless they kick you out, why not?"

A waitress interrupted their conversation. "Here you go boys, one Surfer Special and one Charger Special." She set the hot plates on the table, checked the status of the coffee mugs, and said, "I'll be right back with refills. Enjoy."

Graham looked at the breakfast plate. "Heard from Margo?"

"Wish I had." His voice sounded disappointed.

Graham started eating, and then asked another question. "What's with the dream?"

Riley swallowed a bite of food, and then he answered. "I'll tell you what I remember."

The waitress returned, "How's the food?" She poured coffee into each mug.

"Good, thanks," Graham said.

"Always good," added Riley.

She smiled, and then she walked away.

They ate for a short time in silence.

"It was the craziest dream ever." Riley straightened his posture as he still held onto a fork. "I was driving a sports car, not sure what kind but it was fast. Suddenly a boulder appeared in the road. I thought I was going to crash right into it, but a hand suddenly appeared out of nowhere to lift it away."

Graham looked away from the half empty plate. "That's it?"

"Yeah, what do you make of it?"

"I doubt much of anything. Lots of people dream of a saving hand to rescue them."

"No kidding," Riley was surprised.

"That's what Silvia the Psychic says on television."

Riley grinned.

"Really, that's what she says." Graham returned to eating his breakfast, disappointed in the dream.

With not much more to talk about, the two men

finished off their breakfasts in silence. While Graham was simply curious in the mystery surrounding the old man, Riley had more important interests in getting some answers.

"Anything else?" the waitress asked. With a coffee pot in her right hand, she held onto to the already calculated final check.

"Just top off my mug," Graham said.

Riley put the palm of his right hand over his mug, "I'm fine. Thanks."

She poured a little coffee into the mug closest to Graham, and then said, "Thanks. Here's the check." She set the piece of paper between the two customers, and then walked away.

"Let me do the talking, understand?"

"Whoa! Sure." Graham was surprised by Riley's sudden jumpiness. He'd really like to say something but decided the least said the better for now.

They walked into Serenity House.

Riley led the way as his buddy glanced around.

Graham was surprised the place was as impressive looking as it was. He followed Riley to sign in, and then to a bank of elevators where they waited for an available elevator door to open.

While the time was short, the ascent to the fourth floor made a stop at each in-between floor.

Graham noticed Riley getting more charged up

with each passing moment. This time he decided to say something. "Settle down."

Riley said, "Huh?"

"You're all worked up. Take it down a few notches."

"Yeah. Sure."

The advice took a while to work its way through Riley's system, but by the time they reached room 427, Riley was less ruffled.

He pushed open the door, stopped for a quick second to make sure the old man was there, and then proceeded forward. "I'm back."

"It's what I expected." The old man's voice appeared to have regained some of the previously loss strength. It was amazing the effects of proper medications. "Who's your friend?"

"He's a good buddy. I needed a ride. My car's in the shop."

The old man was not fooled by the tale, but concluded there was no use to challenge him on it, no value in it whatsoever. "I see." He looked at Graham, "What's your name, son?"

Graham glanced at Riley for a quick second as if to ask for permission.

"It's OK, boy. I'm not going to hurt you." The old man felt a little like his old self, but his sarcasm was far from being in full force.

"Graham."

"Got a last name?"

"Bogar."

"Graham Bogar. Hmm. Family from around here?"

"No. Not originally."

The old man said, "I see." He scratched hair stubbles on his chin. "Seems I recollect somebody I knew once with that last name." He paused, "Hmm."

Eager to get past the small chit chat, Riley interrupted. "Wonderful. We're now all introduced to each other." He pulled a chair closer to the old man, turned his back to his buddy.

The old man followed Riley's movements, also without any heed to Graham.

Riley took a deep breath before he restarted yesterday's talk. "The last time I was here you were about to tell me why you needed me, why you picked me, and why you wanted me killed."

The old man gave off a smirk. "I may be old, and sometimes forgetful, but I wasn't about to tell you anything of the like." His hands rested on his chest, one atop the other.

Enough of trying to fool him, Riley thought to himself. Previous thoughts of looking forward to this second meeting did not materialize at first, so he took another approach. "Tell me why you asked me to interview them, why me?" His eyes pleaded for an answer.

The old man cleared his throat. "Simply put, it was purely accidental." He glanced at Graham who sat in a chair in a far corner of the room, and then he reset his eyes to Riley. "When you stopped to ask if I needed help, I figured you were one of those eager beaver Samaritan types, the perfect personality." He snickered just a little, but not enough to let on what was entirely going through his mind.

"So, if I hadn't stopped, you wouldn't have gone to McCarty's. Is that it?"

The old man looked at Graham, "He still doesn't get it." Then he switched to stare at Riley. "You were in the right place for me."

Riley's face reddened. He felt his entire body ratchet up a few degrees. In light of the embarrassment, he continued. "Did you ever really consider giving one hundred thousand dollars to anyone?"

"Definitely not to them, they were going to receive plenty from the irrevocable will. Not a penny more."

"So you knew who they were before I interviewed them? You knew all along!" Riley was shocked.

The old man remained quiet.

An idea sprang to Graham's mind, so he shouted it out. "But if they died before you, then they would not receive anything!"

Surprised with Graham's theory, Riley turned his head in his direction as the old man stayed silent.

Graham continued. "It makes a whole lot of sense," Graham nodded his head as he glanced at Riley and then at the old man. "Then, after Riley played his role exactly the way you wanted it, you had to get rid of him. No one left alive to prove anything." His face lit up with the notion.

"Is that true? Was that your intention all along?" Riley glared at the old man.

He shook his head, no, "Nothing like that."

Riley was more worked up than ever before. He didn't

believe the old man. "How could you plan to kill your ex-wife and two daughters, and then take a crack to kill me; all to save you money? What kind of evil devil are you?" He swallowed hard, almost out of breath from yelling.

The old man remained calm as if he'd practiced his role over and over to perfection. He grinned without saying a word.

Riley took a second breath, not yet willing to let go. "You're despicable, vile, and wicked! I can't wait for you to die to end it all!"

"We're all going to die, one day. I'm luckier than you in that regards," the old man said.

The comment confused both visitors, but angered Riley even more.

"The difference is I know when it is going to happen to me. You don't."

Graham nodded as if he was a good student learning an important principle of life, but Riley had a different reaction.

"Let's get out of here! I can't take any more of this crap!" Riley stood, and then barged out of the room.

Graham followed him but heard the old man say, "You'll be back tomorrow. There's more you want to know."

Later that same night, close to midnight, there was a sound at the front door. Riley sat in the living room, still wound up from the meeting with Smuts. He was not sure what to make of the sound so he turned in the direction of the noise. He saw the door open slowly as someone from outside released the locking mechanism.

Margo quietly stepped inside. She closed the door as if she was trying not to interrupt anyone who might be sleeping. Riley couldn't believe his eyes.

"You look tired," he said. He moved closer to her, slipped his arms around her, and held her body close to his. There was no resistance from her.

"I drove all night. I wanted to get here earlier, but there was too much traffic." She looked directly into his eyes. "Is it OK for me to be here?"

His eyes began to water slightly. "You can't imagine how happy I am to see you."

She gently placed her lips against his, and held them tightly together for a while. Then, she pulled back. "Let's go upstairs."

Once in the bedroom, they sat silently on the bed, fully dressed. Margo made the first move. She inched a little closer so she could begin undressing Riley.

At first, he was taken by surprise, but then he sat perfectly still, enjoyed more than ever her hands removing his clothes. It took her a short time to finish. Then she said, "It's your turn." She gave him a seductive smile to encourage him. Tiredness seemed to have vanished.

He needed no such persuasion, yet he was clumsy. Finally, once he finished, he knelt in front of her as she spread her legs. He hummed something to himself.

"Oh, that's nice." She closed her eyes, tilted her head back just slightly, "Very nice." She reached for the top of his head to hold on. She knew within a short time she'd need something to keep her steady when it came. She heard him savoring. Ooh! Her stomach muscles quivered. Then she giggled.

"I missed you," he said in between nibbles.

She stayed quiet but kept her hands tight on his head. She readied herself for another jolt. This time the feeling rocked her over on her back.

He was very happy he pleased her. Then, he stood and gently pressed himself against her. He felt her wetness as he prepared to enter her.

"Jesus," she said.

The phone rang four times before Riley picked up, "Yeah."

"Mr. Riley Sullivan, nephew to Mr. Alfred Smuts?"

His head jerked forward temporarily forgetting Margo was by his side, still asleep, "Yes, who is this?"

"This is Mrs. Bruce at Serenity House. I'm sorry to bother you today, but your uncle is asking for you. It seems it is rather important, and he won't tell anyone here what it is about. I'm sorry."

While still confused, he was still drawn into the unexpected call from the old man. "Can you put him on the line?"

"Oh, no, I'm so sorry. He made it quite clear he wants to see you in person. You know, your uncle can be quite demanding when he puts his mind to it."

Riley puffed out a few breaths of air. "Yes, I know." He felt Margo move, so he looked her way to notice she had simply turned over to her other side. He hoped he hadn't awakened her. Then, he said to Mrs. Bruce, "I can be there this evening, say, around five."

"Oh, I hoped you'd tell me you might be here earlier, perhaps in an hour. He's really head-strong about seeing you sooner."

Another puff of air helped Riley calm down. "OK, then. I'll be there in an hour, perhaps a little longer."

"Please, not too much longer. I'm sure it would upset your uncle if it was too much later."

"Yes, yes. I understand."

"Oh, just one more thing," she paused.

Riley waited for the next rule.

"He wants you to come alone, no one else."

He shook his head sideways, "Understood, only me."

"Thank you so much Mr. Sullivan. I'll tell your uncle. I'm sure he will be quite pleased."

Riley heard the phones disconnect, so he placed the headset back onto its cradle. He sat upright in bed wondered what it was all about. Nothing came to mind, but he was resolute to find out.

"Who was that?" Margo's voice sounded sleepy.

He turned to her. "I'm sorry the phone woke you."

She moved closer to him, placed her arm around his midsection, and then she slowly slid her hand to his groin. "I love you."

As he felt her hand squeeze him, he began to stiffen. He thought he was now stuck between doing what he wanted to do and what he'd just promised to do. Then, he decided the two choices were able to coexist.

The bed's mattress moaned and groaned as it noisily exhaled through their passionate love making.

He drove faster than normal to get to Serenity House, his mind wandered to Margo. Maybe she'd brought him good luck. At least, that was what he hoped for. He looked in the rearview mirror, pleased to see a smile shine brightly back his way.

Then his thoughts turned to Alfred Smuts. Riley's mood quickly changed. A dark side of his personality started to ooze out. He reminded himself to be on his toes, the old man couldn't be trusted. His hands were fastened like clamps to the steering wheel. The traffic signal light up ahead turned yellow, he pressed down on the accelerator to beat the change of color to red. The engine responded to successfully accomplish the deed. Vehicles in back of him were left behind, stopped to wait for a change in color to green.

Riley pulled into the parking lot, parked in the visitor's section, and then made his way inside. The walk was becoming more familiar each time. He wished it would all stop so he could get on with his everyday life.

He walked towards the large circular desk in the middle of the lobby. He noticed the woman looking his way recognized him. She seemed to be relieved to see him. "Hello, Mr. Sullivan. I'm so pleased to see you. Your uncle is waiting upstairs."

He controlled his emotions. "Yes, yes." That's about all he was prepared to say. She was not the target of his anger, so why take it out on her. He waited to be handed the sign in document.

"I'm really very sorry. I really am." She handed over the paper for him to complete. Her sad-looking eyes matched the sound of her voice.

He forced a smile that did not fool anyone. Without any comment he completed the form and returned it to her. As he walked away he heard her say, "Have a good day."

For a moment Riley stood motionless. He faced the elevator as if he was studying it for a final exam. He noticed for the first time a diagonal scratch on the door. He wondered if it was there before. Then, the door opened.

A few people dressed in official looking clinical uniforms stepped out. They talked to each other about something that was of no interest to him. He waited until they passed by, and then he entered the compartment alone, pressed **4** and stepped away.

Moments later the door opened. He hesitated before stepping out as if to consider changing his plans. *Keep the old man waiting* he said to himself. He backed off the idea, and advanced towards room 427.

There was a good deal of confidence in his stride. He figured the old man wanted him more than the other way around. He decided to play it nonchalant and distant.

"What the hell took you so long?" Smuts sat up in bed. His voice was surprisingly forceful. "I don't have much time to piss away, if you haven't already figured that out!"

Once inside the room, Riley did not move. Silence might be the right decision. He stared at the old man.

"Get your ass over here! I've got a job for you."

He told himself, if he had a gun handy, he could do it. He'd blame it on temporary insanity or something else. He thought he could get away with it. It wouldn't matter. It'd be all over, finally.

"You deaf, boy," his face reddened with emotion. Smuts wiggled his index finger for Riley to move closer.

Riley considered replying with his middle finger accompanied by two choice words. He dismissed retaliating, no value in playing the old man's game. He stepped closer to the old man.

"You might want to write this down." Smuts wiped saliva forming at the edges of his mouth. "There's paper and pencil on the table."

Riley shook his head, no.

"Have it your way. I'm only going to say this once."

Riley stared his way without saying a word.

"I've got a place in Temecula, 302 Milkweed Road. There's a key to the front door inside a flower pot on the porch. In the bedroom, there's only one, you'll find a metal container. Bring it here. Don't open it. There's something very important inside." His voice suddenly was less vigorous. "Now go. Don't tell anyone." He coughed, and then let his head flop back on a pillow. His eyes closed.

Riley continued to remain silent. He noticed the old man's breathing to be deep but difficult. Right then he was not sure what it all meant, but he had little to go on. With no one watching him or overhearing the conversation, it was essentially up to him to carry on the directive. Two things were for sure. The old man didn't have much time left and there wasn't going to be any further discussion right now. Slowly, he turned around to leave.

As Riley passed the large circular desk in the middle of the lobby, the same woman who greeted him said, "I hope everything went well."

He replied, "As well as expected."

Inside the BMW, he silently sat to make up his mind. Should he let Margo in on it and even Graham, or should he simply head out to the place on his own?

He stopped for gas, surprised the price per gallon had risen another four cents since the last fill up, just a few days ago.

Headed towards Temecula on his own he began to conjure up all sorts of ideas for what might be inside the metal container. His immediate answer was money. The trip took him about ninety minutes.

The house was at the far end of a narrow and bumpy dirt road. There were many vacant lots with overgrown weeds. All sorts of debris were everywhere, mostly likely, he concluded, the result of people indifferently trashing stuff into the environment. He spotted a few plastic oil canisters, a tire here and there, and lots of empty fast food containers. *So much for taking care of the environment*, he said to himself.

The place at 302 Milkweed Road looked bleak.

Most of the front wooden steps were rotted, and the whole exterior needed a good paint job. The trees, he couldn't make out the type, drooped as if they could use additional nourishment to get back into shape. There was a depressing smell all around. There were no other vehicles he could see.

Riley avoided parking in the driveway that at one time might have been safe and useful. He wasn't sure what hazards might be hidden that could damage the tires of his car.

He walked up the pathway towards the porch. He was careful to avoid stepping on cement fragments that were everywhere. The pathway was more like a trail in the woods. He almost stepped in a pile of excretion left by an animal of some sort.

Shortly, he lifted his right foot to place on the first step. The pressure from his foot released a squeaky sound that reminded him of an old scary movie with eerie music in the background. He measured the next few paces carefully until he reached the top of the porch. Immediately he spotted the flower pot Smuts mentioned. He peered into the pot to make sure he knew where he was about to plunge his hand. It seemed all clear so he swept his fingers inside the clay pot to find the door key. Bingo!

Strides on the wooden porch produced the same type of sound as the wooden steps. He was used to it by now so he picked up his pace to get the job done as quickly as possible. The key did not insert easily into the door lock, too old and most likely filled with dust. A little oil would make the lock seem new. He turned the metal object clockwise, heard a click, and opened the door. So far so good, he was pleasantly surprised everything was going so easily.

He stepped inside and was almost overtaken by a foul odor that set him back on his heels. A little cough helped clear it up. He looked around the shadowed living room. Nothing seemed unusual or strange to him so he took a few steps inside. A bedroom appeared to be to the far left, the location of the metal container. Since he had no interest to buy the place, he did not take the time to inspect the other rooms. He moved quickly to the bedroom.

The double bed was bare to the mattress and box spring. Two pillows were set on top of each other in the center. There were a few suitcases on the floor as if someone had just arrived but had not yet unpacked, or someone was preparing to take a trip. Nothing else resembled the metal container. He made his way to a small closet that was mostly empty except for a few metal hangers on the wooden floor. His eyes returned to the bed. It must have been the new angle of view because then he noticed something underneath the bed.

He moved quickly, bent over, and pulled out a metal container. His heart started to race a little. Curiosity tempted him to open the container to discover its contents, but there was a small padlock in place. He'd have to break the lock or somehow damage the container to meet his interest. Then an idea struck him. He smiled, concluding Smuts had the key safely in his hands. Just the same, he'd like to get a sneak preview of its contents. He stared at the metal container at his feet a little while longer. Then, he bent over to pick up the container, but found it much heavier than expected. Riley slid the container along the floor to the still opened front door. He was surprised who he saw.

"Sort of weird meeting you here," she said. Her face was without noticeable emotion. She stood erect, seeming prepared to block him from moving further. Arms were crossed over her chest to emphasize the point.

He stared at Detective Cabo, taken aback by her unexpected appearance. Yet, he was determined to stay in control of his emotions. No sense letting on what he was up to.

"What have you got there?" She looked at the metal container with an unchanged expression. There was a little smirk peeking through.

It took Riley only a short time to answer. "I'm taking it to Smuts. He asked me to."

"You don't say?" Her voice inked of sarcasm along with a facial twist.

"Yeah, that's the truth." Riley held his stance. He heard himself breathe through his nose.

"I find it odd that you've become the delivery boy for the man who allegedly tried to kill you." She paused, and then she added, "Don't you?" She forged on thinking she could outlast his persistence.

"It's all how you look at it."

"Hmm," she puckered her lips. "What's inside?"

"I have no idea. See, it's locked." He pointed to the locking mechanism in place.

"Need any help?"

"No thanks. I can manage on my own." His face stayed effortlessly composed. He was now convinced he was finally winning the battle of wits.

"Care to know how I found you here?" She sensed Riley had changed his ways since they last met. He seemed to have his act a little more together. Still, she felt she had the upper hand.

"No, but I'm sure you're going to tell me."

"Been keeping an eye on you since the first time we met." Her eyes opened for emphasis. "Surprised?"

Riley shrugged his shoulders. "What else is there to say?"

Cabo took in a deep breath, and then let out the air slowly. "Don't get in over your head."

He nodded, and then took the door key from his pocket. He closed the front door, relocked it, and dropped the key inside the flower pot. He looked at Detective Cabo. "Just where he told me it would be." Riley bent over to grab the metal container, and started to drag it off the porch.

Detective Cabo held her position, figured to come away with a small win.

Riley stepped around her to avoid a physical confrontation with the law. He knew better than to mess with the law.

She remained at the front door, watched him move

closer to the car. She vowed to find out what he and Smuts were up to. She had her own suspicions.

Once Riley was out of sight, she moved to the flower pot where he dropped the door key. She wiggled her fingers a little inside the vessel until she found the metal object. She took one more look around to see if anyone was nearby. Satisfied she was alone, Cabo headed for the front door.

As she pushed the door open, she got a whiff of odor from inside. "This place has been unoccupied for a while," she announced aloud. Then she scanned the area, immediately noticed foot marks on the floor. "Most likely from Sullivan," she concluded. There was little furniture, all of it old and worn out. The windows had brown coverings made from grocery paper bags, yet there was a little light coming through slits between the bags. Dust was everywhere.

She walked towards the kitchen for some reason to check if anything jumped out at her. Nothing in particular was of interest, so she returned to the living room to follow the footsteps.

Inside the bedroom she spotted the bed and an opened closet door with a few metal hangers. She noticed the suitcases, but ignored their importance. "Smuts wasn't one for luxury items." She moved closer to the bed where the footprints ended. "This is where he must have found the metal container." She nodded her head a few times staring at the spot. Then she circled the bed hoping to uncover something that Sullivan overlooked. It took one clockwise circle and then a counterclockwise circle to notice something.

Something stuck out from between the mattress and box spring. She separated the two pieces just enough to pull out a partially sealed brown envelope. The envelope was unmarked. She removed a small flashlight from her pocket to shine on the paper to determine if she could make out its contents. No luck, the paper was too thick and too dark colored. Gently, she felt the envelope with her fingers, thought there might be a key or some other hard item inside. If the item was a key, then the key might open the metal container.

Cabo decided the only way to find out what was inside was to tear open the envelope. She wavered. The legal part of her mind set in motion a series of thoughts, so she put off opening the envelope to think a little more about it. In fact, she admitted to herself, she probably shouldn't have snooped around in Smut's house anyway, maybe broken a few laws so far.

Finally, she inspected the envelope more closely. It became clearly visible to her that the glue holding the envelope sealed was weak. If she was very careful, she just might be able to peel away the flap to provide enough space to shake out the contents, or at least get a closer view of what was inside.

She got to work, cautiously moved her finger along the flap's edge to separate it from the rest of the envelope. The process was slow. She dealt with it as gently as possible. It took her about ten minutes to make enough room to shake out whatever was inside the envelope. She carefully moved the envelope up and down, jiggled it just the right way to move the item into the hole she had created. A small key fell on the floor. She stooped down to inspect it.

Cabo laughed with joy, and then she kissed the metal object. Then she thought about her next move. She considered taking the key, but that would be stealing evidence if a criminal charge was filed against Smuts. She looked around the place for a few seconds, her mind was traveling faster. She decided to return the key inside the brown envelope and hide it somewhere other than between the mattress and box spring. The opened closet door invited her to use it as the best place to put the key out of sight.

Cabo rested the envelope containing the key on the top shelf. Then she stepped back and stretched her neck to find out if it could be seen.

Satisfied, she left Smut's house to request a search warrant for the place. She returned the house key to the flower pot. She reasoned she'd outsmarted them all.

Elsewhere, another person talked on the phone. She was cheerful.

"I think he's the one."

"Really," she was not convinced. It was only a short time ago her sister was going to dump him.

Margo walked around Riley's place in panties with no bra. The graceful curve of her bare back ended with a tattoo of a small green cat. "Really," she replied. Her voice was animated.

"What's changed?" Elie sat up in bed. Sandy was by her side in a chair. She turned to her sister, "Margo thinks she's in love."

"I heard that. Tell Sandy it's for real this time." Margo put one hand on her hip. "I've given it a lot of thought about what we said before, you know, our promises. Remember?"

Elie relayed the message to her sister who sat alongside her bed, and then responded back to Margo. "Sandy still feels like shit from the other night at Saddles. She hasn't told me everything, but I'm going to pry it out of her."

Margo said, "I learned my lesson. I hope she's learned hers." She stared down at an arbitrary point on the floor.

"Have you met his parents yet?" Elie continued to wonder about the dramatic change from her sister.

"I think they're both dead," Margo said sadly.

"That's tough."

"Yeah, but I think it's made him stronger."

"Hard to say," Elie said and then paused. "He's never been married before. Is that right?"

Margo replied, "That's right. No kids, no baggage, just him."

"That could make it work." Elie paused again, this time to listen to Sandy. "Sis says it could make it worse."

"Of course she says that. Sandy's always sees the dark side of things." Margo shook her head as if the movement would settle the debate.

Elie defended Sandy, "That's not fair. Everybody's got a history, skeletons in the closet."

"I agree." Margo heard her voice quiver a little. "But I just want both of you to be happy for me. That really matters." She stood motionless. "Just be happy for me." She heard the breathing of her own voice, and then she sniffled.

"We just don't want you to do something you'll regret," Elie said. Gone was the edginess of her voice. "Sandy says that we love you no matter what happens."

Margo said, "That's what I was hoping to hear. I love you both so much." She held back a cry, but the effort was short lived. "I think it's going to work with him and me. I really do."

Sandy took her turn on the phone. She wasn't fully recovered from the other night. "Sis, we'd love nothing more than for you to be happy even though we can't seem to find it ourselves. One out of three isn't so bad, four if you include mom."

Margo tried to blink away the tears, but they were persistent. With watery eyes, she managed to say, "No one is born to be unhappy."

Sandy was not convinced. "I wish I could agree."

Elie echoed the same sentiment, "It's probably in the family blood."

"But don't you want to beat the odds?" Margo was determined to convince her two sisters. "Don't you want to find out how it is to be happy, really happy?" She took in a deep breath. "Remember our promise."

"Look, let's just table this conversation for now. OK?" said Sandy.

Margo relinquished, "OK. Maybe I got carried away a little, but I'm going to make it work between Riley and me." Her still body was carefully balanced upright on her toes. She heard silence at the other end. "I love you and Elie." She let her stance return to both feet firmly placed on the floor. "I'll call again soon."

Riley drove away feeling energized. He was convinced everything was about to fall into place once the old man saw what he had brought. He drove a few more miles in silence. Then it entered his mind that talking it out with Graham before he met up Smuts might be a good idea. His buddy usually had his own unique perspective on things. He grabbed his cell phone to give Graham a call.

"Hey, what's up?" Graham stood in the center of Surf's Up, a retail shop he co-owned with a few other surfers.

"Can you get away to talk?"

He heard Riley's excited voice. It whipped up some emotion himself. "No can do, it's busy today with tourists who have money in their pockets. You seem pumped."

"There's got to be a better word, but yeah, I am pumped. I think I've got a ton of money looking straight at me but not sure what to do."

Graham was not sure he'd heard the message clearly. "Let me get this right. You've got money that you don't know what to do with. Is that what you're saying?"

"Yeah, that's the short version of it."

"Why are you asking me? Do you want to give me some of it?" Graham walked around a few racks of colorful Hawaiian shirts. He fiddled with a few of them to occupy his free hand. He was still unclear about what was going on.

"How about it if I stop by the shop? It shouldn't take more than a few minutes. I'd like to talk with you about my predicament."

"Fine with me, maybe you'll buy something for a change."

Riley said, "Yeah, maybe I will. Catch you in about twenty minutes." He disconnected the cell, and then tossed it on the passenger seat. Out of the corner of his eye he spotted a police vehicle. He wondered if he'd get a warning ticket for using a cell phone while driving. He kept looking straight ahead as the police vehicle passed him without notice.

Riley pulled off the Pacific Coast Highway - 101 into a dirt parking lot that was shared among a few retailers. The city of Solana Beach owned the property and had promised to pave the lot for some time now, but with the City's revenue down it was unlikely to happen soon. The retailers refused to pay the entire costs themselves, so the dirt lot remained unchanged.

He got out of the vehicle, covered the metal container with a blanket, and locked the vehicle. He hustled to get to the shop to talk the situation over with Graham. He passed a tall heavy-looking man with a potbelly smoking a cigarette. His hands were pudgy and his nose was veined but his gray hair was neat and perfectly combed in place. Maybe he had a hairpiece. The guy did not look happy.

Now inside, he looked around to see Graham talking with a couple. He felt some tension build up inside, so he strolled around looking aimlessly at the collection of clothes, boards and accessories.

A few more customers entered the shop while Riley hung out. He wondered how long it would take before Graham was free.

Suddenly, his thoughts were interrupted when a woman approached him. "Excuse me. I wonder if you'd give me some help in deciding which one of these to buy my husband." She held up two Hawaiian shirts, one blue and white, while the other was green and yellow. She stared at him with undecided eyes.

He lifted his shoulders. "Is he here?"

"No, he's waiting outside. Why do you ask?"

"I was just wondering, if he was here, you could ask him which one he likes." Riley took a glance outside to see the same man he'd previously seen smoking a cigarette. He wondered if that was her husband.

"Oh, he doesn't know what he wants, especially clothes. I've got to buy him everything he wears or else he'd look awful."

Riley looked at the frumpy looking woman who might have been attractive at one time, but not now. He wondered if that's what marriage did to people, and if that's the way it would eventually be if he and Margo married. He shuddered at the possibility.

"They're both very nice, typical of Hawaii." He gave

the impression of being interested in her dilemma. "If it were me, I'd buy both. I think your husband would like both." He smiled.

"Well, I wasn't planning on buying two shirts. But ... well ... I guess ... I am in California. OK, two shirts it is." She seemed to be pleased with the decision. "Thank you very much." She moved toward the cashier.

Riley wondered where she and her husband came from. Probably some place in the mid-west. Wisconsin or Michigan, he conjectured without any facts to support the guess.

Then Riley heard, "I'll be right there." He looked over to Graham hoping the remark was for him. No such luck. He saw Graham talk with two different customers at the same time. He looked at his watch, not even sure when he arrived. Then he glanced around the store and then back to his watch. He decided to give it ten minutes longer before he left. He heard his stomach growl.

Riley stepped outside to take a quick walk before he was asked for any further advice about shirts and stuff. He was just not in the mood to give assistance to others, too many other things on his mind to worry about. He was the one who needed the help right now.

The air was fresh, except for the occasional tobacco smoke that drifted his way. He moved upwind to avoid the smell. The guy smoking the cigarette was either unaware of the effect of tobacco smoke on non-smokers or just did not care. Riley was not interested in finding out which was true, maybe both were. He glanced towards the front window of the store. The sun shined at just the right angle for him to see a partial reflection of himself, someone who was tense and worried. He extended his hand to his face to verify it was his own image. He took in a deep breath. "You look like hell," he said to the reflection, "but then, I've also seen you worse."

He stared a little longer in the same direction, and then heard, "Who you looking at?" The man smoking the cigarette held the tobacco stick between his index and middle finger, glared at Riley.

Riley blinked once, "Oh, sorry. I was just staring off thinking about something. Sorry." He turned around, embarrassed.

"Freaking weirdo," he quickly took another puff from the cigarette.

The next second, the frumpy looking woman carried out two bags. She glanced around. "John, I bought you something. You'll like it."

Riley waited until the couple moved away from the store before he re-entered. He stuck his head inside the shop. The place was still crowded, but he spotted Graham close by, "Maybe a little later." He saw Graham nod his head, yes.

Riley entered Serenity House, metal container lugged with some difficulty. He checked in. The routine was getting far too comfortable for his liking. He was anxious for it to end as soon as possible. He made his way to room 427 where the old man waited.

"Are you irresponsible or what?" The old man sat in

a padded chair. Nightclothes were replaced with typical casual clothes most men wear during the daytime. He was angry.

Riley stopped after only stepping one foot into the room. He frowned, "What?"

"Was it the traffic, was there an earthquake or a fire, or did you just take your sweet little time to get it? It sure as hell took you long enough to get here." He smacked his lips.

"You're sure feeling your oats today. Died and came back as the devil himself." Riley tried to outdo the old man's cutting remarks but was quickly shutdown.

"Bring it closer to me." He pointed to a place on the floor just a few inches from the cushioned chair, "Unless you're too weak to finish what you started!"

"What is your problem?" Riley shouted.

"What's my problem?" He coughed once, "Let me start with the main one. I'm dying, unless you hadn't noticed. Two, I'll be quickly forgotten after I'm gone. Do I go on?"

The two men's eyes locked on each other as a long silence sliced through.

It took a while, but eventually things changed as both men seemed not to be agitated with the other, not bothered by the recent outbursts or the present silence. For all the blasts made against each other, it seemed they were more comfortable with one another. It all happened before they realized it. Then, slowly, a discussion began as if they had been close friends for many years. The change took Riley more by surprise than the old man.

The old man started it off. His voice was uncharacteristically soft. "I haven't always been this way. I turned from being a relatively good person to a greedy man ready at the drop of a dime to take advantage of anyone. Now I've become someone who feels sorry for himself. I have my good spells when I'm physically and mentally alert, and then my bad times when I can't remember what I ate or even if I did eat earlier in the day. It happens just like that." His eyes got moist.

Riley wasn't sure what to say, or if anything was needed to say, so he kept quiet. He tried fighting off the compassion he was starting to feel about the old man. He also thought that this might be another set up for another round of insults.

"I'm sorry I brought you into all of this, but you were ... well ... quite convenient. I knew when I first met you I could count on you to do what I asked." He looked at the metal container still by Riley's side. "Come sit, take a seat nearby. Bring it to me." His voice was controlled and peaceful sounding.

Still unsure of the turn of events, Riley dragged the metal container to be close to the old man. It seemed lighter now than before. He wondered why. He pulled a chair nearer to him and the container.

"It might be better if you just said something rather than for me to do all the talking."

Riley still wasn't convinced the old man was genuine. He'd been fooled many times before. He nodded his head no to push the conversation back to Smuts.

"At first, I only wanted to taunt them. I knew they

would quickly realize you were not who you claimed to be. You see, I've upset, insulted, and outraged them before. I've enjoyed making their lives miserable since she left me and took the two girls." He cleared his throat. "Then I wanted to do more to them than just taunt. It became addictive."

Riley figured now was a good time to repeat the same questions he'd asked before, but not gotten what he believed were truthful answers. "Who killed them and why was there an attempt to kill me?"

"You can ask those questions as many times as you want, but you'll get the same answer from me. I have no idea." His eyes remained steadfast focused on Riley. "I know you don't believe me, and there is nothing else I can do or say to convince you otherwise."

Riley did not believe him for one second. He took in a deep breath, and then he heard his stomach rumble. He decided to switch to another topic. "What's in it?" He glanced towards the metal container close by.

"What do you think is in it?"

Was this another round of taunting and teasing?

"Don't you ever get tired of annoying and goading people?" Riley felt himself get worked up all over again.

However, the old man stayed calm and under control this time. "Is that how you feel?"

"Take a guess."

"Huh. My guess is you feel that way."

"Now that's one thing we can agree on."

"Can you now see how easy it is to do? You're doing it with me. How do you think I feel?"

Riley swallowed deeply. "Don't turn the tables. You're the master."

"And I suppose you are the victim. Is that how it works?"

Riley decided to stop the ping pong dialog. "Let's just stop this bullshit. I think there is money in it. Is there?"

The old man answered more or less, still in control, "Not exactly cold cash." His eyes moved from Riley to the box, "Things of value for sure."

"Now we're getting someplace, but not far enough. Why did you want me to bring them to you? And don't ask me to guess." His voice quivered. It was desperate sounding and lacked the compassion he had felt just a short while ago.

"That's simple enough. I want you to help me decide how to divide it up. I won't need it where I'm going."

"Oh," was about all Riley could think to say. He suddenly felt guilty for turning on the heat toward the old man.

"Do you have the key?"

Riley frowned. "You didn't tell me anything about a key. All you said was to bring me the metal container."

The old man let his chest droop. Quietly he clarified, "There is a key in a brown envelope between the mattress and the box spring. You didn't spot it?"

"Evidently not," he felt his heart's beat pick up.

"Then, you must return to get it and bring the key to me. That's the only way I'm going to open it, the only way."

It seemed to Riley that the old man was pleading for

help. He thought he had a better solution, "Break the lock!" The resolution seemed obvious.

Smuts shook his head no without comment.

"Why not, just break the lock!" He was insistent.

Another head move from the old man reinforced the same reply.

Riley took in a deep breath and let the air out slowly. The move seemed to calm him down. He wondered if he was going on another senseless exercise that would surely extend reaching the finale. He was really not sure he had enough steam left to move forward, and he was ready to put an end to it. However, before the words reached his mouth, he conceded. "I'll be back tomorrow with the key. Don't go anywhere."

"You know where to find me." The old man rested his head on the bed's pillow and closed his eyes.

Riley wondered if he should mention meeting Detective Cabo at the house. He decided against the idea, and left the old man alone.

Riley left Serenity House with a mix of confusion, anger, and compassion, so he drove to his place to be with Margo. Surely, she'd have a more open mind. At least, that was what he hoped for.

After he pulled into the garage to park the car, he moved quickly to be with her. She opened the door before he had a chance to touch the handle. They grabbed hold of one other and embraced as tightly as they could.

"I missed you." Her voice was heavenly to his ears.

"I missed you more." He wished he could think of something more original. Then he pulled away from her. Suddenly he saw her eyes give him a surprised look as she put her hands to cover her mouth. "What's the matter?"

For a second she was not able to say a word, just thoughts swirled through her mind that arrived at a sad conclusion - he doesn't love me. She thought it was the end of the world, and then started to cry.

He repeated, "What's the matter?" He took hold of her, pulled her as close as he could. "Margo, I love you. You can tell me anything." He didn't see her sad face turn bright, yet the tears and sobs continued for a short while.

"All I want is you," she managed to say. "I don't care about anything else."

He echoed her desires, "Me too, and forever and ever." Inwardly he felt his stomach growl. Then, a few seconds later he said, "But I really need your help. You're so good at figuring things out that elude me." Slowly, he let his hands drop to his sides, and then reached to her shoulders.

She sniffled a little, and then asked, "What is it?" She'd gotten accustomed to him shifting away from deep emotion issues, especially when they affected her. She knew all relationships consisted of compromises and she figured this was one she'd have to make.

"It's the old man."

They walked to a nearby couch to take a seat.

"Talk to me," Margo said. Her voice was pensive as she looked him directly in the eyes, felt more relieved than just a few moments ago.

"You know I just came from seeing him." He swallowed a little. "I think there is something terribly wrong with him."

She wanted to interrupt but listened on.

"I know he's dying and all that, but his personality changes so quickly from one extreme to another. It's like he is two people moving between one and the other. It's actually kind of scary."

She waited to make sure she did not interrupt. "Give me an example of that."

He paused to collect some thoughts. "The first time I met him at the side of the road he was pleasant and cooperative. He bought me a few beers at McCarty's to thank me for stopping to help him out. Then as I went about doing his dirty work, he became abrasive and downright arrogant with me. I almost tossed in the towel because I felt so angry and frustrated." He paused, and then continued. "And now, he seems to be someone who is pleading for help. He's, in a way, but not totally, somewhat gracious and understanding. He's ...." Riley struggled to end the thought.

She filled in the blanks, "Jekyll and Hyde?"

His eyes opened wide, "Yeah, just like that."

"What about hearing voices that aren't there, thinking someone is out to get him, or having some sort of special powers beyond those of humans? Is there anything like that?"

"I'm not sure." He puckered his lips. "Why are you asking that?"

"I'm not yet a nurse, and I've only taken a few

intermediate psychological courses. However, it sounds as if he might be suffering from a mental disorder."

Riley listened on without comment.

She continued, "Or maybe, because he's dying, he's starting to see himself for who he's become, and he's trying to make right for what wrong he's done in the past."

Riley was silent. Things had suddenly stopped moving as fast as before, as if he too saw things more clearly.

She rested a gentle hand on his face, "I know how difficult this is for you. You know I'll by your side all the way."

10

The next day Riley returned to the old man's house. Last night's talk and love making with Margo calmed him down a little, but there still was pent up anger and resentment towards Smuts. He reached into the flower pot to grab the door key. The door lock opened more easily this time around, probably due to recent repeated use.

He stepped inside. Without much hesitation he headed for the bedroom to grab the key in the brown envelope. With little effort, he slid the mattress away from the box spring. The anticipation of finding the prize quickly evaporated when all he saw were a few dead bed bugs. He swallowed with a little discomfort, and then turned over the mattress to see if anything was stuck to its bottom. Nothing! He got to his knees to inspect the floor but again he came up empty handed. He got off his knees to stand, and then bent over to lift the box spring away from the metal bed stand to see if he misunderstood Smut's directions. The same result, nothing!

At last, he stood motionless looking around the room as if the simple action might tell him something important. All he heard was his own breathing. He was stymied at first, but then considered this was just another of the old man's way of taunting him. "Fuck you!" It was about all that was left in his vocabulary.

"Was that for me?"

Riley turned. His face froze suddenly like how a cold wind can turn water to ice. He couldn't believe his eyes.

"I'm flattered, but I don't think it would work out between us."

Riley managed to say, "What are you doing here?"

Detective Cabo answered, "I could ask you the same question." She looked at the mattress and box spring on the floor. "Are you trashing the place?"

"Smuts told me to find something for him."

She already knew the answer to the question before she asked it. "Did you find what you were looking for?"

"Not exactly," his voice sounded dejected.

Cabo whispered to herself, "No surprise." Then aloud she said to Riley, "A search warrant was just issued to Alfred Smuts permitting me to search the house. You'll have to leave now. This place is off limits." She stared at him. "You need to go."

"But ...."

"No buts, you need to go, now."

He dipped his head in defeat, and started to walk around her. Before he got too far, he heard her again.

"I'll take the key to the front door. I wouldn't want you tempted to return and break the law." She extended her hand towards him, palm up.

He dropped the front door key in her hand, and then left her alone. He was not keen on telling Smuts what just happened, but he reckoned he'd already gotten the search warrant and knew what was going on.

Cabo gave Riley a minute to leave the house. She waited to hear him pull away before she grabbed the key she'd hidden in the closet. She took her time to walk around the place in case Riley was watching from a distance. She wanted him to think she was really doing a thorough inspection. Cabo set the alarm on her wrist watch for fifteen minutes to make it convincing. She took a seat on a chair in the living room for the time being.

Smuts couldn't believe his eyes, a search warrant. "This is crap! I'm not hiding anything in that old house. I haven't used it in years!" He was angry, back to his old ways.

The tall thin man dressed in a business-like blue suit remained quiet. He had nothing else to say or further to do. His job was now done. He turned to walk away.

"Hey, come back here! I want a word with you!"

The bravado did not work this time.

"Don't you dare leave me," his voice quivered ever so slightly.

The man in the business-like blue suit was now out of eye sight.

Smuts realized his time was running out. He shook his head but said nothing. Not even a grin or a smirk dared to peek out. His eyes slowly glanced around the room, believed this was the place where it would all end. He pressed a small button at bedside. Within a few minutes a caregiver stepped inside the room.

"Get me something to write with." The order was given, but his voice was feeble.

She left and soon returned with some writing paper and a ball point pen. "Will this do?"

"Yeah," he grabbed the paper and pen. "Stay here. I want you to witness this."

She frowned, unsure what was going on.

He wrote something on one piece of paper, signed and dated it. Then he said to her, "Sign here and put today's date there." He pointed to where he wanted her signature and date.

She read over the short message, and then put her hand to her mouth. "Oh."

"That's right. Just sign and date it."

The caregiver complied and then handed back the document and pen.

"I don't need you anymore. Go."

She left the old man alone.

A few minutes passed. The piece of paper remained grasped in his hand as the pen fell to the floor. He felt a sudden change take over his body that he did not resist. His normal animated hands were now stationary. He wondered if he was still able to pronounce some words or would they stay stuck in his throat. He'd like to move his shoulders but that movement seemed now to be too physical a task. He rested his head back on the bed's pillow and closed his eyes. A dream crept into his final thoughts.

The cold wind slapped his nine year old face as he stood quietly at the grave. Not many people attended the funeral. Why would they? His family had few friends. He looked around, head still tilted down.

He saw his cousin Alex standing next to his Uncle Frank and Aunt Peggy. They seemed uncomfortable.

Then there was another Uncle and Aunt from out of town. He'd never been able to remember their names since they rarely came around.

Of course, there was the priest and his father.

He watched as dirt was shoveled into his mother's grave. A few words from the priest and then a few flowers were tossed into the grave to finalize the ceremony. Everyone looked in poor health.

It was all over within a short time.

No one asked him how he felt. He wished someone would ask, but nobody did. Silently he cried.

Margo picked up her cell. **Sandy** appeared on the screen. She connected but only heard sobs. Startled, she asked "What is it?"

"Elie died." Her voice was weak. "I got to the Hospital as quickly as I could." She wept for a few more seconds. "There wasn't anything I could do," crying returned.

Still shocked, Margo remained quiet for only a short

time to get in control. "I thought she was recovering." Her throat felt raw and constricted.

Sandy gave out a deep breath of air, only partly settled down. "That's what everybody thought. Then she got a severe headache last night." She sniffled. "They did a scan, found an aneurism, but it was too late. It happened so fast."

"I can't believe this!" Margo felt her body shake.

"I need you here."

"I'm leaving now." She cleared her throat. "Stay strong. I love you."

Margo suddenly felt exhausted, too tired to want to do much of anything. Yet, she pulled together everything emotionally she had. She wrote a quick note to Riley figuring she'd have time on her hands to call him during the drive. She dashed out of the house to make her way to Chino.

Riley took his time driving, putting off telling the old man what just happened. He wondered what else could possibly go wrong. His mind drifted to Diego and his mother. He was still unsatisfied how that all ended, and wondered if there was anything else he could do. He thought about it for a few more miles, and then unexpectedly he turned to head toward the kid's home. An idea popped into his head. At least he could offer another apology and maybe even get back to tutoring him. He figured he had nothing to lose.

He pulled up to the house. It seemed nothing had

changed since he was last here. As he approached the place, he heard a voice.

"Do something for you?" The voice called out his way.

He did not recognize the person standing at the door step. "Hope so." His voice was as pleasant as he could make it. "I'm looking for Diego and his mother."

The heavyset man wore a black T-shirt pulled down over his large midsection. He had black knee length shorts on and was barefooted. "Not here." He did not appear to be a happy person.

Riley stopped at the base of the steps. "Oh, when will they be back?"

"Who wants to know?"

He introduced himself. "Sorry. I'm Riley Sullivan. I was tutoring Diego to read. Been gone for a while and now I'm back. I thought we'd get back into it again."

"Huh, tutoring." The heavyset man was suspicious. "You're not from Human Services, are you?"

"Oh, no, I'm a teacher. Diego helped me with something so in return I'm tutoring him."

"Not here," he repeated.

"Yes, I know. You told me that before. But can you tell me when they'll return?" Riley kept a positive tone to the conversation as difficult as it was.

"No, left me in charge."

"Oh, I see."

"I don't think you do. They're gone."

Riley shook his head. "How long have you been here?"

"None of your business," he seemed uninterested in carrying on the conversation any further. He turned around, ready to leave Riley stand along.

"Are they OK?"

"Yeah," the heavyset man said as he closed the door behind him.

"Wait! Will you tell them that I stopped by?" The plea went unheard. Riley stood motionless for a short while, unable to bring it together, to make any sense out of it. Then, he returned to the parked car, and headed for Serenity House to give the old man the bad news. He prepared himself for what he thought Smuts would say, but was shaken up when he arrived.

"Momma knows right. We be better off starting all over again." She looked at Diego sitting next to her knowing he'd rather stay put.

The packed bus moved along nicely, headed for its next stop in Las Vegas where passengers either found their destination spot or transferred to another bus to continue their trip. Diego and his mother fell in the last category, although she still had to buy two tickets to travel to San Antonio where her sister lived.

She wondered if she'd find a job to help pay for expenses during the stay in her sister's home, then, find a place just for her and Diego to live. She knew her son would make friends easily. There was a good church nearby to keep him off the road of self-destruction.

She showed reluctance to conclude whether or not

Diego's reading tutor was the right person to be with her son. Something about the man caused her to be indecisive. She was not sure exactly what it was, maybe just a gut feeling.

Diego gazed through a window. His sorrowful eyes gave away his true feelings. He knew she was right, she had always been right, but still, he was going to miss a few things. Mr. Sullivan, the tutor, was one person whom he will not forget. Maybe he shouldn't have told his momma about the arrangement they had. It didn't seem to be dangerous, and he didn't think they would have a run-in with the cops. He felt someone touch his arm. He knew who it was.

"Everything's going to be right. You're my baby." She leaned over to kiss him gently on the cheek.

"Yeah, I know momma." His genuine smile warmed her heart.

"Need something to eat? I got a few things in my bag."

He shook his head, "No." A wet spot formed at the corner of his eyes. He felt the love from his momma.

She sniffled a little, and then after regaining control asked her son a question. "That man, the tutor."

Diego's eyes lit up.

"Is he a good man?"

"Yeah, he was good to me." He shook his head. "He was teaching me to read real good."

"You liked him, didn't you?"

"Yeah," he seemed certain of his answer.

She paused, looked away and then returned to face

him. "About him asking you to help him out, why did you tell your momma?"

He shrugged his shoulders as the answer was a no brainer. "I knew you'd want to know that I was helping him. I thought you'd be proud of me."

She put her hands to cover her mouth, but a groan escaped. "Oh." Then she said, "My baby." A few tears soaked through.

"What's wrong momma?" Diego looked frightened.

"I made a bad mistake, a real bad one."

He wasn't sure what she meant, so Diego kept silent.

"How would it be if we return to our house? I'll call Mr. Sullivan, ask him to come back to tutor you." Her face was full of hope. "Would you like that?"

Diego matched her optimism. "Yes, I would momma."

She told herself that since she was on vacation, she'd simply return to her job without anyone knowing the difference. "When we reach Las Vegas, we'll catch the next bus back to San Diego."

After an hour or so on the road, Margo called Riley.

He picked up quickly, "Hi, my love." He was in his car to meet up with Smuts, and had not seen the written message she had left at his place.

She felt his affection as if he were sitting next to her. "I love you too." She paused. "But, I've got bad news."

He felt his throat constrict, perhaps a sign she wasn't convinced their relationship would work out in the end, that she was not the marrying type. He hoped he was wrong. "What is it?" The words almost did not make it out of his mouth.

"My sister, Elie, died." She started to sob.

"Oh, I'm so sorry." But his mind raced to something else. The expected shipwreck relationship disappeared. Selfishly he was relieved.

"She was improving so well. Then she suddenly died of an aneurism." Talking it out helped reduce her distress a little, but not nearly enough. She needed much more comforting.

"I'm so sorry." It was the only thing that came to mind, yet important for her to hear. "Where are you?"

"I'm driving to Chino, should get there sometime tonight." Margo inhaled deeply, and then she slowly released the air. She sensed a modest amount of strain fade away.

"Should I come?"

A smile made its way out. "You've got things to worry about yourself."

"They're insignificant compared to being with you."

"Really," she loved hearing the words.

"Totally," his answer came quickly.

Silence, then Margo said, "I love you so much, but, I'd rather Sandy and me do it together. It'll be much simpler that way." She knew he wouldn't be thrilled with the idea of joining her and Sandy.

Riley wasn't interested in pursuing it any further, in some regards relieved of her decision. "OK, you know best, but if I can do anything call me."

"I will." Her throat was dry so she swallowed. Then she said, "I'll call you when it's over. I love you."

"I love you too."

―――――――

Riley drove on. The unexpected death of Margo's sister caused him to think about life and death.

He believed that everyone knew they were going to die one day, but that few people accepted as true it would really happen to them. He wondered if people believed they were really going to die one day, would they live their lives any differently. He wasn't sure, but he now believed the old man was coming to that conclusion.

He didn't know if Margo's sister ever thought about it. Maybe it had to do with age. The younger you were the less significance you placed on it.

He thought about himself, in what category was he in. He paused in thought, and then he concluded he was not sure. *I'm going to die one of these days, but will I be ready for it?* The internal dialog was too disquieting so he decided to turn on the radio to avoid further reflection.

He made a face, obviously more interested in avoiding the topic at that time. With music in the background, he shifted to next week's academic classes, a less threatening thought.

He continued to drive as he mentally hid in plain sight universal truths about life and death.

―――――――

Detective Cabo turned into the parking lot, found a

suitable spot in no time. She grabbed her hat, and once outside the marked police vehicle placed it firmly on her head. She looked official as she took long strides towards Serenity House.

Inside the building she quickly assessed the lobby, and headed towards the main reception area. Her hat was placed under her left arm, short brown hair neatly trimmed. Her face was firm as she stared ahead.

She waited for a professionally dressed woman behind the counter to finish a phone call, and then she said, "Hello."

For a moment the woman was startled to see someone from the police department. It took her only a short time, however, to recover. "Hello, how can I help you?"

"I'm Detective Cabo. I'd like to see Alfred Smuts."

"Is something wrong?"

"It is a police matter." Cabo squeaked out a slight smile to lower any anxiety the woman behind the counter might feel.

"Oh." She looked down toward a directory of patients that had not been updated yet. "That would be room 427. The elevators are behind me."

"Yes, thanks." Cabo was about to leave but was disrupted.

"You'll have to sign in." She passed a clip board with a sign-in sheet attached and a ballpoint pen. She let a faint smile appear on her face, more from nerves than anything else. "Everyone needs to sign in. That's just how it is."

"Of course, I understand." Cabo took the items, and promptly completed the task. Then, she moved towards the elevators. She heard the woman say, "Have a good day."

Cabo whispered to herself, "I wish they were like that."

Now at the bank of elevators, she noticed all elevators were in use. There was nothing to do but wait for the next available one. A brief time passed before a pair of doors slid open. "Bing." She moved back a few steps as passengers exit.

A few glanced her way, curious why a police officer might be in the building. She took a quick glimpse of each person to make sure Smuts was not one of them. Finally, she stepped inside the compartment, pressed **Four**, and then let the rest automatically happen.

Seconds later, she stepped onto the fourth floor, looked around, and made her way to room 427. She was surprised when she arrived.

The room was vacant. Cabo frowned. She stood motionless for another second or two, and then she quickly moved to find someone from the facility. It didn't take her long to find a young looking man dressed in a green colored uniform. "Excuse me. I'm on official business. I'm looking for Alfred Smuts. I was told he'd be found in room 427."

"Uh, I'm only here one day a week, a student doing field work. I really can't help you." He looked at Cabo's name badge, and then completed the sentence, "Detective Cabo." He paused, and then continued. "But I'll take you to someone on the floor who can help you. Follow me." He moved quickly as Cabo followed close behind.

"Nurse DeWyle, this is Detective Cabo. She is looking for the patient who was in room 427."

DeWyle showed no emotional response, looked back and forth between the two facing her. "Thanks, I'll take care of this," she said to the young man. Then, to Cabo, she said, "Come with me." Another fast pace took them into a small room.

"Have a seat." DeWyle removed a pile of paper stacked on a wooden chair. "My official office," she gave a slight grin, and then she took a seat herself. "So, you're looking for Alfred Smuts?"

"Yes, where is he?" Cabo was all business.

"Did you know he was served with a search warrant?"

"Yes, I was responsible for that. Where is he?"

"I see. Well, I'm sorry to say that he died of a massive heart attack." She too was all business.

Cabo was temporarily taken aback with the news, but recovered quickly. "Yes, it's going to happen to all of us whether we like it or not." She kept her shoulders stationary. "Did he leave any personal belongings?"

"Some. Not much. People who come here don't have much time left to live, so they bring very little. That was the case with him."

"I am most interested in a metal container that he had."

"Oh, yes, the metal container," she kept an inert look about her.

There was enthusiasm in Cabo's voice. "So, you know about the container."

"Well, Detective, I am aware that a young man brought him the container just recently."

"Can I see the container?"

"I don't think you can do that."

"Why not," Cabo was confused, her voice no longer as positive as just a short time ago.

"Well, Mr. Smuts turned it over to the young man, along with a very old pocket watch. It now really belongs to the young man."

Cabo's thoughts suddenly spiraled downward. She couldn't believe what she heard. "The search warrant grants me authority to know what was inside his house. So, I am authorized to see the metal container." She knew she was bluffing, but the story was worth it if it worked.

"Hmm, I don't think so. I'm no attorney, but since the young man brought Mr. Smuts the metal container before the search warrant was issued, it seems to me that it no longer was inside the house."

"Yes, but I found the key in his house that opens the box. I have it with me now."

"I think I need to refer this to our legal department. I'm sorry I can't help you."

"Do you really want to do that? All I want is to see what's inside the box. That's it."

"Detective Cabo, the metal container and Mr. Smut's pocket watch have been willed to the young man. That's his decision, not mine. I'm sorry."

Cabo took in another deep breath, decided to try one last time to convince her to help. "Just a peek inside the box, you can observe. It will take less than a minute." She was so sure of finding out its contents she didn't want to leave any rock unturned. She patiently waited to hear what DeWyle had to say.

"As much as I'd like to help you, my hands are tied. Sorry, no."

Cabo left without further talk. She exited the building to sit outside in her car to think things over. Then, she decided to make a call to her Captain to explain what had happened. She hoped to convince him more was needed to get her access to the metal container. However, he didn't seem persuaded.

"It seems you've lost legal control of the metal container. Sullivan removed the metal container from the house before the search warrant was in force. If the will is legally binding, then he owns whatever is inside. What am I missing?" The Captain's voice was flat.

"We need to challenge the legitimacy of the will. I don't think Smuts was mentally capable to make the decision to grant Sullivan anything. Hell, he was dying and probably incoherent most of the time. We can challenge his mental condition."

"This is really a long shot. It could take the legal department a while to create the brief. I don't know if it is worth it?"

"What do you mean, worth it? He probably had killed his former wife and two girls, and most likely tried to kill Sullivan. Who knows what else he's done that we don't know about!"

"It's all conjecture. We have absolutely nothing to go on, no hard evidence. Zip. Do I have to remind you what strings I pulled to get you the search warrant for his house?"

"So, you're going to let the case drop. Is that what you're telling me?"

The Captain took in a deep breath and then let the air slowly slide through his lips. "OK, I'll talk to the head attorney."

"Thanks, Captain. I knew I could count on you." She waited for him to disconnect, and then she closed her cell phone. She knew it was a long shot, but she had nothing to lose. She started the car's engine, and pulled away only a few minutes before Riley pulled into the same spot she occupied.

Riley let the elevator take him to the fourth floor, then he walked to room 427. Like Cabo, he stopped in his tracks when he saw the room empty. He quickly turned to find someone for help.

Coincidently, he bumped into the same student whom Cabo talked with. "Where's the patient who was in room 427?"

He pointed to DeWyle who stood a few yards away. "She can help you."

Riley hurriedly moved her way. "Excuse me. Can you tell me what happened to the person in room 427?"

She looked at him carefully. "You're the young man who's been seeing him recently, aren't you?"

"Yes, why do you ask?"

"What's your name?"

"Riley Sullivan."

She smiled, it appeared genuine. "Come with me. I've got something for you."

Riley followed DeWyle who took him to the Reclamation Department, a place where patients' possessions were temporarily secured for safe keeping until reclaimed by family members or other designated persons. On the way, her back turned to Riley, she said, "I'm sorry to say that Mr. Smuts suffered a massive heart attack. It happened very quickly."

Riley stopped in his tracks, stunned by the sudden announcement. "I didn't know."

She kept walking. "You've been the only one who's visited him. I guess he had no family or other friends. This way," she pointed to a place for them to talk. "I'm sorry for your loss."

She seemed mostly all business-like to Riley as he caught up to her. "I - I really didn't know him that well. I mean, we only met a short time ago." His voice was somber along with a mix of emotions.

"Yes." She quickly moved to the next topic. "He left you something, actually two items."

"What?"

"It seems very shortly before he died, he wrote out a will that granted you two specific items. An employee from Serenity House witnessed it all, signed and dated the document. Our attorneys say it is valid."

"I see," Riley said, although he was still quite baffled by it all.

DeWyle continued to speak in a matter-of-fact manner, the previous smile completely gone. "Serenity House will retain the will unless there is some legal reason why we should release it, but the two items are yours. You'll just need to sign for them." She paused. "I just need to see some proof of identification, such as a driver's license."

He met her emotionless looking face with continued confused eyes. He slowly removed his wallet from his pocket to hand her his license.

She took the license from him, nodded, and returned the document to him. "Thanks. Don't put it away yet. You'll need to refer to it as you complete paperwork." She paused to determine if he was following all of it. Satisfied, she continued. "Is there anything you want to know before I request the two items?" She looked at him.

Riley opened his eyes wider, puckered his lips, and asked, "What did he leave me?"

"You'll find out when the items are delivered." She waited another second or two for any other questions. "OK, then, I'll ask for the items to be delivered here now." She swung around to a wall phone to make a call. "Bring the items given by Alfred Smuts for Riley Sullivan. Thanks." She returned the instrument to its wall cradle.

A brief silence took over, comfortable for her but not for him.

Then there was a knock on the door. DeWyle and Riley looked towards the sound. She said, "Come in."

A man dressed in a one-piece brown uniform brought in a metal container and a paper bag into the room. He set both items on the floor, handed DeWyle two slips of paper.

He didn't even look at Riley, but directed his comments to her. "Complete the form and sign both copies at the bottom with today's date. Give him both to complete, sign and date. Return one copy to me. He keeps the other one." He'd given the instructions many times before. It was automatic. He waited with some impatience. It was close to his break and he didn't want to miss out.

She did her part, and then she handed both documents to Riley to do his part. Finally, he returned one copy to her and kept the other for himself. She gave the man dressed in a one-piece brown uniform his copy. The entire transaction was completed in silence. The man hurriedly left to take his break.

Riley stared at the metal container, and then the bag, not entirely sure the contents of both items. His heart's beat picked up a little faster than normal.

"Do you want to see what's inside now?"

He frowned, "Yeah, I'd like to but I don't have a key to the lock."

"Oh," she seemed surprised. "What about the bag?"

Riley hesitated.

She picked up on his reluctance. "I understand." She puckered his lips. "Well, I suppose you want to take the container and bag with you now." She stood to prompt him to follow.

It took him a little longer to get the message. Finally, he said, "Yes. I should go now." He forced a smile but it was far inferior to what he was capable of doing, although not a surprise under these conditions.

"Do you want some help getting these to your car?"

"No thanks." Then he remembered how difficult it was to lug the container in the first place. He reconsidered for a second, but then did not alter his answer, "I can manage."

Pleased by his comment, she said, "Follow me. I'll show you an easier way to leave the building." There was no need to tell him about Detective Cabo's visit only minutes ago since she felt it was not any of his business. She opened the door, headed toward an elevator dedicated to moving supplies and equipment from place to place.

She pushed the button with an arrow directed down, it opened quickly. "Use this freight elevator."

He stepped inside with both items, pushed the button for **Ground**. The doors slid slowly to close as he heard her say, "Good bye."

He didn't bother to reply. The elevator reached ground level. He stepped out, looked around to readjust to a new place. He spotted a sign on the wall, **Parking**, with an arrow pointing in a specific direction. He followed markings on the floor that took him outside.

He spotted his car a short distance away. However, the metal container was sufficiently heavy that he had to set it down one time at the midway point before he completed the walk.

Finally, at the parking spot, he put down the container, and then he looked at the bag on top. He bent over to find out what was inside. He almost lost his balance with surprise.

It was the old man's pocket watch. He stared at it in an almost fixated way. Right then, at that very moment, the watch piece took control over him such as would a powerful drug or a magnificent looking woman. He gave a closer look at the object, noticed details he had not seen before. The watch was decked out in what he thought was gold along with gems that he suspected were rubies and pearls, but he was not sure. The cover was as ostentatious as the tail fins of a 1959 Cadillac Sedan De Ville. Its weight was heavier than he had ever imagined. Slowly, he lifted open the watch's cover. Inside he thought it was gold, but again he couldn't be sure. The dial's second hand moved peacefully without a sound. To Riley, it was the most breathtaking article of any sorts he'd ever seen, much less held in his hand. Now it belonged to him. For the first time in his life he couldn't believe his eyes that he had such an item in his hand.

Several more seconds passed without much recollection of his conscious thoughts, and then he carefully returned the jeweled clock piece to the ordinary looking brown bag. Next, he turned his attention to the larger object still on the parking lot's pavement. He couldn't imagine what the container held, but he was determined to find out its contents. He heaved it into his car that took him a good amount of effort.

By the time Detective Cabo reached the police station, her Captain had something to tell her. "Our request was denied. There's nothing else we can do."

"Shit," it's all she could come up with then, yet she

knew she was not through with the case. There were other ways to get to the bottom of the mystery.

———————

Riley carefully drove. Thoughts tossed around in his head over and over again, like laundry in a dryer. No one could have predicted it would have turned out this good. All the problems he'd been through since meeting the old man seemed minor now. The inner dialog put out of his mind other thoughts as he made a final turn into his driveway. If Riley could see his face, he'd see a very happy man. Then, he snapped out of the mentally imposed condition to press the electric garage door opener. He pulled into the garage, shut off the engine, and got out. He felt jumpy for good reason. He was close to uncovering the contents inside the metal container.

His neighbor, Jack Bilcini, was tinkering in his garage as Riley approached him. "Hey, what's up?"

Jack turned around. "Hey." He wiped his forehead with the back of his hand. "Not much, just trying to put some order into this mess." He waved his hand around the insides of the garage.

"Yeah," Riley had something else more important to ask him. "Say, do you have any cutters to hack through a padlock?"

"I've got lots of tools. It wouldn't surprise me if I had something that would do the job. Let's see what you've got."

Riley said, "Follow me. I'll show it to you."

Within a minute or two, both men looked down at the metal container on the garage floor.

Jack stepped forward to touch the box and inspect the lock. He then made an effort to lift it. "Whoa, this puppy is heavy. What's inside?"

"Don't know. That's why I need something to pry it open."

Both men looked at the same object in silence as if they were assessing something very important but unsure what it was.

Then Jack spoke up. "Yeah, I've got the right tool. Be right back."

Riley nodded his head, grateful the mystery of the box's contents would soon be unveiled.

A few minutes passed before Jack returned. "You might want to keep the box. It looks very old. I sort of like it." In his hands was a gas torch. "Do you think there's anything inside that would ignite?"

Riley shrugged his shoulders, "Like what, oil or gas?"

"Sure. And anything else."

There was another shoulder motion, "I have no idea, but I doubt it."

Jack cocked his head to one side. "Maybe I should use something else to cut it away." Then he looked between the torch and the metal container's lock on the garage floor, and finally to Riley. "What do you think?"

"When in doubt, don't do it. Find something else to use."

Jack replied, "I wish you had the key. It would be a lot easier."

"Yeah, I understand. But, I don't have the key, never did."

"Be right back." Jack left for a second time, and then returned with a few other hand tools. "It'll take a little longer. I'll try not to damage the box, but, I might have to."

"That's all I'm asking, just get it opened."

Jack set down on the garage floor the hand tools to begin dealing with the job. Riley watched on in silence.

Fifteen minutes passed before both men heard the padlock pop open. Jack shook his head. "I was beginning to think there for a minute that this was not going to happen." He stared at the lock, dangling from the box's top. "It's all yours. I don't think I put a scratch on the box itself." Jack stepped back, proud of the accomplishment.

Riley stared motionless at the box for a few seconds as if he was trying to predict the contents. Then, he slowly stepped forward, bent his legs so both knees touched the floor. With one hand he put aside the busted padlock. Then, he reached with both hands to swing open the top of the box. His body's position interfered with Jack having a clear view.

Jack moved to one side for an uninterrupted line of sight. He too looked on with great anticipation.

Riley was dumbfounded at what he saw. His surprise lasted for about fifteen seconds until Jack shook him loose.

"Hey," Jack said as he touched Riley's shoulder.

"I don't believe it." Riley's voice was subdued in spite of the surprise, and a wee bit unsteady. The contents were not what he expected, and for that matter hoped for.

Jack wasn't sure what all the commotion was about so he stepped closer. He saw several concrete-looking bricks stacked alongside each other. There was a black bag in one corner. He spotted something else. "What's that in the upper right corner?"

Riley's eyes slowly moved to the same spot. He noticed something sticking between the inside of the container and the bricks. He pulled out an old photo and gazed.

Jack said, "Looks like an old black and white photo of a family."

Riley arrived at a quick conclusion. "My bet it's the old man, his wife, and two children. I wonder when it was taken." He flipped over the photo to check out a date, but the back was smudged beyond recognition.

Jack asked, "You know him?"

Riley quietly nodded, yes.

Jack continued, "He doesn't look that old, same with his wife. The two girls can't be more than fifteen years old."

Riley stayed quiet. Any further statements were purely conjecture and he was really not interested in guessing about the photo.

Jack asked, "Did you find the box someplace?"

"No, he gave it to me." He shook the photo in his hand. "I really don't believe this."

"Let me be the first to confirm it. The box and what's inside are real. Believe it." Jack patted him on the shoulder but had no idea why Riley was dumbfounded. Then he said, "Aren't you going to open the black bag?"

Riley had almost forgotten. The bricks threw him for a loop. He stretched his arm to grab the black bag, and then he carefully untied a knot at the top. Slowly, he spread open the bag to reveal a collection of what appeared to be white pearls that averaged in size to about one - half a grown man's thumb. He stared at the treasure in his hand, and then grabbed one to hold. His previous disappointment with the contents turned to joy.

Jack chimed in. "Wow! They look awfully expensive, but I'm no gem expert. You could be a rich man right now."

"Can we keep this between us?" Riley turned to face Jack.

"Of course, silence." Jack ran his fingers across his lips as if to zipper his mouth closed.

"I'm not sure if I'll keep it."

Jack's eyes opened wide. "You're kidding, of course."

"No, I'm dead serious."

"Why wouldn't you want to keep the pearls? You said the old man gave them to you. It's not like you stole it." Jack was still baffled by the sudden comments.

"But you didn't really know this old man."

"Who cares about him?"

"That's it. I care how he made his fortune. It wasn't always legal and ethical."

"So, you should turn it over to the police. Maybe they will give you a reward." Jack continued to be confused with Riley's comments.

"Maybe I will." Riley looked off to no place in particular and then he repeated. "Maybe I will." He stood up, kept the pearl in his hand, and continued looking at it.

Then Jack reached over to inspect one brick, curiosity took over. He looked at it as if it was a strange thing, perhaps some sort of rare novelty. Then he turned it to check out the four sides and finally the bottom. He frowned. "Hey, there's something written on the bottom of this brick." He gave Riley a frown.

Riley's attention was now turned toward his friend, and then to the brick Jack held. A pucker in his brow was noticeable. "Huh?" He replaced the pearl inside the black bag.

Jack set the brick on the garage floor, bottom side up. Then, he reached for the adjacent brick inside the metal container, turned it over, and placed it alongside the single brick on the floor. He repeated the process until all bricks were transferred to the garage floor, tops down and bottoms up. He stepped back a few paces, a grin appeared on his face. "I'll be."

Riley moved closer to Jack, tilted his head in the same direction. "Is it what I think it is?"

"It sure looks like a map."

Riley joined in. "The old man drew a map on the bottom sides of the bricks. Can you make it out?"

"Not a place I'm familiar with." Jack raised his shoulders.

"Me neither. It doesn't help that some of it is smudged and worn away."

The two men continued to stare at the same spot in

silence, each wondered if it was possible to figure out what it meant.

Jack asked, "Got a camera?"

"Sure."

"Get it. You should take a picture of the map to do some research."

Riley returned shortly with a digital camera. He clicked off several shots.

"If I were you, I'd keep the bricks bottom side up and cover them with plastic so whatever you now have doesn't deteriorate any more. Put them back into the box for safe keeping."

"That makes sense."

"I wish I could help out with the research, but I've got too many other projects I've got to get to.

"I understand. But, hey, thanks for your help. I owe you."

"Nah, don't worry about it."

Riley dipped into the black bag, "Here, take one of the pearls. Don't know what they're worth, but it's something."

Jack puckered his lips. "Sure, why not. Thanks."

Later the next morning Riley dialed a phone number.

"Hello, Maps, Charts, and Drawings. This is Billy." His voice was monotone without much enthusiasm.

"Billy, I've got some digital images of a partial map.

I wonder if I showed you the images you could tell me something about the location."

"Hmm, how old is the map?"

"Well, I don't really know but I imagine no more than fifty years."

"Is it in good condition, paper and so forth?"

"Actually, the map is drawn on bricks." Riley had doubts Billy was interested at all.

"Oh, cool. Like a jigsaw puzzle." Billy now seemed more fascinated.

"Yeah, like a jigsaw puzzle." Riley felt a wee more confident of Billy's appeal to the map.

"OK, let me have a look at the digital images, and by the way, bring a brick or two. Maybe there is something about the composition of the brick that will help."

"OK," Riley said. "Thanks, I'll see you shortly." He disconnected and hurried to meet up with Billy at Maps, Charts, and Drawings.

Inside the place was cluttered with old wooden tables and a few chairs. There were perhaps hundreds of maps, charts, and drawings everywhere, some of which hung on the walls, some framed and others not. A stale crusty smell permeated through the large one room work area. A man, much older looking than his real age, face freckled with black and gray colored stubbles, leaned over a large piece of paper. A magnifying glass was held up close to his left eye. He wore worn out jeans and a checkered long sleeve shirt to keep him warm in the unheated room.

His feet fit into a pair of worn shoes that should either be thrown away or repaired. He didn't acknowledge the front door's bells ringing as Riley entered the place. The wooden floor creaked from the pressure of each step. Riley waited a few seconds before announcing himself.

However, before Riley spoke, the man said, "Take a seat. Be right with you."

Riley recognized the voice to belong to Billy. "Take your time."

A few minutes passed before Billy gently lowered the magnifying glass to the table. He looked towards Riley as he reached for a pair of thick lens glasses that he put on his face. His nose curled upward and then lowered. "What can I do for you?"

"I called earlier about a map drawn on bricks."

His eyes lit up, "Oh yeah, the puzzle." He stepped forward. "Come closer. Did you bring the photos and a brick?"

Enthused with possibilities, Riley moved closer, "Yes, here they are." He placed a brick on a nearby table. "Here's the brick." Then he unfastened the digital camera to place alongside the brick. "Here's the camera."

Billy took hold of the brick, examined it closely, and then moved to replace his eyeglasses with the magnifying glass. He carefully inspected the item with a great amount of detail, turned it over and over in his hands in order not to miss anything of importance. He repeated the process two more times, and then he lowered it to the table. He easily recognized the import of the item, but decided to hold off telling Riley anything of significance. Someone else needed to know about this find.

With pent up expectations, Riley waited for Billy's finding.

"Show me the images." He pointed to the camera, and then he returned the eyeglasses to his face.

Riley moved quickly to pick up the camera, and then in slow progression, he advanced the images he photographed the other day.

"One more time," Billy now more fully attached greater importance to the treasure.

Riley repeated the process again. He felt his heart accelerate as he waited for the final verdict.

Billy minimized the worth of the item. "The brick is probably from a chimney nearby. Not many homes around here have working fireplaces these days. I suspect this brick came from a building that was bulldozed down and replaced by a newer home. Contractors buy and sell these bricks all the time. They're used for sidewalks and driveways to give an old traditional look and feel. There's nothing very special about them."

Riley was disappointed, wanted to ask him if he was certain, but Billy cleared his throat, and then continued before he had a chance to say anything.

"Images are clear but the map or whatever it's supposed to be is not. There are too many missing parts. I can't tell if it is of someplace nearby or far away. I'd really like to know myself. Whoever drew it had some imagination to put it on bricks. Clever, whoever he was." He cleared his throat again. "Sorry I don't have any more to tell you." He figured he'd cloaked the truth well enough to put off any challenge from Riley.

Riley's face showed his disappointment. Billy sounded credible. "That's OK." He pulled in a breath of air. "There's another favor I need from you."

Billy frowned.

"I wonder if you'd look at something else for me."

He shrugged his shoulders, "Sure, what is it?"

Riley pulled out one of the white pearls from his pocket, and handed it over to him. "What do you think?"

Billy took the gem in his hand, and then he tossed it lightly a few times. "Good weight." He exchanged the eyeglasses with the magnifying glass. "You know I'm not a gemologist." He looked painstakingly at the item, turned it over a few times in his hand. "No cracks or blemishes I can detect." He placed the magnifying glass on the table, and then he returned the pearl to Riley. "You should have it appraised by someone other than me who is licensed. Might cost you a few bucks, but it may be worth it."

"Thanks again for your help. I really appreciate it." He extended his hand to shake. "What do I owe you?"

Billy waved his hand. "Don't worry about it. Glad I could help. I'll charge you the next time."

Riley put away the pearl and grabbed the camera, ready to leave. He turned to walk away.

"Hey, you forgot something."

Riley rotated his head to look at Billy.

"You forgot the brick. I'd only use it as a paper weight or get rid of it."

Riley laughed, returned, and grabbed the brick before

he finally left. He was no closer to finding out any more about the map that was drawn on the bricks. He wondered if he ever would.

Once out of the building, Billy made an important phone call.

The next day Margo called. "Hi, I miss you."

Her voice sounded strange to Riley. Something was different, but he was not sure what it was. "I miss you too."

"Elie wanted to be cremated. She always told Sandy and me that's the way she wanted it. There won't be a funeral service. No need to come up here."

He kept quiet. He knew she had more to say.

"Last night I had a terrible dream. It wouldn't go away as much as I tried to wake up. It just continued."

His eyes widened. "What was it about?"

He didn't see her head shake from side to side. "I really want to forget it, but I know I should talk it out." She didn't see him smile, but sensed he was listening, so she continued. "It really shook me. I was dying and there was no one by my side. I was all alone. I didn't want to die alone. I wanted someone by my side."

She hesitated long enough for Riley to jump in. "As long as we love each other, we'll be by each other's side forever."

His voice was suddenly a bit hoarse, something Margo clearly heard. She smiled and then tears wet her eyes. "I love you so much. Promise you'll always be with me."

"In sickness and in health, for richer and for poorer, forever and ever, I promise." He paused for a deep swallow, and then he continued. "There is no way I'll go back on that promise."

She felt her body tremble, not a cold shiver, but a warm feeling over her body. She changed the topic. "I don't know what to do about Sandy. I mean, I don't want to leave her and her child Katie all alone here in this small town."

Riley quickly surmised Margo was about to ask him to move to Chino. He was not sure he could do that. He hoped his guesswork was wrong. He waited for her to continue but when she didn't he added, "Why not ask them to come here? She and Katie would be with you and me, and we'd all be together." He took in a deep breath. "You know, Sandy and Graham might be a good match." He wondered where that thought came from, but liked it just the same.

"Hmm, that might be a good idea. I wonder what she'd think of it."

Pleased the suggestion made sense to her, he continued. "We wouldn't put any pressure on her or Graham. There'd just be you, me, Sandy, Graham, and Katie to spend some time together."

"I'll talk with Sandy about moving. Secretly, I think she'd be relieved to leave this place and start a new life."

"When do you think you'll have an answer?"

"I'll call you tomorrow one way or the other."

"Super. Love you."

"I love you more."

Moments after Riley and Margo ended their conversation, his phone rang again. He quickly picked up.

"Mr. Riley Sullivan."

The caller's voice was familiar, yet he still asked for identification. "Who's calling?"

"Detective Cabo, is this him?"

He grinned a bit, enjoyed the little hassle he put her through. "Yes. What can I do for you?"

"A little birdie told me you were recently interested in discovering the details of a certain map."

Riley frowned, wondered what interest she had in the item and how she found out about his visit to Billy's place. "What birdie?"

"A secret one," she enjoyed knowing more than him.

"I don't like secrets."

"I do, especially when they help me solve an opened case. So, back to my question, what's with the map written on bricks?"

He heard air passing out his nose, tired of the cat and mouse game with her. He just wanted to get on with his life. "The metal container that you wanted so badly, but that was given to me from Smuts, is filled with bricks. On the bottom of each brick is part of a map. I brought one brick along with several digital photos of the map to someone named Billy at Maps, Charts, and Drawings. He told me he couldn't figure out the map since there are too many missing parts. He said the brick was nothing special. But I guess you already know that." He paused. "Is he the one who called you?"

She wasn't interested in confirming or denying anything. "What else was in the container?"

Riley suspected she knew about the pearls but not the photo. He decided to tell her everything. "You probably also know about the pearls. I haven't gotten them appraised yet but I intend to do that shortly. There also is a black and white photo. I'm guessing it is of Smuts, his former wife and two children girls taken several years ago. There is no date on the photo. I think the woman and the girls are the same people I interviewed and who later were killed, but I can't be positive. That's it. Got nothing else I'm hiding from you." He felt amazingly relieved right then.

"I very much appreciate your cooperation. I wish it was forthcoming earlier. Would you mind if my people had a look at the metal container, bricks, pearls, and the photo. We've got expertise and technology that most organizations only dream of having." She paused. "At least I can tell you if the pearls and bricks were stolen and what their value might be." Another pause, and then she added, "If you are in possession of stolen merchandise you could be sent to prison and fined."

The feeling of relief was only temporary as he felt tension build up again. "Sure. What the hell." He sounded as if he'd tossed in the towel after losing a long drawn out debate.

"Wonderful. Can you bring all of it to me at the station?"

"Sure."

"Can you do it today?"

"Sure." He let out a whiff of air, "Anything else?"

She thought for a second. "Is that everything Mr. Smuts gave you?"

He gave it some thought and was about ready to say yes, but at the last second remembered something. "Well, he gave me a pocket watch that is very old."

"Hmm, you should bring that along as well."

"Why?"

"Just to take a look at, police work, you know how it is."

"Sure."

"Thanks."

He waited to hear of any last second requests. "Is that it?"

"Yes, that should do it for now. If something else comes to mind I'll contact you." She waited for him to disconnect, but when he didn't she continued, "See you in a little while." She severed the phone connection. She couldn't wait to have a look at the items.

Within an hour Riley entered the police station lugging the metal container containing the bricks, bag of pearls and photo. The watch was in his pocket.

Detective Cabo spotted him immediately and hurriedly walked his way, still wound-up by it all. "Glad to see you. Here, let me help you with it." She reached to take away the container, but he resisted.

"I've got it. Just tell me where to put it down."

"Of course, I understand, this way." She turned to walk towards a room with large interior windowpanes. As she entered the area, she pointed to a place on the floor, "Put it over there while I call my people."

Riley thought to himself that everyone these days seemed to have people available to them. He wondered who he might refer to as people. A few came to mind immediately, but he decided to let the idea slide away just the same. Standing alongside the container he looked at it as if he was about to say goodbye to an old friend. His inner thoughts were interrupted.

"We'll start in few minutes. Can I get you something to drink?" Her voice was calm in spite of all the excitement.

"Yeah, a cold Stella sounds about right just now."

"Well, I'm sorry about that. I'm thinking more of a soft drink, water, coffee, or tea."

"You can't blame a guy for trying." He looked at her to wait for a response that did not come. All he saw was her blank stare. "OK, water is fine."

"Be right back."

While Detective Cabo was absent, he sat in one of the stiff chairs. He temporarily forgot about the watch still in his pocket. He looked around the room for nothing in particular, twisted his neck to loosen up a little. He heard a few cracks during the movement that relieved some tension. He saw Cabo return holding two water bottles. There was a plainclothes man by her side carrying a satchel. He wondered if he should comment that her people meant more than one, but decided against it, just not worth it.

"Here's your water." She handed over one bottle to Riley. "This is Detective Forensi. He's a specialist in artifacts who can tell you almost anything about relics, works of art and so forth."

Forensi stepped forward, "Good to meet you."

"Same," Riley said. He had no interest in getting chummy with the expert.

Both men waited for Cabo to start if off. She looked at Forensi. "OK now. Mr. Sullivan has a few items that I want you to take a look at, determine if you can figure out their origin, if they are authentic, or anything else that might help in the investigation I've already briefed you on." She turned her eyes towards the container on the floor. "The items are over there."

Forensi stepped towards the container, bent over to hoist it onto the table. The weight surprised him. "Ooh, heavier than I thought."

No one offered a helping hand as he managed to transfer the container to the table top by himself. "Let's see what we have here." He lifted open the lid, and then gently he took one brick at a time from the container to the table top."

Riley said, "The inscription is on the other side of each brick, so you have to place them bottom side up."

Forensi followed Riley comments until all bricks were transferred to the table top, bottom side showing. He stepped back to appraise the pattern, grunted a few obscure words that were difficult for others to understand. He made his way around the table to determine if a different angle might help him decipher the image. "It sure looks like a map of some sort, sketched several hundred years ago is my guess. The markings appear to be Modoc, a small tribe of native people who lived closer to the Oregon border than around here. Perhaps they fled this way for safety." He stared at the bricks without blinking.

"Their leader, Kintpuash, was also known as Captain Jack." He smiled as if the tiny bit of information was relevant.

He circled the table again, this time in reverse. "I'd say this is a map to show his followers where to hide from the U. S. Army, but I don't think the map represents anything in our area. It would be more Northeast California in the lava beds, not here. I'm almost positive of that."

He moved to his small bag, pulled out a sharp pointed instrument, and then scratched the side of one brick. "Not from around here, not a brick as we're accustomed to seeing, definitely chiseled from lava. I'm sure."

He turned to look at Cabo and Riley, nodded once, and then returned to the brick.

Riley's confusion as to the different interpretations of the bricks between Billy and Forensi cleared up all of a sudden when he concluded that Billy must work for the cops and therefore must have made the phone call. He wanted to tell Cabo and Forensi he knew about their tactics, but settled for the time to ask another question. "How did the old man get hold of them and why would he want them?"

Cabo let Forensi answer Riley's bewilderment. He was the expert in these matters, not her. She looked his way to give him the OK to reply.

"I have a probable answer to one question. These items are rare and are sought by collectors of Native American artifacts to include museums and individual collectors. If one person owned these particulars he was quite wealthy." Forensi kept his eyes on the items as he talked.

Riley added, "Or he stole them somehow."

"Yes, that's always a possibility. But, he could have purchased them," Cabo said.

Forensi lifted his head. "Well, if he purchased them in the open market, a lot of heads would have turned. These are quite rare. There would be many interested parties looking into who was selling them and why."

"Including the U. S. Government," added Cabo.

"Precisely," Forensi said.

"I don't think he bought them. No, the old man probably swindled them from some unsuspecting person or else he stole them. This guy," Riley shook his head sideways, "was ruthless."

"Detective, I suggest you make an inquiry of the national data base to determine if anything like this is on the hot list."

Without comment, Cabo nodded her head to agree with the idea.

Forensi asked, "OK, then, what's next?"

Cabo said, "Mr. Sullivan brought us pearls. I guess they're in the black bag."

Riley began to wonder if anything he'd brought would be returned to him.

Forensi opened the bag, and gently he shook out one pearl into his palm. His eyes opened wide from the size of the gem. "Simply amazing, I've never seen a pearl this proportion." He removed all the pearls onto the table top.

273

"They're all about the same size!" He shook his head in amazement. Then he pulled out a magnifying glass and a miniature scale from his satchel. He placed one pearl on the machine to weigh. "I've never seen anything like this in my life." Lastly, he put the magnifying glass close to the gem, and took his time inspecting it as Cabo and Riley silently looked on. He set the pearl on the table top. "It is genuine, but I have no idea where it came from. I can only imagine its worth."

Riley jumped in, "How much?"

"Easily, twenty-five to thirty thousand dollars apiece, and that's just an estimate. I'd want to peer review them to get a more accurate value. I'm probably on the low side."

A broad smile appeared on Riley's face but his positive feeling got tampered with when he heard Cabo ask a question.

"Could these be so rare that they too could have been stolen?" As she looked at Forensi, she also got a dirty look from Riley.

"It's always a possibility. I'd do the same thing with the pearls as you do with the bricks. Make an inquiry from the national data base."

"Shit," Riley whispered to himself.

"What's next?" asked Forensi.

"There's a photo," Cabo replied.

Forensi looked it over, shrugged his shoulders with disinterest. "It's nothing more than a black and white photo of a man, woman, and two children." His voice was significantly less enthusiastic this time around.

"Anything else?" asked Forensi.

Cabo looked atop the table but did not see the old man's pocket watch. She turned her head towards Riley. "Did you bring the pocket watch?"

He let go a big breath of air through his nose, and then he reached into his pocket. Gently, he placed the time piece on the table. "Yep, here it is."

Forensi reached for the item. "Beautiful." He held the pocket watch in his palm as if it might break, like an egg if handled too roughly. He turned it over a few times, and then gently lifted the cover. "Simply beautiful," he said. His eyes got dreamy as if he was falling in love for the first time. "It's a Glashütte Original Pocket Watch No. 1. There are probably less than one hundred worldwide and I'd guess each is valued at around twenty thousand dollars."

Riley corrected, "Specifically twenty-five. There are only twenty-five in the world, and each is worth over fifty thousand."

Forensi said, "Really? I didn't know that."

"That's what Smuts told me. He was real proud to own it." Riley felt as if he was defending the old man.

"I really wasn't aware of that. Thanks for correcting me." Forensi seemed genuinely thankful for the updated information. "Each watch has its own serial number. I'd have to lift off the glass to get to the mechanism inside where the serial number is found. But, honestly, I'm hesitant to do that since it might decrease the value of the piece."

"Simply opening and then closing it like you found it would decrease its value?" Cabo asked.

"Yes. Anytime you tinker with those tiny screws and

snoop around inside the watch, there's bound to be a scratch left behind. Even if you avoid scratching it, once opened it is no longer the same watch. You can never return it to its original condition. It has been corrupted," Forensi answered.

Silently Riley pleaded to leave the watch out of the picture.

Cabo hesitated, and then said, "OK, don't mess with the watch." She turned to Riley, "Happy?"

He nodded his head, yes.

She continued to look at Riley. "Is there anything else Mr. Smuts gave you, even if it was an old shirt?"

"Nothing else, you've got everything."

She turned to Forensi, "Is there anything else you can tell us about these items?"

"I think I've covered it."

"OK gentlemen. That should do it." She turned to Riley, "I need to keep the bricks and pearls until I receive an answer from the inquiries. We need to complete some paperwork to document the transference of items. You can keep the photo and pocket watch."

"How long will that take?"

"One day, two at the most."

"What are the chances I'll get them back?"

She nodded her head sideways, "I don't have a clue." She turned to Forensi, "Any idea?"

"The odds are the bricks belong to a museum or have been reported as stolen. As to the pearls, I doubt if there will be any information about them. Whoever originally owned them probably acquired them illegally and also sold them illegally or had them stolen and didn't report it."

"So there's a good chance I'll have the pearls returned but not the bricks."

Cabo said, "If what he says is true, then yes."

"That's fine with me."

Two days passed before Riley received a phone call. "Hi. I can't wait to see you."

"What's up?"

"Sandy likes the idea of moving. She wants to get out of this town and start over with Katie."

"That's great."

"Yeah, me too, her apartment lease is up in another day or so that should give us enough time to pack her stuff. I'm going to stay here until that happens."

"Oh. What can I do?"

"Nothing for now, she'll drive her car with Katie while I follow behind in my car. I think you'll see us in about two days."

"Where will she stay?"

"She and Katie will stay with me until we figure out living arrangements. But, I'd like to move in with you as soon as possible. Maybe I can sublet my place to Sandy."

Riley took a deep gulp of air. The realization of he and Margo hooking up was about to become a reality.

"Are you still there?"

"Oh yeah, I was just thinking how great this is all

turning out." He wondered if she heard a wee bit quiver in his voice.

"It is going to be great. I just feel it."

Riley decided to keep quiet everything about the old man's stuff until he heard from Cabo. The least said now the better it was. "Yeah, I feel it too."

"Got to go now, love you."

"Love you too." He heard the phones disconnect. Slowly he flipped close the cell phone, his mind not focused on anything in particular, random thoughts bumped around not making any sense. Then he heard a sound that was familiar to his ears, another call.

"Hello?"

"This is Detective Cabo."

Riley felt his heart skip a few beats.

"I've got answers to my two inquiries."

He heard his own breathing, nothing else. "Yes, what did you find out?"

Her voice was monotone without any noticeable emotion. "The bricks were stolen from a Native American museum in Oregon. They have to be returned." She paused for a response from Riley but there was only silence. "There might be a small reward, but I wouldn't count on it." She paused again. "There were no hits from the data base regarding the pearls. I suspect they are stolen goods, and like Forensi mentioned to us, no one is about to come forward. The pearls are yours to keep. You can come by anytime to claim them. One out of two isn't too shabby."

Riley was lost for words, unable to say anything for a few seconds.

"Are you there?"

"Yes, yes. I'm so ... I don't know what to say."

"Maybe you should thank Mr. Smuts. He gave them to you, along with his pocket watch."

"You know, it's hard to thank him. I mean, he wasn't a good man. He lived a rotten life and treated people like disposable parts of a machine. He tried to kill me! He probably had those three woman killed, and who knows how many others. Come on, thank him?"

"Then why did he give you the metal container with the bricks, pearls, and photo, as well as the watch that collectively are worth a small fortune?"

Riley paused, not able to come up with an answer at first. Then he said, "Maybe he just didn't want to die alone." He didn't see her roll her eyes. "I mean, do you want to die without anyone remembering who you were and what you did in your life?"

"Since we're all going to die one of these days, I'd prefer to have people care about me when I'm alive, not when I'm dead and put in the ground. This guy is a mystery to me."

"That's probably because you're a cop."

He didn't see her frown as to say, *what's that got to do with anything?*

Riley said, "Maybe he didn't want anyone else to inherit his wealth and I was the least of the undesirables?"

She gave out a slight chuckle. "Could be, but I suspect there's more to it."

"Like what?"

"Like, I don't know, but there's more."

"Do you believe in coincidences?" Riley asked.

She replied, "Like luck and twist of fate?"

"Exactly," he answered quickly.

Her answer was flat and definitive. "No."

Riley probed further. "So you don't believe in just being at the right place at the right time, as well as being at the wrong place at the wrong time?"

She repeated the same answer as before, "Exactly."

"Well, I do. Being at the right or the wrong place just happens sometimes."

Cabo interrupted. "That's the easy way out. Don't believe that for a second."

"What do you mean, easy way out?" His curiosity was peaked although he sensed where the conversation was headed.

"There's one important thing we were taught in the Academy."

"And what's that?" He felt himself getting defensive.

"If you let me explain without interruptions, I will." She paused. "There is always a reason why you or anyone else is someplace, and why people do or don't do something. You may not know the reason or even care about the reason, but there is a reason. Things just don't happen. They happen for a reason. Someone who robs a convenience store at midnight is doing it for a reason. What I'm trying to figure out is the reason for him giving you the bricks, pearls, photo, and watch. That's what's driving me crazy. It is more than you were the least of the undesirables, much more." She paused. "And assuming he had his wife and two girls killed, and further, tried to do you in, why did he do that? There's got to be a reason or reasons for it all. It didn't just happen."

She waited for Riley to respond, but he was silent. She continued, "Anyway, come by at your convenience to pick up the pearls. You can take the metal container as well, or leave it with the bricks. Forensi says there isn't much value to the box."

Riley was happy the conversation had ended. "OK, I'll stop by tomorrow morning, probably early." He heard the phones disconnect.

The next morning, Riley got another call.

"Hi, it's me."

He smiled at the sound of Margo's voice, "So good to hear your voice." He let out a deep breath.

"You sound a little down, anything up that I should know about?" She wondered if he'd become so-so on Sandy and Katie relocating, and her moving in with him. Maybe everything was happening too fast for him.

"Oh, no, everything is fine, In fact it's great. I guess my mind is someplace else."

She wasn't convinced, but she let it go. "We're about to leave now and should be there tomorrow mid-day."

He swallowed deeply before he said, "That's great." He paused and then continued, "I'm so glad you called now. I've got some great news."

She felt her breath taken away. "Can you give me a hint now?"

Riley thought for a second and wondered how much

he should tell her. "The situation with the old man is complete. I don't want to get into it now, but he died and left me some valuable things."

She frowned. "Left you something valuable?" The beat of her heart picked up a little faster.

"Yeah, it's hard to believe, but he did. After we talked yesterday, the police called to confirm it all. I am about to pick it up at the police station."

"Amazing, why do you think he left you anything? Didn't he try to kill you?"

"Yeah, that's what I suspect, but I can't prove it. Anyway, I'm still having a hard time accepting that he actually left me anything. I mean, he put me through hell." He paused. "What do you think?"

Her voice was a wee bit high pitched, "I have no idea why he would leave you something, but people do strange things at times."

Riley was about to say something but instead he heard Sandy nudging her sister to finish off the call.

"As soon as you two love birds end we can start driving."

"Good idea," Margo said.

"Uh - uh," Riley agreed.

"One more thing before I go," Margo said.

Riley listened closely.

She said, "If it wasn't for him, we wouldn't have each other now."

He listened, searched for the right words but came up empty handed. He got a welcomed reprieve when he heard Sandy prod Margo to bring to an end to the conversation.

"Sis, we've got to get going."

"OK, OK." Margo answered.

Riley picked up on the signal. "She's right. The sooner you start, the sooner we'll be together."

"I love you."

"I love you too. Drive safely." After he heard the phones disconnect, he replaced it in its cradle.

He swallowed the remains of the coffee, now tepid, and walked towards the kitchen sink to set the empty cup inside. About to clean the coffee pot the phone rang again. He stared at it as it rang a second and third time. He reached over to pick it up, thought Margo had something else she forgot to share.

"Riley Sullivan."

He did not recognize the voice. It sounded foreign. "Who's this?"

"Is this Riley Sullivan?" The voice was persistent.

He listened more closely but still could not identify the caller. Finally he said, "Yeah, who's this?"

The phone disconnected.

Riley frowned, unclear as to what just happened. He returned the phone to its cradle, and then he finished off cleaning the coffee pot and cup.

Voices from a morning radio talk show continued in the background. There was a discussion on the pathetic results of the Chargers' season with a nonstop battering of the coaching staff, players, trades, and close games that were lost. A few jokes were tossed about that only covered up the fact that the expectations for the team's season far exceeded their dismal performance. It almost made you want to give up on the team forever. He shook his head agreeing with most of what was said but didn't hear the front door's locking mechanism picked-open.

A few seconds later, he heard, "Don't move."

Riley felt the cold barrel of a gun pressed against the back of his neck. The coffee cup dropped from his hands into the sink. It broke into a few pieces. "I won't." He raised both hands, and figured one squeeze of the trigger would send a bullet through his body to end his life.

"Don't turn around."

"I won't." The right response had been memorized very well.

"Where's the pocket watch?"

Riley thought the guy had an accent but couldn't place it and for the time being was not interested in figuring it out. All he wanted was to stay live, "In my bedroom."

"We're going there together. Turn around nice and easy." The voice was definitely that of a man and it seemed to belong to someone who was late in age.

Riley still felt the gun barrel against his neck. Slowly he turned to match the intruder's movement not interested for the time to get a glimpse of the man's face. He did not want to do anything that would upset the man with the accent. He made sure his eyes angled towards the floor. Then, he followed the man's instructions to head towards his bedroom.

He accidently kicked the first step of stairs and almost fell over, but Riley recovered quickly by grabbing onto the handrail to his right. He took the rest of the steps more carefully.

The man stayed very close behind.

Soon Riley entered the bedroom with the gun still stuck like glue to his neck. He moved towards a night stand and then stopped. "It's there on the top."

"Bend over real slowly and pick it up." The man's voice sounded anxious with a slight quiver of excitement.

None of this was what Riley had in mind when he awoke this morning. He took in a deep swallow before he leaned over. He felt a little dizziness come over so he blinked a few times to steady himself.

The man was impatient. "What are you waiting for?"

Riley was about to say something but he only got out a few words, "I'm trying ...."

His response was cut short, "Shut up. Just do what I say."

Riley complied. He grabbed hold of the timepiece. His hands felt clammy.

"Now, turn around slowly. No unexpected moves or they could be your last."

The thought of coming face to face with the man with the accent sent a shiver through Riley's body. He froze.

Why would this man let his identity be known to Riley unless the man with the accent had the intention to kill him? Riley wanted to plead for his life, to tell him of his future plans with Margo but nothing came out of his mouth. The words were stuck deep inside his throat.

Then a flash passed through his mind. Maybe the man

wasn't going to kill him. This was a good thing. Riley managed to move to face him but just in case he kept his eyes lowered to be on the safe side.

"Kneel." A one word order gave Riley the shivers.

Riley rethought his previous thoughts. Maybe his time was up. Slowly, he lowered his body so his knees touched the floor. All he saw was the man's black scuffed shoes. He remained quiet. He couldn't think of anything to say, and if he could, he was not sure it would mean much.

"Hand me the watch."

Without reluctance Riley gave up the pocket watch. If he got out of this situation alive, Riley figured the timepiece was an excellent exchange for his life.

The man with the accent mumbled something that only he understood. Then, more clearly, he said, "I've taken back what is mine."

Riley's eyes were closed and his mouth was bone dry. He could no longer bear the fright he felt. His body jerked and then twisted as he rolled to the floor. He no longer heard his own lungs take in and let out air, nor his heart pump blood throughout his body. He didn't struggle to make sounds with words. He felt no sensation at all. He remained still on the carpeted bedroom floor.

A nudge from the man's foot did not get a reaction from Riley. He shouted something that did not reach Riley's ears. The man with the accent shrugged his shoulders as if he had no care in the world. Finally, he turned to leave Riley alone. He'd finally had what he came for.

Sixty minutes passed before Detective Cabo made a telephone call that was not answered. She wondered why Riley hadn't come by yet to pick up the pearls and metal container so she decided to pay him a visit.

As she approached the front door she noticed a crack where light shined through. She reached for her revolver, gently pushed the door open a little wider. It moved with ease. She stepped inside.

Her eyes quickly scanned the immediate area, and then she yelled out, "Riley Sullivan. This is Detective Cabo." There was no response, so she moved further inside the house. She repeated, "Riley Sullivan. This is Detective Cabo." Still there was no answer.

She carefully inspected the first floor. The kitchen was the first place she checked. She noticed the broken coffee cup and dirty coffee pot. Then she turned towards the stairs that led to the second floor.

Step by step she advanced to the master bedroom where she saw Riley motionless on the floor. Cabo rushed to his side, put her thumb to his neck to detect a faint pulse. Quickly she called in for an ambulance.

Later that same night, sleeping in a hospital room, Riley dreamed.

His arms flailed and his heart leaped in all directions. He flew through the air headed towards the ground with amazing speed that he couldn't control. His body hit the earth's surface with a thud.

It was difficult for him to see but he felt bloodied and

bruised. His skin was badly scraped. While his injuries were so severe he couldn't endure the pain, he wasn't about to give up. He stood but then fell down. Another attempt resulted in the same effect.

Then he heard a voice off in the distance, "I love you. I love you with all my heart." He recognized her voice.

He pushed himself again. This time he stood, and suddenly Margo was in his arms. Her touch affected him in a way that he'd never felt before, "And with all my soul, forever and ever."

A sudden white flash circled their bodies as they stay clutched together.

He suddenly woke up, eyes wide opened. At first he was not sure where he was. His body was sweaty and his mouth was dry. He looked around at the unfamiliar surroundings. Then slowly he realized he was out of harm's way, it was only a dream. His heart slowed down to a normal pace as he took in some needed air. A smile slowly appeared on his face, tiptoeing delicately, until he felt it was safe.

- End -

About the Author

Antonio F. Vianna is a prime example of someone who's refashioned both himself and his career to stay in step with the changing times. In fact, you might say he wrote the book on it with "Career Management and Employee Portfolio Tool Kit, 3rd edition" along with his "Re-Careering At Any Age" and "Career Strategies" workshops, all of which have enjoyed much success. With a M.M. from Northwestern University's Kellogg Graduate School of Management, and a B.S. from Union College, Vianna is a faculty member with a myriad of San Diego, California universities. He has been able to professionally re-brand himself from a former U.S. Air Force officer into a professional human resources position within the private sector, and now as a phenomenal storyteller. Today, he is a professional writer, speaker, and educator with 18 published books —both fiction and non-fiction—since 2003. His non-fiction works are up-to-date, relevant, practical, and easy to use. His fiction works are written with an appetite to tell intriguing, credible, and unique stories. He sets a quick pace with his dramatic language. Vianna's frequent television and radio guest appearances, plus his membership in Publishers and Writers of San Diego, Read Local San Diego, and the Military Writers Society of America are testaments to his lifelong commitment to the writer's craft. Vianna lives in Carlsbad, CA. His books are both in paperback and electronic, and are available wherever books are sold. For more information about Antonio F. Vianna and his other books, go to his website at www.viannabooks4u.com.

Also By Antonio F. Vianna

Non-Fiction

Career Management and Employee Portfolio Tool Kit Workbook, 3rd edition, (2010) (ISBN: 978-1-4107-1100-7)
Leader Champions: Secrets of Success (2004) (ISBN: 1-4184-3684-4)

Fiction

A Tale from a Ghost Dance (2003) (ISBN: 1-4107-1384-9)
The In-ter-view (2003) (ISBN: 1-4107-0876-4)
Talking Rain (2004) (ISBN: 1-4140-6648-1)
Uncovered Secrets (2005) (ISBN: 1-4208-1795-7)
Midnight Blue (2005) (ISBN: 1-4208-6397-5)
Veil of Ignorance (2006) (ISBN: 1-4259-1695-3)
Yellow Moon (2006) (ISBN: 1-4259-5112-0)
Hidden Dangers (2007) (ISBN: 978-1-4259-9710-6)
Haunted Memories (2007) (ISBN: 978-1-4343-2852-6)
Bound and Determined (2008) (ISBN: 978-1-4343-7450-9)
Stranger On A Train (2009) Book 1 (ISBN: 978-1-4389-1490-9)
The Hiding (2009) Book 2 (ISBN: 978-1-4389-6206-1)
The Vampire Who Loved (2009) Book 3 (ISBN: 978-1-4490-2488-8)
Second Son * (2010) (ISBN: 978-1-4490-7473-9)
Unintentional Consequences (2010) (ISBN: 978-1-4520-5901-2)

  * Novel and Screenplay